# Nightingale

*Books by Eric Pace*

NIGHTINGALE
ANY WAR WILL DO
SABERLEGS

# Nightingale

## Eric Pace

Random House New York

*This book, being fiction, takes some liberties with fact. For example, an eight-eenth-century platinum-and-sapphire brooch—a turban ornament—is said to be among the crown jewels of Iran. Actually, however, platinum jewelry was rare before 1900, and the platinum pieces among the crown jewels were all made after 1920.*

E. P.

Library of Congress Cataloging in Publication Data
Pace, Eric, 1936–
Nightingale.
I. Title.
PZ4.P113Ni   [PS3566.A24]   813.5'4   78–11269
ISBN 0-394-48420-7

Manufactured in the United States of America
2 4 6 8 9 7 5 3
First Edition

TO SUZANNE

*Teheran, Iran—Some nations back their currencies in gold. Others link currency to the Special Drawing Right, an accounting unit created out of thin air by the International Monetary Fund. Backing the Iranian rial, however, is a treasure that no other nation can match: the crown jewels of the Persian empire.*

*The collection includes gems extracted by slaves from the diamond pits of India's ruined city of Golconda, ruby-red spinels from mines high in the Hindu Kush, and lustrous pearls from the warm waters of the Persian Gulf. There are hundreds of thousands of stones in all.*

*Today, the treasure serves as collateral for the equivalent of about $3.75-billion—or 75%—of Iran's currency, according to Bahman Homayoun, vice governor of the central bank. (The remainder is backed with gold and foreign exchange.)*
— Ray Vicker, the *Wall Street Journal*,
November 6, 1975

While it is somewhat impractical to consider going to Teheran to see gems, there is no question that their collection is the finest in the world today. Because the gems are collateral, the Shah of Iran has taken great pains to make them accessible to his people as well as to tourists, with a view to bolstering confidence in the fiscal integrity of his government.
— Benjamin Zucker, certified gemmologist,
*How to Invest in Gems*

PART

# 1

"TALES OF THE VIENNA WOODS" CAME TO AN END. THE DANCE
band paused for a moment. In the lull, Harry Arloff could hear
distant sirens wailing somewhere in the east of the city. The
sound was faint, barely audible over the clink of china and the
babble of voices at the American ambassador's dinner dance.
But it made Harry uneasy.

What bothered him was not so much the thought of what
the tough Teheran police might be up to at midnight on a
Thursday night; like most Americans operating in the Iranian
capital, he had tried to put the stories about official brutality out
of his mind. What bothered him more was the thought that the
sirens might dampen the spirits of the Iranian guests who were
living it up around him, their dark eyes glittering in the glow
of the chandeliers. That would be too bad, because Harry found
his work went best when his potential clients were in a good
mood. His long experience at ambassadorial parties had taught
him that the best time of any evening to ply his trade was now,
when the crêpes suzette were finished, the dancing was warming up, and the waiters were moving among the tables dispens-
ing the ambassador's tax-free brandy.

And so Harry took leave of the friendly but unpromising
women who had sat next to him during dinner, at one of the
candlelit tables along the walls of the ballroom in the ambassador's residence. From the dowager on his right, Mrs. Mehdri,
the wife of a well-known Iranian archaeologist, he got a mater-

nal smile. The only fancy jewelry she was wearing was what looked like a turn-of-the-century garnet-and-gold bracelet. Chicken feed, Harry had concluded. From the high-strung American woman on his left he got a nod and a hurt look. Mrs. Karthian, her name was, and she said her husband was the U.S. agricultural attaché. Mrs. Karthian wore heavy gold-colored earrings, but they were almost certainly costume jewelry. And the diamond in her engagement ring was only the size of a BB shot. Harry was sorry to hurt her feelings by rushing off like this, but he had a living to make.

His first stop was the coatroom, where one wall was hung with the Arab daggers the ambassador had collected during a long career in the Middle East. Harry ignored them—the hilts and sheaths were at best only silver—and checked his appearance in the big mirror, like a policeman preparing to go off on his beat. He remembered to straighten his secondhand signet ring. He adjusted his Paris-made necktie, plucking at the fine silk. He got out his comb and tried to make his hair hang in a nonchalant way above his face, which looked all too bony and eager. It also looked too tired after too many late nights like this one, and too much fighting for hotel rooms in the crowded oil capitals of the Middle East. And it looked too old, years older than his actual age, which was thirty-seven. Some Americans, especially the self-employed ones, age early if they work too long in Iran and Saudi Arabia and the other rich oil-producing countries. The life is exciting, but it wears on a man to deal all the time with people who are much richer than he is—to know that a nod from one of them can make him a millionaire, and that a misstep by himself can make him lose out on a fortune.

If Harry had been in a simpler country tonight—Kuwait, say, or Abudhabi—he would have tried to look merely prosperous and neat. But to impress Iranians, he had found, it helped to try to look elegant and a little rakish. So he made sure the handkerchief in his breast pocket had a floppy look. He checked the black leather case that held his calling cards; it made a sleazy impression to carry them around loose. Then he took out the snapshot of his daughter, Emily, holding the hand of her expensive Scottish governess. He looked at it a moment, and he was ready for the night's work.

The sound of sirens not far away made Pegano say good-bye to his two Iranian friends. But the noise ended quickly, and the neighborhood, in the east of the capital, was quiet by the time he walked through the gate of his friends' rented villa. He turned left and began to stroll down Chaman Street toward Ayendeh Avenue. He could see by the glow from the street-lights that police cars had arrived at both ends of Chaman Street. He did not see policemen standing around; perhaps they had all stayed in the cars. Perhaps—who knows? He concen-trated on walking easily, keeping calm. As an American citizen with a valid passport, he had little to fear. The name on his passport was not known to the Iranian police, and, anyway, the Iranian police treated Americans kindly. Most of the time. To help himself relax he began to hum an old marching song from prouder days, in Europe thirty years before. The words ran through his mind:

> "Oh, Mr. Tru-man,
> Why can't we go home?
> We have conquered Afri-ca,
> We have conquered Rome;
> We have subdued
> The Master Race,
> But now they say,
> 'No shipping space.'
> Oh why can't we go ho-ome?
> Oh why can't we—"

Pegano hummed more softly when he noticed the two foreign hippie girls standing under a streetlamp forty yards ahead of him. At least, they looked like foreign hippies, with their fair hair, jeans, shawls and bandannas. They might have stopped off in Teheran while hitch-hiking to Afghanistan. But as Pegano walked closer, he saw that their faces were too old and hard for hippies. He stopped humming. He was sorry to give up the tune. Its beat was reassuring. But he did not want these women, whoever they were, to think he was a little crazy or drunk. Drunk the way the American oilmen and helicopter-pilot instructors got on their visits to Teheran.

"Hi, Tex, got a light?" the taller of the women called out, in English with some sort of an accent. Okay, Pegano thought to himself, if they aren't hippies, what are they? They could not be whores, he thought, not in this quiet side street in eastern Teheran, and not now, at midnight. They must be Iranian detectives or intelligence agents.

"Sorry, I don't smoke," he called back with false heartiness. He kept on walking toward them, hitching the strap of his plaid canvas shoulder bag. He wanted no problems, and he hoped that Iranian detectives, even Iranian intelligence agents, would not make trouble for what looked like just an ordinary, clean-living American, well into middle age.

"Got any hashish, Tex?" the other woman said. Her voice was also accented, but deeper. Her mouth was unsmiling. She was not enjoying her role.

"Not today," Pegano said, trying to keep things friendly. He gave an awkward wave. He walked faster.

"What are you doing in Teheran, Tex?" the bigger woman said. "Came up here to get yourself a little hash?"

Pegano gave another false smile. "No, honey. Not me. Not here," he said, and he tried to make a little joke: "Too many cops around here. Too many sirens."

The two women didn't bat an eye. They must have instructions from officers somewhere, maybe looking down from the windows of one of the dark buildings along the street. The women might have been staked out here for a long time to watch people coming in and out of the house where Pegano's Iranian friends were staying. They might have summoned the prowl cars. As he approached the streetlight the women moved out from under it and toward him.

"Hey, Tex, you want to buy some good stuff? Afghani stuff?" the smaller woman said. She and her companion were fifteen yards away from Pegano now, and even in the weak light he could see that they were thin and stringy. They probably did calisthenics at their barracks every day. Their hair looked dyed. He glanced at their bodies under the fringed shawls: there was no sign that they were carrying arms.

"You like looking at my body, Tex. You not so square, after all," the big woman said.

"I'm pretty square," Pegano said, walking quickly now.

"Come on, Tex," the big one said more boldly, "let's you and me go to a hotel and crash. I been on the road a long time." She poked at the canvas bag. "You got a bottle in there, Tex?"

Pegano flinched. "Leave that alone," he said a little too sharply. Then more softly: "That's something for my wife."

"Oh, Tex," the smaller woman said, smiling now. She was warming to her work. She grabbed his right arm and tried to rub her face against his shoulder. "You got something for me, too?"

Pegano wanted to play it cool. He put his arm around her and said, "Now, honey, beat it; I've got to go home."

But the big woman grabbed his left arm with one hand and began fumbling quickly with the canvas bag with the other, trying to seem playful.

"Hey," Pegano said as she unsnapped the cover. She peered inside.

"Look, Vida!" she said in Farsi, the Iranian language. "Look—"

A loud explosion echoed through the neighborhood. It sent scraps of plaid canvas and other things sailing into the air. For an instant all was still. Then Pegano's friends stuck their heads out an upstairs window of their villa. From nearby rooftops, police marksmen opened fire.

Moving slowly to hide his slight limp, Harry took a quick tour of the ground floor of the ambassador's residence. You never know where you might find a customer, he told himself for the ninety-ninth time. In the entrance hall he passed an antechamber where U.S. marine guards in ill-fitting tuxedos were sitting beside a walkie-talkie and a red plastic telephone. He assumed the telephone was connected with the guardhouse at the gates to the residence, or perhaps with Teheran police headquarters. He visited Teheran only every few months, but he knew the ambassador was highly security-conscious—which was natural, because there were continual shootings, shoot-outs and bombings in the capital and elsewhere in Iran. The outlaws involved were terrorists opposed to the country's wildly wealthy ruler, Shah Mohammed Reza Pahlavi. A marine guard was using the telephone now, speaking softly, confidentially. He looked over his shoulder to see if strangers were within earshot. Harry moved on.

In the reading room, Harry paused to light a cigarette. A pockmarked Iranian retainer was manning a portable bar in one corner, and around it were standing a half-dozen expensively dressed Americans. One was a beefy man in flashy clothes whom Harry had already met: his name was Buddy Something-or-other, he was a visiting television producer, and he had reached the age where he found it important to comb long hairs over his balding scalp. The other men were also middle-aged, also beefy, but more conservatively turned out. From their loud jokes about Iran, Harry knew they were some of the hundreds of traveling American businessmen who came to Teheran every month, hoping to pry loose some of the country's oil wealth—despite the fact that the Shah's huge military spending had put the budget into the red. These travelers knew well that Iran's large population—over thirty million—would make the country a lucrative market for decades to come. And so, Harry reflected, they streamed into Teheran, unfazed by the occasional, much publicized murders that were carried out by the terrorists—left-wing dissidents who wanted to make trouble for the Shah. The killings did not weaken the Shah's main power base, the loyalty of the armed forces. Nor did they affect the country's wealth, which had grown enormously since 1973, when world oil prices began their sudden rise.

Buddy and the other men began swapping the current rumors of the Teheran expatriate community: the Shah was taking a tough position in negotiations toward an agreement to supply vast amounts of Iranian oil and gas to the Soviet Union, and the Russians were said to be furious; an American colonel, once an adviser to the Iranian army, was about to be arrested here for hanky-panky in obtaining military sales contracts for American firms; such-and-such a luxury hotel was being built without adequate safeguards against earthquake damage; such-and-such a prison was overcrowded now with captured terrorists and other political prisoners. The conversation turned to rumors about the Shah's sex life. Old rumors, Harry noted with disappointment. The pockmarked retainer looked uncomfortable.

Harry finished the cigarette on the veranda, where clusters of Iranian matrons were roosting on the settees, chattering away in Farsi. Their menfolk were scattered in little groups among them. Many of the men and the women were drinking nothing stronger than tea. These were Teheran sophisticates, people who were fluent in foreign languages as a matter of course, people who were at ease with foreigners. But at parties like this, many of them tended to remain cozily among themselves.

The Iranians here tonight were dressed in elegant Western clothes, but they were set apart from the Americans by their dark eyes and hair, their strong-boned features and their complicated good manners. These were part of a system of courtesies that grew up during many centuries of absolute monarchy, when extreme politeness became a way to avoid having your head cut off by a wrathful ruler or vizier.

Harry surveyed the scene before him carefully, his eye lighting on a diamond brooch here, a pair of earrings there, on women's well-turned ankles and shapely shoulders left bare despite the coolness of a spring evening. But his heart sank; among all these elegant people, he had seen no one whom he knew to be a promising business prospect. What to do? Hoping for the best, he positioned himself by the French windows that connected the veranda to the ballroom. They gave a useful view of the festivities inside. The band was playing another waltz— Mrs. Fraser, the ambassador's wife, liked waltzes—and the ambassador himself was whirling around the floor in an Iranian dowager's doughy arms. This evening was a challenge, Harry reflected: the non-Iranian guests were not good prospects for him: they were probably not rich enough, or if they were rich, they were not recently rich enough to suit his purposes. And the Iranians here, alas, were not movers and shakers. Among those he recognized were a deputy minister of commerce, a minor general, even the ambassador's own social secretary. That's the trouble with this kind of party, Harry thought, and he could not resist a grin: if it's the kind they invite me to, the other guests are not likely to be the absolute cream of the cream.

"Why the smile, Harry?" a cheerful tenor voice said in his ear. Harry turned and his spirits soared. It was Hobie Stiles, the society columnist for the *Teheran Mail*, a local English-language newspaper. Hobie was someone who could be very useful, although past years of hanging around minor Arab sheikhdoms along the Persian Gulf had left him rather the worse for wear; his face was pink from all the sun and the whiskey. Like many Americans who had become old Persian Gulf hands, he had come to seem slightly English. This was from years of rubbing shoulders with the Englishmen who were hugely influential in the Gulf in the years before Britain's power waned.

Yet Hobie still made valuable use of the skills and connections he had picked up at Princeton two decades before. He danced well. He played the piano deftly and had worked as a piano player in various hotels around the Gulf. He provided himself with an enviable succession of girlfriends. He spelled people's names accurately in his gossip column. And, as Harry had once learned from a drunken American diplomat in Oman, Hobie had been an agent for the U.S. Central Intelligence Agency since a week after collecting his bachelor's degree.

Three years ago, Harry knew, Hobie had moved from the small Gulf sheikhdom of Bahrein to Teheran—which must have meant a big promotion in the spying profession: Iran is strategically important not only because of its oil wealth and its vast area, which is as large as the part of the United States that lies east of the Mississippi river, not counting New England. It is also important because of its sensitive location: bordering it to the north is the Soviet Union, which has spied on and meddled in Teheran for decades; the Shah is implacably opposed to Communism, although on the surface, Irano-Soviet relations are generally courteous enough. And bordering it to the west is Iraq, whose radical Arab regime is largely Soviet-armed and has a long history of feuding with Teheran.

"Learned anything interesting tonight, Hobie?" Harry asked with a grin. "Gossip-wise, I mean." He could afford to kid Hobie a little because the man was always careful to be friendly to him and to other Americans who traveled continuously in the region and might provide useful bits of information.

Hobie gave Harry a sharp look and then grinned back. "Slim pickings in Teheran tonight, I'm afraid; where are *you* living these days?"

"I've taken an apartment in Kuwait, just as a *pied-à-terre*. But I'm traveling most of the time, mainly on the Arabian peninsula."

"Nice of you to pay us a visit, even if Iran is operating in the red."

"My pleasure. Any country with twenty billion dollars a year in oil revenue can't be all bad. But is it safe?" Harry tipped his head toward the embassy garden, where guards were moving among the floodlit pines.

"Well, there are a few terrorists around town, and they manage to assassinate an Iranian government type every now and then. How long has it been since you were here last?"

"Four months."

"They haven't killed any Americans lately, but as you doubtless know, they've been killing one or two American officers every year or so—and the betting is that they'll try to pick off a few more. They're still pretty angry at Washington for backing the Shah, and they think it embarrasses the Shah to have Americans killed in his own capital."

*"Et voilà."* Harry had long ago found that it impressed certain customers to speak a few words of French, and the habit had stuck with him. *"Does* it embarrass him?"

"Yes, it does, rather. I must say it even makes me a bit nervous. There were sirens earlier tonight, far off. And then I was walking in the garden a few minutes ago, and I thought I heard an explosion and shots in the distance. Not good for the digestion, I can tell you. Now, dear boy, tell me how I can help. Who do you want to know?"

Hobie, good old Hobie, gestured toward the ballroom with his highball glass.

"Who do you think I should know?"

"How about little Harnischfeger, the East German ambassador? The one pumping his arm up and down as he dances? Charming chap. Everybody says he's really a count, but he's suppressed his title because he's a Marxist."

Harry observed this worthy without enthusiasm. He was not interested in Marxists.

"And there's old Dr. Jahanbari, from the agriculture ministry. And a certain Miss Olsen, from Buffalo, with no known means of support. See, the young woman in the blue jersey dress. There. The woman with the big—"

"Yes. Nice. But look, Hobie, *mon vieux*. I'm not interested in bureaucrats. Or tourists. Show me somebody who'd be *interesting*."

"Those *are* amusing people, old sport," Hobie said. "Jahanbari knows all about—" He noticed the blank look on Harry's face. "You mean interesting, ah, professionally? For your business, I mean?"

"You guessed it."

"Why didn't you say so? How about that old gaffer in the corner? The one with the carnation falling out of his lapel. Mr. Kashfizadeh. Owns half of Khuzistan. Used to be—"

"Thanks, but no thanks. He's senile. I can tell from here."

"Well. If you're going to be *exclusive*, you might enjoy meeting Mrs. Zadar. The Iranian woman at the table on the far left. Her husband supplies the Iranian railroads with railway ties. Oops. The woman who just tipped over her glass."

"The fat one? She's drunk."

"She might seem a little *merry*, but—"

"Come on, Hobie. I don't work crazies, and I don't work drunks. I'm not a swindler, I'm a technician. I may have an odd occupation, but it has its satisfactions. And it makes me a pretty fair living, when my luck is good."

"Which it isn't just now, unless I miss my guess?"

"It could use a little help." Harry smiled. "I've been getting a lot of competition lately from the British and the French. Unscrupulous types."

"Nobody's perfect," Hobie said, gazing philosophically at little Harnischfeger's up-and-down arm.

"Please help me, Hobie. I promise you, the next missile base I see, you'll be the first to know."

"Now, now, I'm happy to help without any thought of recompense. Just buy me a whiskey-soda now and then when I retire."

"*Merde*, Hobie. I bet there's a couple of trust funds waiting for you in Switzerland. Set up by your friends in Washington."

"One has to think of one's old age, doesn't one? And I have a bit of child support to pay; I haven't led a blameless life, you know. Now pay attention. You see that Iranian woman with the hawknose? And the big gold necklace?"

"I do, I do. It's the size of a horse collar. She looks quite *sympathique*. Just my type."

"Thought so. Now, she . . ."

# 2

AN UNMARKED, FOUR-DOOR DODGE SEDAN RACED NORTH-
ward along Ayendeh Avenue. The muscular Iranian chauffeur
slammed on the brakes when the car came to Chaman Street,
which was now roped off by the police. The driver and an
Iranian bodyguard stayed in the front seat. An American in
rumpled evening clothes clambered out of the back seat and
stared down Chaman Street.

There was little left to see. Ambulances had taken away the
five bodies. A detective was dusting the villa gateway for fingerprints, working by the glare from the police floodlights that had
been set up on the sidewalk. Another detective was photographing the chalk marks that showed where the bodies of
Pegano and the women had lain. Still another detective came
through the gates, carrying a stack of pamphlets that had been
found inside. A couple of curious schoolboys, up long past their
bedtime, looked on with yawns.

The American, a pale and pudgy man in his forties,
straightened his black bow tie and strode over to the police
laboratory van. He asked, in bad Farsi, for the ranking officer
on the scene. A foxy-faced man in a brown raincoat appeared
and made a small bow.

"I'm Feeney from the U.S. embassy," the American said,
speaking English now and making his voice deep and authorita-
tive-sounding. He had been drinking, which made him skip the
courtesies that are so important to Iranians. "Where's the body

of the American?" he rumbled. "Where are the personal effects? We must have his personal effects."

"How do you do, sir. I am Colonel Avali," the foxy-faced man said slowly. He did not identify himself further, which suggested that he was an intelligence officer.

"Hello there. Is the body in the house?"

Colonel Avali looked at Feeney through narrowed eyes. "I am sorry, sir; I can say nothing."

"Nothing? Look, I've been sent here by our ambassador. He's having a party and they called from your headquarters and made him come to the telephone. They said terrorists had blown up—"

"I am sorry." Rank is important in Iranian life, and Colonel Avali did not have the authority to divulge any details of the case. Contacts between the embassy and the intelligence service were generally cordial, but they were carried on at higher levels.

"Come on, Avali. Here's my card. I'm a first secretary at the embassy. We need confirmation of the American's name. We need a look at the body." He glanced at the man carrying the pamphlets. "What's that—propaganda? Political propaganda leaflets at the scene? We'll need to know what they say."

Colonel Avali allowed himself a smile. "You must be from the political section of the embassy. They are always interested in what the pamphlets say. I can tell you that these say the usual 'Down with the Shah,' 'An end to corruption.' The customary Communist filth."

Feeney was new to Iran, but he guessed correctly that the colonel was misquoting the pamphlets somewhat. The colonel wanted to seem to oblige Feeney without actually giving him precise information. But Feeney wanted badly to learn the text of the leaflets. Then he could quote them to the ambassador and show that he had managed to get the confidence of local officials. Then he could prepare a cable to the State Department in Washington. But he knew that if he cabled incorrect quotations, he would look bad before long. In a day or two, the chief CIA official at the embassy would go over to intelligence headquarters, have a cup of tea and some cookies—they served Occidental cookies to visitors—and get all, or almost all, the details, which he, too, would transmit to Washington.

"Come on, Avali, goddammit, take some responsibility." The liquor and the late hour had made Feeney cranky. "We need—"

"I think you are new to the Middle East, sir," Avali said evenly. "I wish you a good tour of duty." He turned and began giving orders to the men. Two of them began to rub away the chalk marks on the sidewalk.

By busying himself with other things, the colonel avoided the necessity of further words with Feeney. He also gained time. And in a few moments, as he had hoped, a Volkswagen drew up at the police cordon. A tall, gaunt Iranian in a Cardin suit stepped out.

Feeney was quick to buttonhole the newcomer, sensing his high rank.

"Feeney, United States embassy," he boomed, fishing a calling card from the chest pocket of his tuxedo.

"A pleasure to meet you, Mr. Feeney; I am General Mehrani," the tall man said, smiling down on Feeney with a benign expression that several Americans had told him was Lincolnesque. "How may I be of service?"

Even Feeney knew who the general was: one of the deputy directors of the intelligence service, an old soldier, nearing retirement, who was not competing for promotion when the present director retired. A good Joe, they said at the embassy —he's been briefing and debriefing the CIA guys for so many years that his English is perfect.

"General, sir, that colonel what's-his-name there has been refusing to cooperate. We need a quick briefing on this tragedy."

"Refusing to cooperate? I shall see that he is reprimanded."

Of course, General Mehrani would do no such thing. His wife's niece was married to the colonel, and the general himself had arranged the colonel's transfer from the army engineers to the intelligence service years ago after some unpleasantness about contracts for barracks construction.

Feeney felt relieved as the colonel came up, saluted the general, and spoke in a burst of quick and idiomatic Farsi, which Feeney could not understand.

"Well, now," the general said to Feeney when the colonel was finished. "As you can see from the chalk marks, three people were killed here in the street. One was the American you are asking about. I am very sorry to be obligated to confirm his death. The other two were our own operatives—women agents, actually. We are not yet sure how the three came to die."

Feeney failed to say that he was sorry to hear that the women agents had been killed. The general noted his discourtesy.

"Two terrorists died in the villa there, resisting arrest," the general went on, a little more coolly now. "They were evidently Iranians, but we have no idea what terrorist group they belong to, or who they are. And we are puzzled. These men are older than the usual left-wing terrorists. They look like educated, highly Westernized men, which makes it unlikely that they would be right-wing, Islamic dissidents. Their identification papers were false and give us no leads."

"How do you know they were terrorists?"

"The neighbors tipped us off that they were acting suspiciously. We found four Swedish submachine guns hidden under mattresses in the villa. And a supply of pamphlets denouncing the government. But these pamphlets don't take the usual Marxist line about corruption and revolution. They denounce His Majesty the Shah for living in luxury, and for trying to spread his power in the Persian Gulf region." The general's voice turned sarcastic. "They say it's wicked that His Majesty always travels by helicopter and doesn't drive around among the people. They complain about his ski holidays in Switzerland, his personal wealth, his letting his family wear the crown jewels. The pamphlets go on and on. But they bear no name of any terrorist group. Only a picture of a bird, the kind we call a *bolbol*. You have a longer word for it: 'nightingale.' "

"How about the American, General? That's what we really need to know." Feeney was not the sort to be interested in nightingales.

"He was carrying a regular U.S. passport, issued at Athens in the name of James Peters."

Feeney had a little black phone-number notebook in his hand now. He was scribbling on a back page. The general watched this exotic behavior. He himself had junior officers to do his note-taking for him.

"Before you write too much, Mr. Feeney, I must tell you that we know this man from long ago. There was enough left of his face for our people to identify it. His real name was James Pegano. He worked with your Central Intelligence Agency here when Mr. Kennedy was your President. Isn't that right, Avali? It was Avali who recognized who he was."

The colonel nodded with a little grimace of pride.

"When this Pegano worked here, he was a fine official," the general went on. "He instructed our people in interrogation techniques, that sort of thing. He had been in your Office of Strategic Services during World War Two."

"What happened to him here?"

"I can tell you, but unofficially, that he had bad feelings about not getting a promotion, as I recall. Or perhaps it was also a question of misappropriation of funds. Or both. And he left your service."

Feeney scribbled on.

"Then, I am sorry to say, we received reports that he had been involved in illegal commerce in this area," the general said.

"You mean crooked dealings with Iranians?"

"No, across the border in Afghanistan—"

"Trafficking in dope?"

"Something more interesting, and almost as universal: smuggling gemstones. You have probably heard of emerald-smuggling in Ecuador and jade-smuggling in Burma. There is also a little-known trade in Afghanistan in a certain blue, semiprecious stone."

"You mean lapis lazuli?"

"Yes, that is the name. Your compatriot Pegano was a large-scale dealer in lapis lazuli. It was carried illegally out of Afghanistan sometimes by plane, sometimes overland to Iran."

"What was he doing here?"

"Your guess is as good as ours; he was presumably involved in smuggling something to the terrorists. The explosive that killed him was nitroglycerin. He must have been carrying it with him. Perhaps he had smuggled it in for terrorists to use against His Majesty the Shah."

"But why would he be carrying it himself around downtown Teheran? If he were just delivering it to terrorists, surely he would have done that someplace else."

"All I can say, Mr. Feeney, is that sometimes we find you Americans inscrutable."

Feeney was not amused. "Where's the body now? And the personal effects?"

"I'm afraid we will have to keep everything for a while, while we start our investigation. But we will hand it all over to the embassy in a few days."

Which meant that the CIA chief would get credit for recovering the material. Feeney looked glum.

"Cheer up, Mr. Feeney; things will work out." The general glanced at his Cartier wristwatch. "Now, if you like, you can hear some news about this incident. In your mother tongue."

He ushered Feeney to the window of the laboratory van, and the driver turned the dashboard radio to the Teheran English-language station. First it played "Tea for Two." Then a newscaster with an Australian accent came on the air. He went on and on about King Hussein of Jordan and the Sultan of Oman, monarchs friendly to the Shah. At last came the news Feeney was waiting for:

"Two Marxist terrorists died in a shoot-out with Iranian police early today after they opened fire on innocent civilians from a hideout in downtown Teheran. The only other casualty was an American tourist. His name is being withheld pending notification of his next of kin. The police confiscated a quantity of Marxist propaganda leaflets and several firearms.

"In Jerusalem today—"

The general nodded, and the driver switched off the radio

"But that's all wrong," Feeney said indignantly, gesturing with his notebook. "That's gross distortion. You know damn well the international news agencies monitor those broadcasts. They'll pick up that false version and report it all over the world. That's what they're going to hear first in Washington. God *damn!*"

The general said nothing. The colonel said nothing. Feeney stood by the van, his hands on his plump hips. His lips moved to accommodate a small hiccup. At length the general smiled his Lincolnesque smile again. Now it was a weary smile. He turned toward his Volkswagen. He said something in Farsi, very quickly and softly, to the colonel. He climbed into the car and drove off.

"Hey, you," the colonel barked at Feeney. "You. Get the hell out of here."

Harry's mind was on business as he strolled toward the table where the hawk-nosed woman sat, talking to a young Iranian ensign in dress uniform. From the corner of his eye, Harry noticed that Miss Olsen, she with no known means of support, was standing now in the doorway to the ballroom. She looked cheerful and bright, although maybe a little hard. The blue dress clung nicely to her body. Harry put her out of his mind, shot his cuffs, and slipped into a chair at the hawk-nosed woman's table, murmuring, "May I join you?"

The woman smiled a warm smile. Hobie had said her name was Mrs. Naghi, and her husband had made a fortune importing rubber tires and automobile parts. But the husband was nowhere in sight, and Mrs. Naghi seemed to be concentrating on eating the mints in the cut-glass dish in front of her. An instant after Harry sat down, the ensign, looking relieved, slipped away.

Mrs. Naghi was in her fifties, too old for her violet off-the-shoulder evening gown—a Halston, perhaps—and too motherly-looking for her necklace, which was probably Van Cleef & Arpels, to judge by the opulent design. She had a wide, amiable mouth, which was overshadowed, so to speak, by her nose. Already, Harry felt some admiration for her: many well-off Iranian women were having their noses remodeled by plastic surgeons, he knew; Mrs. Naghi had shown strength of character by leaving hers in its natural state. Harry took a mint and sat listening to the band play "Begin the Beguine." Then he leaned toward Mrs. Naghi and said, *"J'aime beaucoup le foxtrot."*

"Oh, you are from France," Mrs. Naghi said, also speaking French.

"No, but French was part of my upbringing."

"How is that? You were raised in Paris?"

"In Connecticut. But my parents are White Russian émigrés; they spoke French around the court in St. Petersburg as children; my family served the czars for centuries."

"Ah, the old Russia," Mrs. Naghi said, as though the days of the czars had been but yesterday. As though her husband's having made a million dollars in commissions—Hobie's estimate—on a tire-plant construction contract had given her an appreciation of the finer things in life. Perhaps it had, Harry thought.

Mrs. Naghi took yet another mint. "Then you must be of the nobility," she said between nibbles.

"Permit me to present myself. I am Prince Mikhail Arloff. But titles mean little these days. Everybody calls me Harry."

"Enchanted to meet you. My name is Minou Naghi. It is nice to meet a *real* Russian, not one of those tiresome types from the Soviet embassy." Another mint. "I have a friend who is crazy about *la vieille Russie*. Perhaps you know her, Fatemeh Lajestani? The widow of Manuchehr Lajestani? That was her son I was talking to just now, the man in the sailor suit. Their family has lots of real estate in Tabriz, where the big cement plant is going up."

"I don't think I have had the pleasure."

"You'd adore her; she has a collection of those toy Easter eggs they used to make in St. Petersburg, the enamel ones with all the gold on them, and the little jewels. Poor Manuchehr, she used to make him buy her one every time he took her to Paris. Once she lost one on the Air France plane coming back."

"How awful." Harry clucked his tongue sympathetically, but he was feeling happy. The conversation was going well. Soon he could start making his pitch.

"She was showing it to the stewardess, and she fell asleep with it in her hand. She must have dropped it, somewhere between Zurich and Rome, she thinks. It must have rolled along on the floor. The stewardess was sweet, she says. She offered to make an announcement on the loudspeaker and ask the passengers to look for a gold-and-enamel Easter egg decorated with diamond chips. But poor Fatemeh is so shy. She said, Never mind, she'd make her husband buy another one!"

Harry smiled. "Those Fabergé eggs are pretty. And, of course, they are interesting from the historical point of view."

Mrs. Naghi's attention wandered for a moment. She took yet another mint. History was clearly not her prime interest.

"But there are a lot of false Fabergé eggs around," Harry went on. "In fact, I can assure you there is really no way of proving that one of the eggs is the real thing."

"Really? Then if you buy them it is possible to be cheated?"

Mrs. Naghi's eyes widened. Wait till she told Fatemeh.

"An unpleasant possibility. Even a likelihood, I would say. It means they are not a good investment."

There was a flash of blue at Harry's left, just as he was about to embark on Phase One of the pitch. He glanced leftward and saw that Miss Olsen had sat down next to him. He also saw that her eyes were a fine china-blue, and looking warmly into his. He smiled a small smile. Then, with something of an effort of will, he turned back to Mrs. Naghi, and Phase One.

"Actually, madame, choosing wisely about what things to put money in has been a matter of enormous importance to my family over the years. Life-and-death importance, you might say; we have been through some difficult times." He kept on speaking French, which he hoped Miss Olsen did not understand.

"I can imagine," Mrs. Naghi said. "Those dirty Communists."

"And the inflation in Germany after World War One. And World War Two in Paris."

Mrs. Naghi shook her head. "Awful."

"I can tell you that we have learned a lesson over the years that is still useful today."

"What is that?"

"That it is all very well to buy securities or houses or paintings or fine shotguns, but when hard times come, what really keeps its value is—" Harry paused in mid-sentence.

"Is what?" Mrs. Naghi said. Now the band was playing "From This Moment On." An Iranian youth with long sideburns had seized a microphone and was crooning the lyrics. Mrs. Naghi was leaning toward Harry now to hear his words over the music. Her eyes had a glint of cheerful materialism. The gold necklace, seen up close, fulfilled its mission of distracting attention from her crepey décolletage.

"What really keeps its value—" Harry said. Then he stopped again. It was true, after all; he could definitely feel a foot rubbing, ever so gently, against his left calf, from Miss Olsen's side. When he first noticed the pressure, it was so faint that he thought it was his imagination. But now the moving touch was continuing, so gently that were he to mention it to Miss Olsen, she could say it was accidental. He glanced down and to the left, but the skirt of the tablecloth hid his view. Miss Olsen's legs were crossed. It was evidently her right foot that was making the contact; she must have kicked her right shoe off onto the floor.

Harry shot a glance at Miss Olsen. Her face had a quizzical expression, but she said nothing. Evidently she did not speak French. The dark blond hair was very fine. And the bosom. He tried not to look at the bosom. Even after he had spent—by his rough count—thirty-five nights now, in four countries, without a woman. Well, except for an Armenian widow in Dubai. And that didn't count; that had been business. Speaking of which, he resolutely picked up the conversational thread, still in French. Looking at Miss Olsen's neckline would be all very pleasant, but it would not pay for Emily's governess.

"Jewelry. Fine jewelry. That's what keeps its value better than anything," he said hastily to Mrs. Naghi. But now he felt a tapping on his left sleeve.

"I'm real sorry to interrupt," Miss Olsen said in English, in a voice that was surprisingly resonant and low. "You two must be talking about something that's real interesting. Could you wave at that little man for me? And ask him to bring me a brandy and ginger?" She crinkled the blue eyes in a way that Harry had thought had gone out with the early June Allyson.

Abandoning Phase One for the moment, Harry did so, and asked the waiter for brandy and soda for Mrs. Naghi and himself. There was really no choice now but to switch to English and include Miss Olsen in the conversation, even though he had already calculated that she was a poor business prospect. The blue dress was cheaply made, despite its charms. And she was wearing a skimpy necklace of seed pearls. There were introductions all around—her first name was Gail—and Harry said doggedly, "We were talking about investments."

But now, strange to say, Miss Olsen was suddenly not listening. She was looking out across the ballroom. Harry, curious, followed her gaze. The ambassador had disappeared for a while, but now he was back on the dance floor, dancing with another Iranian matron. A marine guard had walked up to him. The marine was saying something into the ambassador's ear; both were tall men. With a flurry of apologetic gestures, the ambassador steered his dancing partner to a table and strode out of the ballroom. His craggy face was solemn.

"That's a beautiful necklace you're wearing," Harry said, turning back to Mrs. Naghi.

Miss Olsen said, "It sure is lovely." Her foot was still moving against Harry's leg. Very slowly. It felt good, even though it made it difficult to concentrate on Phase One.

"Thank you very much," Mrs. Naghi said. "I wanted a sable coat, but my husband gave it to me instead. He said I had too many fur coats already. What could I say? It's his money." She laughed—a good laugh that pealed slowly, like a bell.

A waiter brought the brandies.

"Your husband has excellent taste, Mrs. Naghi," Harry said somewhat distractedly. Miss Olsen's foot was still moving, moving as though it had a mind of its own. He found himself wondering what her legs looked like. He noticed that two Iranian men at the next table were giving her interested glances. She must be an enormous success with the Iranians, with her hair, her eyes, her bosom . . .

"Your husband has very sound judgment, madame," Harry heard himself say. "That is what my family has found, that fine jewelry is a matchless investment, for beauty, of course, and also for security."

"And these are difficult times," Mrs. Naghi said. "I thought I heard sirens a while ago; I wonder what *that* was about."

"From This Moment On" had ended. The youth with the

sideburns had surrendered the microphone. The band began to play a very slow fox trot, "Mood Indigo." Slow fox trots were all Harry ever tried to dance, because of his bad leg. This fox trot was so slow that he could take a few minutes off and ask Miss Olsen to dance . . . He put the thought from his mind. The ugly facts are that I am a middle-aged man with no real profession, he said to himself. There is nobody in the world I love except Emily and I want to make sure I can give her all the best things in life, which is going to take a lot of money. Let the lawyers and the doctors and the architects and the engineers dance with the pretty girls from Buffalo, he thought, I have to hustle.

"They *are* difficult times, Mrs. Naghi," he said, as Miss Olsen's foot continued its ministrations. He paused again, trying not to laugh or to blush. The pause was too long this time. Mrs. Naghi peered at him as though he might be drunk. He smiled at her. Very deliberately he took a big sip, almost a bite, of his brandy and soda. He thought he could feel the alcohol working inside him, undermining Phase One. Ah well, all work and no play . . . Harry turned to Miss Olsen. Would she like to dance? The answer was a delicious nod. He turned back to Mrs. Naghi: Would she excuse them for a few minutes? *Mais oui, mais oui,* she would.

A moment later, from the dance floor Harry glanced back at the table. Mrs. Naghi was watching him and Miss Olsen with a look not of hurt feelings but of friendly interest. In the Middle East, Harry reflected, most middle-aged women are realists.

# 3

WHAT HAPPENED AFTERWARD WAS LARGELY HARRY'S OWN
fault, though not entirely. It was his fault because he should
have thought more about what motives might lead a self-reli-
ant, desirable American girl in her late twenties to thrust herself on a battered compatriot who could, at best, be called a
soldier of fortune and, at worst, several other things. Yet it was
not all his fault: in succumbing to the pressure of Miss Olsen's
foot, he was succumbing in part to the deep-down loneliness
that gets to many American male travelers in the Muslim Middle East, no matter how many dinner dances they attend. This
is because attractive, available women they can really talk to
are relatively few and far between. And if a traveler wants to
do more than talk to a woman in those semipuritanical countries, he may have to reckon with her brother, father and uncles
and with the detectives stationed in the lobby of the hotel. Not
to mention her husband, if she has one.

And so it was that Harry Arloff found it an enormous pleasure to be dancing with Miss Olsen. Found the friendly pressure
of her foot replaced by the friendlier presence of her torso.
Found, through the glow of brandy, that he had no regrets for
having abandoned Mrs. Naghi to her mints, and no desire to go
back to the table. Found himself happily exchanging routine
information with Gail Olsen over the whining of the saxo-
phones. He began by saying he was a businessman, that he was
from Greenwich, Connecticut—he left out the business about

St. Petersburg—that he was *désolé*—sorry—about his limp, if she had noticed it—why no, she hadn't—and that it was from a polo injury long ago. She said she was from Buffalo—as Hobie had reported—that she had been studying acting in New York, that she was visiting friends of her parents' in Teheran. And that a sweet Englishman named Hobie Stiles had told her she absolutely must make sure she got to know Harry.

Good old Hobie, Harry thought.

Somehow, apropos of friends, Gail soon suggested they go on to a couple of other parties she knew of, and Harry found himself unquestioningly accepting; it was going to be another rowdy Teheran night. So they got their coats from the mirrored coatroom and slipped out through the main entrance to the residence, past the marine guard's telephone room. Its door was now closed. They stood for a moment on the marble steps of the residence while a doorman summoned the Mercedes taxi that Gail had hired for the night. Harry, watching every penny, had let his own cab go when he had arrived.

Then Harry nestled in the back seat of the Mercedes, happily watching the tall pine trees slip by as they drove through the embassy compound. Happily taking a nip from the fat silver flask that blossomed in Gail's hand. Happily watching her blow a kiss to the guards when the taxi purred out through the gates.

It's a strange city, Harry thought then, as they drove past a spotlit statue of the Shah's father, Reza the Great. It was he who began modernizing the country and changed its name from Persia to Iran. If you don't look hard, Harry reflected, you think Teheran is like a European capital. It has high-rise buildings, modern traffic lights, even some churches here and there. But when you look closer, you realize that it is deeply Iranian —the modern center of a Muslim but non-Arab culture that inspires a heady pride in the Iranians: they are proud of their sumptuous mosques, matchless caviar, nightingales, roses, jewels and poets. And proud, too, of their thousands of years of history, symbolized by the ancient ruins at Persepolis—the site that the Shah chose for the celebration, a few years ago, of the 2,500th anniversary of the founding of the Persian Empire.

The Mercedes sped southward down Ferdowsi Avenue, a European-style boulevard adorned with a statue, not of a general but of an old-time Persian poet. The shop windows that were still lit at this late hour looked European enough—yet they were displaying not cars or clothes but carpets, thousands of Persian carpets.

"Fabulous, aren't they?" Harry said.

Gail's mind was on other commodities, however. "Look there," she said, "that big building on the right. Know what that is?"

"Sure, it's a government bank building."

"It's where they keep the crown jewels, isn't it?" she said, peering through the rear window as the building receded behind them. "Wow. Just think . . ."

The jewelry that interested him most at that moment was the ridiculous seed-pearl necklace at her throat. "Just think what?" he said. Her ear was close. Wild horses could not have prevented him from giving it a nuzzle.

She giggled. "Quit that. A minute. Just think, those jewels are worth a lot more than a billion dollars, a man told me tonight. A deputy minister of something. Dr. Fa— Fa—"

"Fakhur. Deputy minister of commerce. A dirty old man."

"Speak for yourself," she said, giggling again. She gave directions to the silent driver, and the Mercedes swung left into a neighborhood of chunky brick villas and apartment houses, built in the days before the oil boom, where, Harry knew, non-Iranian teachers and scholars liked to live. They stopped there in a narrow side street and made their way down a brick staircase into a basement apartment. It looked Western, but it reeked gloriously of cheap Iranian red wine. It was jammed with Bohemian-looking Iranians—"I love those big black mustaches," Gail said—and raffish foreigners.

There seemed to be other people from Buffalo, including a fat, professorial man who could curse in Farsi. There was a haggard German who was in the carpet trade, a gang of Englishmen, drunk as lords, and an Italian who stirred the bowl of red-wine punch with his hand. There was much loud, hilarious conversation; and, for some reason, they all sang, or tried to sing, the Eton boating song. By this time, Gail was sitting in Harry's lap.

Then he and she got back into the Mercedes, and they sped back uptown, while Gail's quick hands plied him with more brandy and, now, played jokes with his body, switching from tickle to caress. She unknotted his fancy French necktie, tossed it with an odd brusqueness onto the taxi floor, and began playing her hand-jokes again. Had Harry been younger perhaps, or soberer, or braver, or prouder of himself, he would have made her put the flask down, would have busied himself seriously with her hair and her lips and her dress. Would have told the driver to turn off toward his hotel, the Bristol. As it was, he simply put his arms around her.

"You're not—not like the others," she whispered in his ear, and he foolishly accepted that explanation for why she was here with him. She must be lonely, too, he thought, after too many lecherous Iranian playboys, too many fat men from Buffalo.

Gail straightened up again when they drove through a tall iron gate. A manservant in a white jacket grinned a welcome —his face was teakwood-colored in the headlights—and waved them on up an asphalted driveway, past a swimming pool. Harry could make out the heads of swimmers, two by two, on the obsidian surface, and much splashing toward the shallow end.

"An underwater orgy," Gail said, laughing. "We sure don't have them back home."

They parked beside a big house that was mostly dark, and Gail and Harry picked their way along shadowy corridors, littered here and there with towels. They came into a candlelit library decorated with Georgian oak paneling that was so finely carved that Harry decided it must have been imported from England. Iranian men were standing around in various stages of undress, mingling with towel-clad French girls with wet hair who were making conversation imperturbably, as though they were in cocktail dresses. Harry gathered the girls were stewardesses. From other rooms came shouts, in French and Farsi, and bumps and thumps. Once, before Harry and Gail left, there was a soprano cry that was almost a scream.

Then came more time in the taxi, more brandy, more probings of his body, until—pretty drunk now—Harry found himself at Gail's side in a stifling nightclub somewhere nearer the center of town. A turbaned male performer, dark and fierce, swallowed fire. A belly dancer writhed and whirled, the sweat glistening on the small of her back. A fistfight broke out in the audience, with much shouting, and the next thing Harry remembered was being in a cellar saloon, where grim-faced Iranian bar girls were talking to the male customers from behind the bar. He and Gail were waited on by a bald Iranian bartender with dirty fingernails who poured the brandy without measuring it out in shots.

And then Harry found himself in a drab bedroom, like one of the dormitory cubicles at the military school he had gone to long ago. The light bulb overhead was the same, but here it had no shade. The feel of the coarse coverlet was much the same, but now there was the feel of Gail's quick hands undressing him. And now there was the sudden appearance of her body—less pretty than he had imagined—and the bobbling of the big breasts. She was all over him, being brisk but very skillful. Dazed by the brandy, and the light, and the different things she was doing, Harry began to laugh, until she put her mouth hard on his. There was no sound then except the clanking of the bedstead—and from the floorboards a sudden squeak. Harry sat up and looked around him. The bald bartender was in the doorway with a hand-held movie camera, filming the scene.

Faiz Kiani, a versatile Pakistani, was surprised to hear loud knocks on the door of his room in the Darius Hotel in Rezaiyeh, a small city in the northwest corner of Iran near the borders of Russia, Iraq and Turkey. It was well past midnight.

"Sir! Sir! Telephone call from Teheran!" the night clerk shouted.

Faiz put down the book of mystic poetry he had been reading. He trotted down the stairs in his dressing gown.

"Cabin two, sir," the clerk said in Farsi.

Faiz shut himself into one of the evil-smelling wooden booths where guests received their telephone calls. The Darius was a third-class hotel, not the sort of place where international tour guides like Faiz usually choose to stay.

It was half a minute before a man's voice came on the line.

"That you, Charley?" the voice said, although Faiz's name was not Charley.

"Yes."

"Have a good trip?"

"Yes, thanks." Faiz had driven into Rezaiyeh from Turkey the day before. But he did not discuss the trip over the phone line, which might be tapped.

"How's, um, the project?" The caller had an odd accent. He seemed to be a Central European who had spent many years in England.

"Fine. The cabinets are in, all the fixtures are ready."

"That's just fine, Charley. How are you enjoying it up there?"

"Fine," Faiz said, although in fact he was bored stiff. He couldn't even get the BBC on his portable radio up here, although the airwaves were full of broadcasts in Russian (the Soviet border was only a hundred miles to the north).

"Um, Charley, look here, we've had a little accident down

~ *33* ~

here, which may create some problems unless we act quickly. So we're going to need your delivery as soon as possible. *Just* as soon as possible. Not in three days, as we'd planned."

Faiz frowned into the old-fashioned telephone receiver. His caller was talking too much over the phone.

"I have things pretty much all arranged up here," Faiz said with a trace of pride. "I could probably leave here in an hour or two. That means with luck I could drop by your office in the early afternoon. I'll check out here now and be on my way, and if there's any sort of hitch, I'll give you a ring."

"Tip-top, Charley. Hope to see you in a few hours. It's, um, it's pretty important."

"How so?"

"Um, your American friend has gotten hurt; we're having to replace him."

"Isn't that hard to do at short notice?"

"Not too difficult, actually; we're already getting another chap. But things may get, um, a little complicated. You'd better hurry."

"I see. Cheerio, then."

The caller, perhaps even more tense than he seemed, hung up without saying good-bye.

Faiz went back to his room, dressed, checked out, and piled into his dusty Plymouth Voyager Maxiwagon, a kind of passenger van. Then he drove, with imprudent speed, through the darkened streets.

"Cut it out," Harry said. He wrapped the coverlet around his waist and moved toward the bartender, who stopped filming and stepped back down into the hall. The bartender's place was taken by a square-faced man holding a small object in his hand. At first Harry thought it was a camera. Then he saw it was a gun. He sat back down on the bed. There was a flash of blue as Gail grabbed her clothes and bounded into a side room. That must be a bathroom, Harry thought. His head was suddenly clear, but it ached. He shut his eyes an instant, then opened them. The gunman was still there.

"Prince Mikhail Nikolaevich Arloff?" the gunman said. His tone was flat.

"Yes." Harry squinted a little in the bright light. "Only everyone calls me Harry."

The gunman did not seem inclined to call him Harry. "They will call you worse things than that back home when they see our film of you." he said. He was a European, perhaps a Frenchman, who spoke American English well, as though he had spent years working, say, in an overseas branch of an American bank. He moved forward into the room. The floorboards squeaked again. He stood solidly on the balls of his feet, and the jacket of his cheap gray suit hung open, showing a wash-and-wear shirt over a flat belly. His square jaw was gray with stubble. He must have had a bad night, Harry thought. Or he must have been waiting hours for this moment.

"What do you say to that, Arloff?" the man said. The barrel of the gun gave a jerk upward in his hand. It was a revolver, probably .38 caliber. Too big for this sort of work, Harry thought.

"Not much I can say, I guess." Slowly, so as not to make the gunman nervous, Harry looked around for his clothes. He could not see his underpants, and so, still moving slowly, he reached for his trousers.

"Hey, Gail," the gunman called. "Does he have a knife in his clothes or anything?"

"Nope, not even a key ring," she said evenly through the door. Her voice was harder now. She was running the faucets. "All he's got in his pockets is a wallet and an address book and a little leather thing, to hold visiting cards, I guess."

So much for the caresses in the taxi, Harry thought. So much for going to the other parties with her—so he could not possibly be tempted to return to Mrs. Naghi. So that, perhaps, the gunman and the bartender would have time to set all this up. So that there would be time for the brandy to dull any suspicions he might have. He put on his trousers.

"You are from Greenwich, Connecticut," the gunman said. "You are a man of affairs. You have a reputation to protect. Your title. Many things." Harry nodded. He buttoned his shirt. It smelled of brandy. He put on his socks and took one shoe in his hand. In the bathroom the faucet noise had stopped. The toilet flushed. The gunman's eyes jerked briefly toward the bathroom door. In that instant they had a hungry glitter, which Harry recognized. I wonder how long it's been since *he's* slept with a woman, Harry thought.

"You are married," the gunman said. He gestured with the revolver muzzle toward Harry's right hand, where, affectedly in the Continental fashion, he wore his wedding ring. He found that wearing it made women trust him more. "You know your life can very easily be ruined now," the gunman said.

The bathroom door opened. Gail came out, wearing jeans and a tight silk blouse. She must have stashed the change of clothes in the bathroom hours ago, Harry thought, or maybe one of the goons put it there for her. This was a well-organized operation, whatever it was.

"Morning, honey," the gunman said, giving her a lingering look. "You okay?"

"Hi, Marcel. Yes, sure," she said. "You think I could get a cup of—"

Harry threw the shoe, sidearm but hard. It bounced off Marcel's jaw with a thwack. Harry bounded out the doorway, which led to a flight of steps. He hopped down them, using his strong leg. The hall turned right, and there stood the bald bartender. He got Harry in the solar plexus with a left jab. Harry fell down. When he got up, the bartender was standing close. In his right hand was a knife. The bartender's breath reeked of scallions, a favorite food in Iran. "Go back," he said in English, adding a rush of Farsi words which ran together in a growl.

So Harry went back up the stairs, stumbling only once. In

the bedroom there was a small armchair flecked with cigarette burns. He set himself down in it, holding his stomach. Gail was sitting on the bed. She was pale now without her makeup, pale from fatigue and who knows what emotions. Harry's mind was working quickly, but he had no idea what was going on in her head. He found himself wishing he knew. She saw he was looking at her, and bit her lip.

Marcel was standing where he had stood before. The shoe had not marked him, but Harry could hear him breathing more quickly. Boy, I'm really going to get it, Harry thought.

Yet Marcel began talking again as though nothing had happened.

"You came here as a businessman. You have high-society connections in your country. You are invited to the American ambassador's parties as a matter of course. At least to some of his parties. You have a certain limited access to Teheran society. From all this you make money, but your livelihood depends on your good name." Marcel was speaking bitterly now; he clearly made his money in other ways.

"Suppose we develop this film," he said. "Showing you having rather complicated sexual relations with a woman with the body of a chorus girl, whose face is not visible. Showing you drunk but obviously having a wonderful time. Showing you sucking on her breasts like a little boy with lollipops."

No blush appeared on Gail's skin. She was keeping her face impassive, a pallid mask. She's tough, Harry thought, but not quite tough enough for the people she's in with, or for this guy at least. She can't smile when the talk starts to get dirty.

"Suppose we show this film around Teheran," Marcel said. "We don't even have to do that; we can just print up a few frames and mail them out. Like postcards. We send one to Mrs. Fraser. Boom, no more invitations to the ambassador's parties. We send one to Fakhur and his wife; they know a lot of people. Boom, half the government will think you're a dumb degenerate who doesn't know enough to keep from getting himself photographed. We send a few more to some of those rich women who were at the ambassador's house tonight. Boom, they won't let you in the door, prince or no prince. And your business has a lot to do with women, doesn't it, *Your Highness?*" He almost spat the two words.

"Yes."

"Exactly what do you do, anyhow?" Gail asked. So they didn't tell her everything.

"You fill her in," Harry said to Marcel. Harry wanted to know what the man knew about him. What it was that had made him set up this trap. He thought that if he only kept his wits about him he could come out of this all right.

Marcel began to speak crisply, as though reciting from a police dossier. "This man is a diamond salesman, on a commission basis," he said. "It's as though, in your country, he was selling encyclopedias from house to house. He operates on a pretty high level. He travels around these oil countries and he tries to sell stuff to the rich people. Especially the ones that have just made a lot of money, so they haven't had a lot of jewelry before, and now they want to buy themselves some."

"Where does he get the diamonds?" Gail asked.

"From his father-in-law, Jules de Kirsch."

"Gee, I know that name from someplace," Gail said.

"Sure. He's a big-time diamond trader. He has a big family firm. It has offices in New York, Paris and Amsterdam. Isn't that right, *Your Highness?*"

"Right."

"Okay. Listen," Marcel said. The room had a vanity table, painted battleship-gray. He sat on it, resting his gun hand on his thigh. The muzzle was pointed at Harry's waist. "We want your cooperation in a business venture. And you are going to give it to us, or we are going to ruin you. First off, we will arrange to deliver a print of this film to your wife."

Harry glanced at the gun. It looked well taken care of. Whatever the business venture was, it must be crooked as hell. He looked at the gun some more, saying nothing. Then his shoulders began to shake. He was laughing.

# 4

AS FAIZ KIANI GUNNED HIS MAXIWAGON—A VEHICLE DE-
signed to carry groups of passengers over long distances—toward the heart of Rezaiyeh, he became aware of a worrisome
rattle. The noise bothered him; he glanced back over his shoulder to see if there was something lying loose in the vehicle that
might account for the sound. There was not. He grimaced
under his fine gray mustache, tugging abstractedly at his fou-
lard neckerchief.

As it happens, rattles are not unknown in a Maxiwagon,
despite Plymouth's painstaking engineering, especially after a
Maxiwagon has covered scores of thousands of miles toting tourists around the Middle East and the Indian subcontinent as
Faiz's sage-green model had done—and after its body has been
repaired and altered now and then to suit the operator's rather
specialized needs.

Faiz turned down Pahlavi Street, a main boulevard. He
passed the floodlit town hall and the local monument to the
Shah's father. He made two left turns and pulled up in front of
a building that had its ground-floor windows lit despite the
hour: it was a small hospital.

Faiz parked the Maxiwagon in the dark side street.
Through the hospital windows he could see patients waiting
outside the emergency room: wrinkled farmers, black-clad
women, and men wearing brightly colored sashes and baggy
pantaloons: these were Kurds, members of a stateless, perenni-

ally dissident ethnic group that lives in Iran, Iraq and neighboring countries.

A tall, plain girl in Western dress was sitting at the main reception desk.

"Is Dr. Ali here, please?" Faiz said in English. "It's an emergency."

The girl made no reply; she evidently spoke no English. Faiz hesitated a moment, smelling the smell of disinfectant, listening for a doctor's voice among the noises coming from the emergency room. He waved when he glimpsed a stooped, tired-looking man in a white smock, who was shuffling toward the desk.

"Dr. Ali, I must see you; we must deliver the material now," Faiz said, taking the man by the elbow.

Dr. Ali pretended to be studying the clipboard in his hand. "But this is three days earlier than we had planned. And late at night; I cannot be sure that my associates will be available."

"Please."

The doctor nodded. He said something in Kurdish to the girl receptionist, and she disappeared down the hall. She had on a modishly short black skirt; she must be a member of the Kurdish elite, Faiz thought; she must be a Kurd from Iraq, just west of here, who had fled when the Kurdish revolt in Iraq had fizzled. She evidently had to do night work to support herself. Her legs were really not bad at all. As a man of the world, Faiz asked himself what it would be like to sleep with a Kurdish girl. Then, as a good Pakistani, he asked himself whom that girl's family could find as a husband for her; they had probably lost all their property when they fled Iraq. Anyway, he decided, she was probably sleeping with Dr. Ali.

Acting on this assumption, Faiz turned to the doctor with something of a leer and said, "She has pretty legs, doesn't she?"

"She is my sister; her husband was killed during our war in Iraq," Dr. Ali said. Faiz winced inwardly; the delivery was getting off to an awkward start.

The girl came back escorting a young man with long, Beatles-style hair. He had powerful shoulders under his coarse sweater, which was obviously locally made; he looked sleepy and sullen. Faiz distrusted him on sight.

"This is our cousin, Mustafa," the doctor said.

"Pleased to see you," Mustafa said. "Now we go, yes?"

Faiz hesitated; it was always this way in these deals. You were fobbed off from agent to underling so that if anything went wrong, only the underling would be in trouble. But the underlings, Faiz had found, were generally more avaricious, more crooked and less intelligent than their leaders.

Faiz was going to say something to Dr. Ali, but the man had disappeared back into the emergency room. That's what I get for that crack about his sister, Faiz thought.

Mustafa took the seat next to Faiz's in the Maxiwagon and guided him through a succession of dark streets. They pulled up in front of a drab brick building. Mustafa rang the doorbell over and over until a light went on behind a shop window; it was a tailor's shop, evidently with living quarters upstairs.

A fat man in pajamas greeted them with a torrent of Kurdish and repeated bows. Mustafa spoke to him in Kurdish in a soft, urgent voice. The fat man smiled, beckoned them into a back room, and turned on a lamp. Mustafa shut the door behind them. There were endless shelves covered with boxes and scraps of cloth. Very gingerly, with his careful tailor's hands, the fat man took down a European shoe box. He held it while Mustafa worked the lid off cautiously with his fingertips.

"You okay?" Gail asked Harry. "You want a glass of water?"

He was laughing uproariously now, here in this room with the dust and the cigarette burns and the smell of a woman's body.

Marcel's mouth began to move, as if to ask "What's so funny?" But his lips tightened into a thin line. His jaw seemed grayer. He was worried.

Harry laughed and laughed. He coughed a few times. He cleared his throat and wiped his mouth on the coverlet. His headache was worse now from the laughing. But he was smiling.

"Well, funny man?" Marcel said.

"You've been badly briefed," Harry said. He was a little hoarse. "Whatever you're up to, you planned this party well, but you didn't check me out well enough. If you think my wife would care, you're crazy. We're separated. She's moved out of Greenwich; she lives in Manhattan, God knows where. She moves in and out with different people. If you can find her there, the chances are you'll find she has scabs on her elbows. You know what that's from? At school we used to call them mat burns. We got them from wrestling on rough canvas. Only she gets them from swinging. From making love on rough carpets. A lot of carpets. A lot of lovers. Go ahead and send her that film. She'll probably have it projected on her ceiling, to turn her friends on."

Harry reached for his jacket.

"And if you think her father and her uncles would care, think again. If they trusted me an inch, they'd have brought me into the firm with them."

Gail was taking this all in. Clearly, business was what turned *her* on.

"They have me out on the road like this because they want to keep me away from the important part of the business," Harry said. "Show them the film if you want. They think that's what I do all the time anyway. They *know* that's what my wife does. Anyway, one of my uncles-in-law would pay *admission* to see that film. He'd envy me."

Marcel said nothing. The gun sagged, although not much.

"Okay now," Harry said. "Time for me to go. *Au revoir.*"

Marcel shook his head. "Nice speech, friend; it sounded good," he said. "The lady here was interested." He scratched under the wash-and-wear shirt with his free hand. "But, you know, you left out something. You left out Iran. If we show that film around, your goose will be cooked here. We can fix it so you never get another visa to here. So if the Iranian police see you at the airport, they'll pop you back in the plane like you had leprosy. You'd never—"

"Never set foot in Iran again? Fine with me. The Iranians are really too sophisticated for my kind of operation anyway. They do most of their jewel shopping in Europe. Some of them even go shopping in New York. And my reputation in Iran has nothing to do with my reputation in the Arab countries, where the real money is. The Saudis and the Kuwaitis don't trust the Iranians much. If an Iranian told them something about me, they'd be likely to think it was lies. And in those countries I make most of my sales to the men. In a lot of different places. You'd have a hard time figuring out who I deal with on the Arabian peninsula, and where. And the kind of men I deal with there are more rough-and-ready than the men here. If you show them that film, they'll shrug and they'll say, So what, I get in my private jet and fly to Vienna once a year to do that. They'll laugh like hell and they'll look hard at Gail's body and make jokes about whether they ever met her or not."

Silence in the room. The seconds passed. It was still early, and no light seeped in around the sides of the window curtains. They were made of green oilcloth with a pattern of roses, the Iranians' favorite flower. There were some traffic noises in the street now, and Harry thought he smelled fresh bread. Maybe there was a bakery nearby. Somewhere a woman was shouting, over and over, the name of a man or a boy: "Parviz! Parviz! Parviz!"

"All right," Marcel said finally. "If you have really no shame, you leave me no choice. This is your final word? You refuse to cooperate?"

"Yes. Now, if you'll excuse me—"

"Wait." The gun was still there.

"Why?" Harry raised his eyebrows. He was feeling almost

jaunty now. He had been in tough spots before and gotten out of them. These people were amateurs. The smell of bread made him want breakfast. He could already taste the croissants at the Bristol Hotel. When he got back to his room, he would put a call through to Emily. He had earned that.

"I'll show you why," Marcel said, and he called, "Alireza!"

The bartender clumped back up the stairs and into the room. Again the floorboards creaked. The camera was gone, but the knife, a switchblade, was still in his hand. Marcel said something in slow Farsi to the man. He nodded. He strode to the window and yanked the curtain to one side. The window had one of those European-made frames that open sideways. Alireza fumbled with its aluminum handle, then flung it wide open. He started to shout through the window in Farsi.

Marcel began to grin. Now, even with the gun, with the gray stubble on his cheeks, he looked almost cheerful. "As you can imagine, Alireza is well connected with the police in this, in this—"

"Precinct?" Gail said, still without expression.

"That's the word, this precinct," Marcel said. "So he has just shouted that a foreigner with a knife is in this room raping a woman. So the police will come here soon. If you still do not cooperate with us, Alireza will tell them more. Soon you will be in prison, with a twenty-year sentence, if you are lucky. In a Muslim country the courts are tough with rapists." Marcel turned to Gail. "Gail," he said, grinning, "Please take those clothes off."

Faiz said in a tense whisper, "But there were supposed to be four bottles. There are only three."

It was true. Nestling in the cotton batting that lined the shoebox were only three blue-tinted glass flasks, each labeled in Arabic with the same word. Even with his limited Arabic, Faiz knew the word was "nitroglycerin."

"Sorry, my friend," Mustafa said stonily. "One bottle became bad. Did not Dr. Ali tell you this?"

"No, he certainly did not," Faiz said, his voice rising in anger. "We will not accept this; we will not be cheated."

"We do not cheat you, my friend," Mustafa said, hooking his hands cockily in his belt. "Maybe our war was no good; maybe the Iraqis killed too many Kurds. Maybe now we must sell the equipments of our war to have money. But we Kurds do not cheat."

"Then where is the fourth bottle?" Faiz asked. "Answer that simple question."

"It became bad only; we are sorry."

Faiz was sure the bottle had been sold to someone else, to some anti-Shah group—to anyone who came along and offered the Kurds a higher price than what he had negotiated with them.

"How could it have spoiled?" he asked.

"The Americans gave it to us; maybe they wanted to hurt us, to make sabotage," Mustafa said.

It was true, Faiz reflected, that the secret U.S. support for the Kurdish insurgents in Iraq had ended before the revolt was crushed.

"I don't care what happened," Faiz said, plucking nervously now at his neckerchief. "The deal is off."

Mustafa only smiled—a smile marred by a gold eyetooth put in, no doubt, by a Kurdish dentist somewhere among the crags of Iraqi Kurdistan. "Never mind, my friend; do not be angry," he said. "Now we shall give you something better instead. Something your men will like very much, if they are brave."

Gail stood up. Her face was reddening. She put her hands to the top button of her blouse. She paused. Harry felt sick to his stomach with sudden fear. Now they had him, he thought. Christ, twenty years in an Iranian jail. Emily would be a full-fledged woman by the time he got out. He would miss her whole adolescence, would never see her as a co-ed, as a beginning career girl. He knew he would do just about anything to stay out of the Iranian prison system. His pulse was racing.

Gail thrust her arms stiffly down at her side. Her whole face was pink; she was blushing all the way down the V of her neckline.

"You're sick, Marcel," she said with loathing in her voice. "I'm not going to do anything more for you. Goddammit, I'm a cocktail hostess—I'm not a hooker, and I'm not a gangster. You can go fuck yourself. Go tell that to your Dr. Gumbert. And if you don't want to, I'll do it for you."

She ducked back into the bathroom for a moment, came out carrying an Iran Air flight bag—evidently containing her dress—pushed past Marcel and Alireza, and slipped out of the room with only a faint floorboard squeak. The two men made no effort to stop her.

Harry's pulse slowed; his panic faded. He realized he had been sweating. Now it was a whole new ball game. Marcel clearly did not know what to do. To Harry it looked as though the man had been following elaborate instructions from somebody else, maybe this Dr. Gumbert. Marcel did not look bright enough to have worked up this plot by himself. Now he seemed to slump forward; the stomach no longer seemed so flat. He blew air out through his mouth, making his cheeks bulge.

Then Marcel spoke: "Let's go. On the double." He gestured with the gun. He looked ready to kill; Harry had no choice but to obey. The floorboards squeaked again as Alireza, then Harry, then Marcel moved out into the corridor.

Alireza led the way: down the stairs, then the right turn, then up three flights of stairs, through a peeling door—and Harry found himself on a tar-covered rooftop. In front of him, in the faint, predawn light, the flat roofs of modern Teheran stretched away northward, toward the Elburz mountains. The rooftops bristled with aerials for the new television sets that oil wealth had brought. In the middle distance loomed the hulking new headquarters building of the Shah's political party, the only legal party in Iran; the Soviet-backed Communist party had long since been outlawed. Pigeons flew up as they crossed the roof. Harry bent to retie a shoelace.

"Move," Marcel said. "Jump across to the next roof."

"Look, I've got a bad leg."

"I see that. Jump, anyway."

Harry did so, with a twinge of pain, and the trio moved across the rooftop of the next building. Alireza unlocked a doorway, and they filed through it and down flights of stairs in what was evidently a small office building. The halls were empty, since it was Friday, which in Iran as in other Muslim countries is a day of rest. Not even a cleaning woman was in sight. But for safety's sake, Marcel had taken off his gray suit jacket and had hung it over his right arm in a way that hid the gun. They went out a side door and into a large courtyard. On the far side was a boxlike two-story brick building with a small spire: a Christian church. With Alireza still in front and Marcel bringing up the rear, they walked across the courtyard.

Harry's eyes switched back and forth. He was looking for possible ways to escape. High brick walls surrounded the courtyard on three sides. A few parishioners' cars were parked near the front gate, to the right. Otherwise the courtyard was empty. Harry thought fast. If he ran off that way, to the right, Marcel would have a fairly clear field of fire. Or Marcel and Alireza could probably catch up and grab him.

Organ music, a hymn being played too slowly, seeped out of the church building, which had narrow, Gothic-tipped glass windows, crudely stained dark blue. Worshippers were visible inside. In Teheran, Harry knew, Christian churches have their main weekly services on Friday, rather than Sunday, for convenience' sake. Alireza began to bear left when they were halfway across the courtyard. Harry saw the man was walking toward a rear doorway leading out of the courtyard. Forcing himself to stay calm, Harry simply headed toward the church's front door, which was ajar. He moved quickly. After a few seconds Marcel said in a harsh stage whisper, "Hey, keep left. Keep following Alireza."

But in another instant Harry had disappeared through the church door.

Mustafa gave a quick order, in Kurdish, to the fat tailor. The man stooped over and flipped back a piece of flannel that had been covering a wooden crate: a case used for shipping the local wine. In the dim lamplight, it seemed to Faiz that the crate was filled with straw. But the tailor gently parted the packing material with his hands and fished out a brick-sized object covered with metal foil. Looking closer, Faiz saw that part of the foil was torn away. Inside it was a solid grayish substance.

"What is that? *Plastique?*" Faiz asked. He had heard of, but never seen, the old-fashioned explosive that had been used to such advantage during the revolt against French rule in Algeria.

Mustafa nodded. "The best. The Israelis got it for us. They gave us more, much more, and we used it against the Iraqis. This is all we have left."

Faiz studied the brick; it showed no signs of having melted or become mildewed, but he was dubious. "How old is that stuff?" he asked. "How do I know it's still good?"

"It is not old," Mustafa said, sullen again.

Faiz shook his head. "The deal is off."

"No," Mustafa said. "We must have the money. We need the money. For our war to begin again."

"Look, I just can't accept this stuff without authorization from, ah, from Teheran."

Mustafa held out a thick hand. "The money, please. We are not cheating you." His voice was hard.

Faiz had been standing with his back to the door through which they had entered the back room. He stepped backward and put his hand on the door handle. He tried to turn it, but it would not budge. While he had been arguing, someone had locked the door from the other side.

When Harry touched the church door, it was opened silently from within, by an elderly Iranian man in a black suit. Harry stepped inside, finding himself inside a church for the first time in years. His bad leg was aching again, but he felt pleased with himself. Now, with a little luck, he could give Marcel and Alireza the slip for good. They would not want to start shooting or to make a fuss in here, in front of scores of witnesses. Harry smiled. It was enough to make a person believe in God.

The nave was a simple rectangular chamber with a high, flat ceiling in the old Persian style. Two fans hung in midair, suspended on long, thin shafts that came down from the ceiling. There must be two hundred worshippers in the pews. They were listening to a clergyman preach. He had a shock of gray hair and a gloomy manner.

Hastily, but not too hastily, Harry found a seat, making sure it was in a crowded pew where Marcel and Alireza could not sit beside him. After a moment it dawned on him that the minister was preaching in Farsi. This must be a service for Iranians whose families had been converted to Christianity in past decades when missionaries were active here. Harry promised himself that if he got out of here in one piece he would give the church a fat contribution.

A slight draft came from behind him. Someone must have opened the church door again. He glanced backward. Sure enough, Marcel and Alireza, evidently after some hesitation, had come into the church. They were staring grimly at him; but they did nothing, made no sign. He turned toward the preacher and pretended to be sunk in reflection.

The sermon stopped, and a second, younger minister rose in front of the congregation, speaking in Farsi. He began what was evidently a rousing Bible reading. Harry felt a draft again;

the candles in sconces on the side walls of the church flickered momentarily. When he looked back, sure enough, Marcel and Alireza had gone. Hosanna, he thought, if I can ever get the money together, I'll give this place a baptismal font the size of a swimming pool, enough candles for ninety years . . .

The organ began to play. The worshippers stood up, hymn books in hand, and began a droning hymn in Farsi. A little Iranian girl with huge chestnut eyes looked naughtily at Harry from the pew in front of him and stuck out her tongue. He gave her a nervous smile.

The hymn ended. The minister intoned what was perhaps a benediction. The organ began to play again, and Harry's nervousness returned as he saw that the congregation was beginning to file out. The men's heavy shoes shuffled over the slate flooring. What to do? Harry slipped out of his pew and moved along in the throng of worshippers toward the door. He was looking, frantically now, for some authoritative-looking person he could confide in, someone who might make sure he escaped. There was the man in the black suit, obviously a pillar of the congregation. He was shaking hands with the worshippers, standing beside the older minister by the door. Harry was about to speak to them when the black-suited man greeted him by name.

"You are Mr. Harry?" he said softly in English.

"Why—yes."

"I'm sorry to have to mention this, but there is a detective who is anxious to see you. He has shown me his credentials. He is waiting outside in the courtyard. I am sure you will want to cooperate with him." The man in the black suit smiled very firmly and put his hand on Harry's elbow, steering him toward the door. Before Harry could figure out what to do, Alireza slipped in through the door. On the lapel of his jacket he had pinned a badge.

IT IS USELESS, IN A POLICE STATE, TO TRY TO RESIST A POLICE-
man, Harry knew. And useless to ask an Iranian civilian for help.
So he moved along, as Alireza now quietly ordered. Quickly,
almost trotting, the three men went out the side gate of the
courtyard and into another office building. Up an elevator
marked with Farsi graffiti. Down a dim corridor, where the
office doors bore, in various languages, the names of firms that
mainly had to do with travel: a minor hotel chain that Harry had
never heard of, an air charter service, a couple of travel agencies. At the end of the hall a light glowed behind a frosted glass
door marked MINARET TRAVEL AGENCY. Alireza knocked.
Harry smelled coffee.

"*Herein*"—"Come in" in German—a man's gravelly voice
said. In they went, and Alireza and Harry paused a moment in
the anteroom—the secretary's table was vacant—while Marcel
went on into the main inner office. There followed a burst of
muttering in some northern European language—German,
maybe, or Flemish. From where Harry stood he could see part
of the inner office: one end of an old wooden desk, and on it a
hotplate, a teakettle, a Nescafé jar and an open can, from which
a man's hand was spooning something.

"Come in, come in," the voice rasped, and Alireza prodded
Harry through the doorway. A fat man with a pepper-and-salt
goatee was sitting at the desk, taking bites from the spoon and
holding a hand under it to keep from spilling on his beard or

vest. Besides coffee, Harry now smelled a fishy smell. He realized that the fat man was breakfasting on Nescafé and caviar, taken straight from the can.

"I am Dr. Gumbert, Prince Arloff," the man said. "Um. How are you feeling?" He did not offer a cup of coffee or any caviar.

"Hello. Fine, thank you."

"I am delighted to see that you are physically, um, unscathed from the rigors of the night."

Gumbert spoke with an accent that Harry had encountered before: he must be a Central European who had lived a long time in England. He also had acquired the British tendency to say "um."

"Alireza is, as you have doubtless gathered, a Teheran detective. Happily for us all, he was able to take today off," Gumbert continued, keeping up staff morale.

Harry nodded. "I thought he might be a cop; he very carefully hit me in the stomach, where the mark wouldn't show."

Gumbert seemed pained by the remark. "Actually, that was at my request. I myself engaged in saber duels in my student days, and I have always regretted that several men have gone through life with their faces scarred because of my youthful aggressiveness. I thought we should show some consideration for you, if you were at all cooperative."

"Thanks—but no thanks," Harry said defiantly. "Your friend Alireza has been using every threat in the book to try to recruit me for what he calls a business venture. It's obviously something crooked, and just as obviously, you're involved in it, too."

Gumbert gave a judicial nod. There was dandruff on his vest, Harry noted, apparently from the beard. "Alireza has spoken to me about your comments to him earlier today."

"I stand by them," Harry said. His fatigue and lack of breakfast contributed to his being more defiant than he should have been—as soon became clear. "You are taking some risks yourself in all this hide-and-seek with me," he went on, starting to bluff a little. "Your people must have told you that I don't lack *piston*—influence—in these parts. My family isn't totally unknown. I have prominent friends in business and government —here and in other countries. So please call off your goons, and let's call it a day." He glanced scornfully at Marcel. Marcel smiled.

Gumbert stuck his spoon into the caviar can with great concentration. He loaded the spoon with the largest possible payload of caviar grains. He delivered the payload. He smiled. "I'm sorry you have that attitude, my friend," he said paternally. "You will permit me to call you Harry, since I am almost thirty years older than you are. Now we are going to have a little talk, and it will convince you that you must join us. It will be an honor to join our enterprise, I assure you; it is an historic venture. If you play your cards right, you stand to make hundreds of thousands of dollars—more than a million if all goes well."

That was a lot of money. It caused Harry to hesitate a moment. It was much more than he would probably ever make in his life, unless he were to be the agent for a large weapons sale to some Middle East government, which was highly unlikely.

"Nothing doing," he said rather loftily. "I like doing business the way I do it now. On the up-and-up."

Gumbert put the lid on his caviar can and set it aside. He leaned forward across the desk. "Harry, your calling cards say 'Prince' on them, I believe."

"Some of them do, yes."

"You know as well as I do that that is what you Americans call horsecrap."

Marcel interrupted. "'Horseshit' is the word, Doctor."

Gumbert ignored the correction. "At any rate, nonsense. We have done some elementary research, and we find there was no princely family named Arloff in Czarist Russia."

Faiz hesitated. He figured the odds. He could shout, threaten, try to make his way back to the Maxiwagon, where he had a pistol hidden. He was in good shape and he suspected that he could beat Mustafa in hand-to-hand fighting, but what about the tailor—and what about the explosives? Any rough stuff in the room would kill them all. And the other Kurd or Kurds waiting silently outside this room, if they survived the blast, would pick over his body for the money.

Sweat broke out on the palms of Faiz's hands. He rubbed them on the tweed of his jacket. Mustafa's and the tailor's eyes followed his hands, then snapped back to his face. They knew they had won.

"Relax, boys, I'm going to reach for the money now," Faiz said softly. He brought out the wad of twenty-dollar bills he had bought in Turkey and had carried with him across the border. With their vast oil revenues, the Iranians didn't worry about exchange controls. He counted the money into Mustafa's hands.

Mustafa said something in Kurdish. The lock turned in the door. Two more Kurds came into the room—big men, in Kurdish dress. They carried the two boxes out to the Maxiwagon. Faiz opened one of the secret cabinets he had had built into its body for the project. Mustafa spread blankets on the bottom of the compartments. The big Kurds laid the boxes on top, and Mustafa laid more blankets on top and around the boxes. Faiz drove off, alone in the Maxiwagon, through the dark streets. He was driving more carefully than before.

At this early hour, the headquarters of Iran's national intelligence organization was hushed. The guards at the stone gateway looked even more bored than usual, as they waited for their shift to end. When an unmarked Chevrolet sedan drove up, they glanced inside, recognized the smiling driver and waved it through. Beyond the gates, the headquarters compound was, as usual, spotless. At this hour only a few men were strolling along the paved paths that led across the lawns: the place looked like an American junior-college campus. The smiling man's cordovan shoes made a *clop-clop* sound as he strode into a low-lying office building, nodding at the guards. He slipped into a small meeting room. A tall, gaunt man was sitting at the conference table, beside a pot of tea and a plate of sandwich cookies.

"Morning, General Mehrani," the visitor said, smiling even more.

"Good morning, Mr. Karthian. No sugar, yes?"

"No sugar. Cream but no sugar, the usual. Thanks." Karthian took a long, slurping sip. "Cup of tea hits the spot at this time of the day. I didn't get one at home. My wife was mad at me for getting up at this hour. We'd been up late at a party."

"Yes, I know."

"Of course." Karthian gave a wry smile. That was the sort of thing that General Mehrani knew about anyone in the country, if he chose to. Matter of fact, Karthian thought, Mehrani probably had a tape of everything that was said at the Karthian household. Well, he was welcome to it. This morning's tape would consist mostly of Darlene's complaints: she was angry that General Mehrani had called at the crack of dawn; she was depressed that only a couple of men had asked her to dance last night; she was feeling old; and she was sure as hell not interested in making anybody a cup of anything at that Godforsaken hour.

"I was terribly sorry to disturb you so early," the general said. "I called you because something has come up which I thought that you, as the CIA station chief, should be made aware of. Immediately. The director general agrees with me. But I am telling it to you now as a friend; this is not a formal communication to your agency. Is that understood?"

"Of course, General."

"It is something extremely serious."

Harry had encountered this sort of challenge before, over the years. "Actually, my father and grandfather were of the untitled Czarist nobility," he said. "But years ago it was not uncommon for Russian aristocrats, traveling abroad, to assume a sort of courtesy title—"

"Utter horsecrap," Gumbert said. "We have had to gather our data on you hastily, most of it within the past few hours, but I'm sure with more time we would find that your ancestors weren't even sergeants under the Czars. Let us pass on to another topic." His gravelly voice grew darker. "Your schooling."

"It's no secret; I was at New Haven, a very pleasant part of my life."

"Horsecrap. Or, um, semihorsecrap. Your statement implies that you were matriculated at Yale University, but the new man at the American embassy—"

"Feeney," Marcel put in.

"This new man told one of our informants that he was in New Haven, at Yale Law School, at the time you claim to have been there. You once had a conversation with this Feeney, it seems, and told him the truth, which is that you were in New Haven for only a few months, learning French at summer school."

*"Et voilà,"* Harry said wearily. He could not see where this unpleasantness was leading.

"Another question: are you familiar with this advertisement?" Gumbert fumbled among some papers next to the coffee cup and came up with a Xerox copy of something. He handed it to Harry.

Actually, it was a Xerox copy of a Xerox copy of an advertisement that had appeared in the Paris English-language newspaper, the *International Herald Tribune,* a few years back. Harry sighed as he looked at it. He knew it all too well. It said:

### Notice
Mr. Mikhail Nikolaevich Arloff, hitherto an assistant manager of our Paris office, is no longer in our employment. De Kirsch and Co.

"Well?" Gumbert said.

"That was just my crazy wife, Alice, getting back after I finally left her." Harry almost explained that he had moved out and taken Emily with him, because it had been getting impossible to raise a little girl in a household where the mother was half the time either missing or stoned on drugs. But he wanted to keep Emily out of this. "My wife got my father-in-law to put that ad in the paper, but it means nothing. Look, as your man Marcel knows, the De Kirsch firm trusts me now with thousands of dollars' worth of jewels, on a commission basis."

"Now, perhaps, but what about your reputation a few years ago?"

"What do you mean?"

"When you should have been attending university, you were idling in Europe."

"It wasn't really my fault. I had been in trouble in one or two American secondary schools, I admit that. It would have been impossible for me to get into a good American university. And so I became an expatriate. A ski bum. That's no crime."

"Trading on your phony title in Swiss hotels."

"I had temporary jobs at a few hotels, yes. That's no crime, either."

"Being a part-time gigolo."

"What you mean is that women, sometimes older women, found me attractive."

"Stealing their heirlooms."

Harry sat straighter in the chair. This session was becoming very unpleasant. He fished in a side pocket of his jacket and found his pack of Parliaments. He took one. Marcel gave him a light. He took a puff and said carefully, "You are evidently referring to a misunderstanding involving a Greek woman. In Gstaad, years ago."

"In 1968. Madame Stavropoulos."

"A fine woman."

"She didn't prefer charges against you, you mean," Gumbert said. He sipped his Nescafé, which must by now be cold. He swished the coffee around in his mouth. Harry knew why: caviar, even caviar of the finest quality, leaves a fishy taste in the mouth if the eater takes too much of it at one time.

"It was all a terrible mistake; she meant to give me that gold snuffbox," Harry said. "She was an impulsive person. Anyone who was in Gstaad in those days can tell you that." He took a deep drag on his cigarette. Thinking about his young manhood was churning up old emotions.

"What you mean is that she was always tipsy as a skunk," Gumbert said.

Marcel interrupted again: "*Drunk* as a skunk."

Harry shrugged. "I can't help what the tabloids said."

Gumbert smiled, flashing the false teeth again. "Another question, your weak leg. You told our woman associate last night that you had injured it in a polo accident as a student."

"I may have said that; I don't remember exactly."

"We understand you injured it in a fall from a second-floor balcony of a hotel in Baden-Baden eight years ago."

"Mezzanine."

"What, the Mezzanine Hotel?"

"No." Harry sighed. He took another drag. "It was a balcony on the mezzanine floor of the hotel. I had had a couple of cocktails."

"And you had also just rifled a steamer trunk belonging to a real member of the Czarist nobility, a Princess—"

"Princess Troubetzine. That was all a mistake, too. She was an old friend of my family's and she was very sick, poor lady. I was calling on her, that's all."

"Friend of her family's? Our information is that your mother was some sort of servant, a washerwoman—"

"A governess-companion," Harry said in a flat voice. The old facts were dragging him down. "Look, Doctor, I've already told your people that you can't really harm me much by blackmail."

"With all this information, we might be able to, um, curtail your sales in the Arab oil countries, where you say you do the, um, bulk of your business."

"I doubt it very much."

"We won't argue about that," Gumbert said. "But that brings me to the point of this exercise." He took another sip of the Nescafé and fussed a moment with the papers on his desk. "What have we here?" he asked rhetorically. "We have the record of a two-bit wrongdoer, as you Americans say, a bad banana."

Marcel put in: "Bad apple."

"A kind of semiswindler," Gumber continued, "who bounced around Europe for years, getting in and out of scrapes. Avoiding, by a miracle, serious trouble with the law."

"That's *right,*" Harry said.

"I concede that. I also concede that you have been behaving properly for the past five years or so. All the indications are that you take a genuine pleasure in your, um, profession, although it brings in only an uncertain income."

"*Voilà!*" Harry leaned back in the chair. He stamped the cigarette out on the floorboards.

Gumbert paused, like a judge about to sum up. He straightened his vest. "At this point an obvious question arises: there must have been something important in your life which changed you. What could that have been?"

Harry turned pale.

General Mehrani rose from the table. "You know about Pegano's death, of course?" He began to pace up and down the room.

"Yes, my night-duty man called me at the party," Karthian said. "We have no idea what he was up to. We'd pretty much lost track of him since he got into smuggling. It was penny-ante stuff. There didn't seem to be anything political—"

"Exactly," the general cut in, still pacing. "Here was a

renegade intelligence man, if you don't mind my saying so, who had become a routine soldier of fortune. We had long ago put his dossier in our inactive file. These types usually make enough money to retire, or they get injured or killed in the course of their work. Or they eventually get picked up by the civil police. The Middle East is full of such men—Americans, Englishmen, Frenchmen, Germans. Many of them are alcoholics, many of them are addicted to narcotics of one kind or another. As far as we know, Pegano was neither. He just wanted to make money and to have a little excitement along the way."

Now the general stopped pacing. "This brings me to the serious part," he went on. "It is clear from the circumstances of Pegano's death that he was in cahoots with an obscure group of anti-Shah terrorists. The existence of a group which we know little about is not in itself so worrisome. New groups are being formed every so often; it takes time for us to gather data about them. But this is the first time in recent years that a terrorist group has enlisted an American—and gone out of its way to enlist him. After all, they apparently brought him here from outside the country. Not only that, but they enlisted an American who is known to be apolitical, who has no reason to oppose the Shah."

"What is your conclusion?" Karthian asked.

"I suspect that the only thing that could procure Pegano's services for this group would be money, large amounts of money. That, in turn, suggests that this little group with a nightingale for an emblem is involved in something important—that it has generous financial backing from some quarter, or that it intends to earn a large amount of money, so that large expenditures are a reasonable preliminary investment—or both. The Russians or the Iraqis or the Libyans or some other Communist or radical regime may be backing this group in hopes of embarrassing or weakening His Majesty's government. Or this group may itself have widespread, relatively sophisticated operations. Or more than one of these possibilities may in fact be true."

Karthian nodded. He was staring absent-mindedly at the highly polished toes of his shoes and running over the possibilities in his mind. "We don't really have much to go on, do we?"

"Very little. But there is one assumption I think we can reasonably make."

"What's that, General?"

The Iranian stopped pacing and leaned across the table. "If this group has hired one foreign adventurer, it seems logical to expect that it will hire others. And it may very well hire foreigners who already reside in Iran, since they would presumably know their way around our country. This makes the matter even more serious. We have scores of thousands of foreigners working and living here; thirty-five thousand Americans alone. These people play key roles in our military and economic affairs, and in our oil industry. Must we now suspect them all?"

"Isn't there some way we can narrow the field?"

"Not really. Pegano had had such varied experience during his career that it would be hopelessly difficult to try to decide what aspect of his, ah, skills led to his being associated with the Nightingale group, and therefore to try to speculate about what other foreigners might be recruited. How could we interrogate or keep under surveillance all the other foreigners who were formerly in the OSS, formerly in the CIA, were experts in interrogation and other techniques that are useful in intelligence work, had become soldiers of fortune, were knowledgeable about Afghanistan, knew about lapis lazuli, and so forth and so on?"

"Okay, General, but you could at least speculate that any organization that wanted to use Pegano's special skills might be working up a plot in one of those fields."

"For instance?"

"It might want to infiltrate your organization—or mine."

"Impossible, Mr. Karthian; you know that. We are constantly on the lookout for that sort of thing."

"It might want to capture someone, a high Iranian official or an American—and interrogate him or her."

"Yes, but who? There is no way of telling who."

"It might be out to overthrow the Afghan government—or to engage in some kind of activity along Iran's border with Afghanistan."

"Highly unlikely. If either presumption were true, why would this group risk bringing nitroglycerin into downtown Teheran?"

"It might want to mount a jewel theft—even to steal the crown jewels, for instance."

"A minor jewel theft would serve no purpose, and an attempt to steal the crown jewels would be suicide. There has never been such an attempt in all the years the jewels have been on display in the bank-building vault. The alarm and guard systems are unbeatable."

"Or it might simply want to mount a coup d'état: to have one or more seasoned foreign adventurers try to lead a band of men against the government's forces at some vulnerable point."

"Out of the question. His Majesty the Shah has been spending billions of dollars a year to build up his armed forces to prepare them to confront many types of threat to our country." The General sighed. "We lack facts; we cannot know what this group may contemplate. But I can tell you one thing, Mr. Karthian."

"What's that?"

"As soon as we come upon its trail again, we shall pursue it and crush it." The General spoke firmly, but he began pacing again.

"What *was* it that altered your character?" Gumbert said to Harry, half musing, "Was it your marriage to a wealthy but dissolute young woman, a marriage which now has evidently gone off the rails? I doubt it. Was it your being employed, one way or another, by her family firm? Most unlikely. Was it your being separated from your wife? Also most unlikely. No. It's obvious that what changed you was the birth, five years ago, of your daughter, named . . ." He riffled through the papers.

"Emily," Harry said, his face stony.

"Don't look as though you were facing a firing squad, my friend," Gumbert said, suddenly cordial. He knew he had Harry now. "It is a fine and honorable thing for a man to reform himself in an effort to be a suitable father to a little girl whose mother is clearly irresponsible. No one can criticize you for that."

Harry said nothing.

"What you could be blamed for is if you were to let something bad happen to that little girl, something bad which it is in your power to prevent."

"Such as what?" Fear was writhing now in Harry's gut. Now that he was under great stress, the habit of using French words had faded.

"Such as if your daughter were to be kidnapped. And if the kidnappers were then to threaten you, to threaten to do dreadful things to her if you did not comply with their wishes. You know the sort of things they do. Amputate her toes, perhaps. Deliver them to you, one by one. Do something to her face."

Harry stood up. Marcel kicked him in the bad leg. Harry went down on the floor. He pulled himself back into the chair. There were tears in his eyes.

"As you have evidently guessed, Harry, our people in the United States now have your daughter in, um, custody. Along with a certain Miss MacDonald, the holder of a British passport. A servant. You will doubtless want proof that this is so. We will provide it. Marcel will go with you now back to the Bristol Hotel. You will wait there in your room or in the lobby, if that suits you better. You know that you will do nothing to escape from us, because that might lead to some disfigurement of the child." A small smile. "As you know, long-distance telephone connections are a bit uncertain between the United States and here. But if you are patient, you will doubtless hear from your daughter within the next few hours. Please tell her not to cry so much. She has been getting on our people's nerves. They are not, um, family men. You may have a chance to talk to Miss MacDonald, but you will doubtless note that she is under sedation."

"What do you want from me?" Harry said softly. "What the hell are you up to? Why is it me you came after?"

"We need you because you are an expert in diamonds and other jewels. We need someone who can quickly make sure that certain jewels are in fact genuine. Make sure that copies have not been substituted for them. And do it under conditions of stress."

"Okay, but there are plenty of jewelry experts around. You could have gotten some real underworld type with a lot less trouble."

Gumbert nodded. "We had another man recruited, with somewhat less expertise than you, but with broad and valuable experience. He was, um, more in sympathy with our undertaking. But he has fallen ill."

"Bullshit. He's been arrested, or he's chickened out or something's happened to him is what you mean."

"Harry, we will not tolerate this discourtesy from you. And you will not be so discourteous to us again. Because if you cannot master your emotions, you may receive another telephone call from your daughter. And, who knows, she may tell you that she is in considerable pain."

"So what *is* your project?" Harry asked, controlling himself.

"We are going to steal most of the crown jewels of Iran. That is step one. Step two is getting them out of the country."

"But those jewels are kept in an enormous vault," Harry protested. "They are under guard day and night, by a whole contingent of specially trained—"

"We are not going to take the second-rate things in the crown-jewels collection. A lot of trash has crept in over the centuries. But we will take all the best things. It will be the biggest jewelry theft in recorded history. Booty worth well over a billion dollars. You will help us."

"I'll cooperate with you, all right," Harry said, in a choked voice. "I don't want anything to happen to Emily; you know that. But I want you to know that there is only one word for what you are about to try to do: suicide."

"Take him back to the Bristol, Marcel." Gumbert said. "I must proceed with the, um, other arrangements."

"Wait," Harry interjected as Marcel motioned him toward the door. "When are you thinking of doing all this?"

Gumbert looked up from the caviar tin. "Soon, very soon. Now get moving, you two. And, Marcel, go ahead with the preparations so our new friend can take the test."

"What test?" Harry said, his face drained looking. "I've *said* I'd cooperate with you fully."

"That's all for now," Gumbert said, dismissing him. "Good luck."

PART

# Two

# 6

THE ANTIQUE DAGGERS WERE LYING AROUND THE COUNTER
like swizzle sticks at the bar at P. J. Clarke's. They fascinated
Buddy Brabham, who had been a weapons buff since his high
school days. But his attention was instantly distracted when he
saw Gail walking into the lobby of the Bristol Hotel. Fabulous
tits that bimbo has, he said to himself, fabulous.

"Please notice how elaborately decorated some of these
items are," the salesman said in his fruity voice. But Buddy was
looking sideways at Gail. She's got to be an American to be
wearing that tight blouse, he thought. She looks pretty smart,
but she looks like she could use some more sleep; too bad,
because she'd be a real honey if she took care of herself.

Gail was examining a display case full of jewelry. After
Buddy had been looking her way for a moment, she glanced
over in his direction. Nice eyes, too, Buddy thought, especially
when she crinkles them in the corners like that. She looks like
she could take care of herself, too, like she knows the score.

"How's that, my friend?" Buddy said, turning back to the
salesman. Buddy's voice had a statesmanlike resonance that he
had acquired from the elocution lessons he had taken twenty
years ago, back when he had hoped to become a network television correspondent.

"These are what we call Luristan bronzes, sir, from the
region of Luristan in western Iran. They are pre-seventh century B.C. As you see, these are very fine items. And very—"

"How much?"

"Well, actually, this longish one is of museum quality. We'd have to charge more than fifty thousand Iranian rials."

"What's that in dollars?" Gail asked. Buddy realized that she had been listening to him talk. She must be interested in antique weapons herself. Or lonely.

"More than seven hundred," the salesman said, smiling at both his customers. "But I think we could let this smaller one go for four hundred or so."

The salesman looked over at a white-haired Iranian man who was sitting in an armchair in a corner, drinking tea. That old geezer must be the owner, Buddy said to himself; he's probably a millionaire—a millionaire from overcharging people like me.

"Aw, come on, save that for the tourists," Buddy said to the salesman. "I can get a piece of shit like that on Madison Avenue, New York, for two hundred fifty dollars; how come it costs more here?" Buddy was getting ready to haggle. You have to bargain with these Orientals, he thought, it's their way of life. Gail had stepped nearer now, and Buddy saw that she was wearing a little smile, as though she thought he was doing the right thing, showing these Orientals that they couldn't pull a fast one on every American who came through their store. But she sure looked tired. Buddy wondered why she was out shopping now, instead of getting some sleep.

"I do not know what is sold on Madison Avenue," the salesman said. He had been eating some kind of onions, Buddy noticed. Boy, these Orientals sure don't know about Sen-Sen. "But this shop is a branch of my family's establishment; we have been in business for sixty-seven years. We give a certificate of authentication."

"Aw, come on," Buddy said again, cutting the man off. "Just yesterday I was up at the palace, talking to one of the Shah's top staff people. He was kind of giving me some tips, and one thing he said I should watch out for is getting ripped off on old bronzes."

Gail seemed very interested now. She moved a couple of steps closer. "He's got some real nice things here," she said in a good, resonant voice. Buddy liked that voice. He was tired of the feathery whisper his wife used back in Mamaroneck when she wanted to nag the hell out of him.

"We don't get complaints," the salesman said imperturbably; he was evidently used to all kinds of chitchat from potential clients. "Some of our things are in the finest museums. See, here, these calling cards." He pointed to a dusty array of customer's cards Scotch-taped to a counter. They were mostly from Europeans, including a lot of Germans from museums in towns Buddy had never heard of and some woman from the Louvre.

"I don't care what you say, Mac," Buddy said. "I'm told these bronzes are ver-ee easy to fake. They tell me at the palace that some of those guys out there in Luristan turn these things out like candy bars; they make them look old by burying them in horse manure."

Gail smiled. She was clearly not put off by horse manure.

"That is an amusing story, sir, but I think you have been misinformed," the clerk said. "It is true that forgers of antique bronze works of art are able to give a piece a surface that is either encrusted or dark and mellow, indicating falsely that the piece is old. But they do this simply with chemicals, according to standard formulas. And we are, of course, always on guard against such forgeries." He paused, his honor defended, and added more softly, "Since you are a friend of the palace, we would be happy to give you a discount of ten percent."

"Yeah. Well, I'm going to look around before I buy anything." Buddy began to look over the glazed tiles in the case next to Gail.

"Is that true about faking the bronzes?" she asked. "What *will* they think of next?" Her voice was a little too nasal for broadcasting, but with some training it would be okay, Buddy thought automatically. She wore no wedding ring, he could see now. He was glad he had put his own wedding ring in his pocket, attached to his key chain, as soon as the Iran Air flight to Teheran had taken off from New York.

"Sure, it's true, at least that's what they say up at the palace. Who knows when these guys mean it and when they don't?"

"You've been visiting the palace." The marvelous eyes seemed to open wider. "That must be real interesting."

"Fascinating, matter of fact."

"Are you a diplomat by any chance?"

"Nope, only a TV producer," he said with false modesty, and he named the network. "I'm here setting up a big documentary. 'The Splendor of Iran.' John Armbruster will come over in a few days to do the interviewing. He's going to spend a day with the Shah, visit the army, play around with the crown jewels, tag along with some nomads. The whole bit."

The salesman had retired discreetly. He was murmuring in Farsi to the old man.

"That's exciting," Gail said. "I'm just here visiting friends that my father has here. I'm in acting school back home."

"That so?" Buddy said. "So we're both in the world of entertainment. We have a lot in common."

She smiled, and from that moment on, Buddy knew it was going to be a cinch. He said his name, she said hers, he said the hotel had this terrific bar with these crazy Iranian pistachio nuts, and how about a drink? She said real fine, it wasn't too early for that, and even if it was, they were a long way from home. That's for fucking sure, Barry thought, thousands of miles from Mamaroneck and the wife, and her voice, and her old appendix scar, and the wrinkles around her nipples. Anyway, she was probably dropping her drawers about now for that skinny commercial artist in her therapy group. What the hell, Buddy Brabham thought, I'm not a monster, and I'm not a sex fiend, but I'm entitled to a little fun in my life, and I think I just lucked out.

Without saying good-bye to the salesman, he ushered Gail out toward the bar, lightly touching her hip. He was glad that Armbruster and the crew had not yet arrived. He wanted this one all to himself; this was as good as anything you'd find at P.J. Clarke's.

The entrance was a surprisingly small and simple doorway in the north wall of the government bank building. Marcel was struck now, as on earlier visits, by the absence of ornamentation around the door and the lack of symbols to denote the importance of what it led to. But he noted that a television camera was mounted on the wall of the building immediately north of, and across a twenty-foot alley from, the bank building. The camera was permanently pointed toward the doorway. Marcel and his colleagues had learned, among other things, that one of the longstanding rumors about the bank building was true: the television camera was designed to perform one specific task—when the alarm went off in the bank's huge downstairs vault, the camera automatically began photographing anyone who passed through the doorway.

Two bank guards, in their brown uniforms, armed only with holstered revolvers, stood by the doorway. They looked remarkably alert and content, Marcel noted, compared with most guards in the Islamic Middle East. This was understandable; one of the many bits of information that had come into his possession was that these guards were paid three times as much as the Teheran city policemen.

Marcel nodded to the guards, entered, and went down the flight of Persian-carpeted stairs, past the coatroom with its suspiciously burly male attendant, and up to the ticket counter, where an Iranian girl in civilian clothes sold him a ticket for a hundred rials, something more than a dollar. Tourists were welcome to enter the vault during visiting hours. Marcel smiled faintly as he read the instructions printed in Farsi and English on the back of the ticket: "No arms and cameras should be taken into the treasury-vault. Visitors are requested to deposit them at the entrance."

In point of fact, Marcel had left his gun behind today. He had also taken the precaution of wearing a pair of dark glasses to make his appearance slightly different from what it had been on his last visit some weeks before. Yet the risk of arousing suspicion by repeated visits, a few weeks apart, was very slight, Marcel and his colleagues had concluded. With thousands of foreign tourists and Iranians visiting the crown jewels every week, the Iranian authorities clearly did not bother to study their faces with any particular care. Today, Marcel fitted right in with the scores of visitors, mostly Americans and Germans, who were waiting to take the tour. In the group there were also a few Iranians, including, Marcel assumed, at least one unobtrusive security man.

The tour guide appeared: a skinny, professorial Iranian wearing a cardigan sweater under his suit. With the crowd clustering around him, he began his spiel in English:

*"Welcome, ladies and gentlemen, to the crown jewels of Iran, formerly Persia. Welcome to the accumulated splendor of centuries of luxury and conquest. The collection includes hundreds of thousands of jewels. Their total value has never been officially appraised, but it is no secret that this treasure has at times been used as indirect backing for currency worth well over a billion U.S. dollars. Now kindly follow me."*

The crowd shuffled along behind him, down more carpeted stairs, past a souvenir stand with an attendant—also suspiciously burly—to a windowless, marble-floored vestibule, which was decorated with more carpeting and a fine chandelier. A gracious chamber, Marcel thought, except that it was more than twenty feet underground, guarded by more revolver-toting guards—and divided down the middle by a steel gateway. At the moment, these outer gates, each about twelve by twelve feet, were open to let visitors pass back and forth; over the years the gates' daily openings and closings had gouged arc-shaped scars in the marble. The group of visitors moved through the vestibule, and the guards discreetly made sure that no one came too close to the gates. Marcel assumed that this precaution was meant to keep anyone from being hurt if the alarm should go off—which would trigger, among many, many other things, the closing of the gates to prevent thieves from escaping.

*"The treasure which you are about to see has been collected by many shahs. Some of them were so proud and excited to have obtained great gems that they actually had their names and the date carved on them, with the result that today, to quote an official publication, 'these inscriptions constitute more accurate historical records than the voluminous literature on the subject, most of which often lacks precision.' "*

So we're not only going to steal the country's wealth and its national pride, we're even stealing some of its finest historical records as well, Marcel thought, without the slightest twinge of guilt. He was a professional, and he welcomed anything that increased the value of the booty that was to come into his hands.

The guide then led the visitors, one by one, through a second, inner gateway in the right wall of the vestibule. This portal was of a different design: it consisted of a massive steel doorframe, six feet high, and a two-feet-thick steel vault door that hung from it on steel hinges the size of bread loaves. This inner door, flanked by uniformed guards, was open now to let people pass in and out. The visitors shuffled through it and then stood still, immobilized by the magnificence of the sight before them.

They found themselves in the crown jewels' display vault, a steel-walled room which measured a hundred by fifty feet. Its ceiling was about eighteen feet high. It was cool—the hum of a powerful air-conditioning unit was audible—and dimly lit, and floored with great squares of marble. The space inside the room was broken up by ten massive, marble-sheathed columns, evidently housing girders that helped to support the bulk of the bank building above. Scores of other tourists, earlier arrivals, were moving now among these columns. They were speaking in hushed tones, as though they were in a cathedral. What made them speak quietly was the impact of what they were seeing in the illuminated display cases lining the chamber's walls and set among the columns. Even Marcel, not a nervous man, found himself sweating slightly. He removed the dark glasses—very briefly—to wipe his forehead. Here, probably more clearly than anywhere else in the world, he reflected, a man could see billions of dollars in physical, stealable form.

The cases were agleam with bejeweled crowns, tiaras, sabers, turban brooches, necklaces, vases, tableware, harness ornaments and endless boxes and bowls of loose jewels and pearls. Over and over, in case beyond case, three kinds of glitter repeated themselves: the blaze of diamonds, the fiery glow of rubies and of spinels—another red precious stone—and the green glint of emeralds. Marcel feasted his eyes; the sight was more sumptuous than the crown jewels of England, more lavish by far than the great cathedral treasures of the European continent.

The only thing Marcel had seen that could possibly match it was the huge display of rhinestones in the great stores of Prague in decades past. Except that the vista before him now was worth hundreds of times the value of all the rhinestones in the world.

Then the alarm went off.

Back in his hotel room, Harry had tried to sleep, but without success. He was lying on the bed, his hands under his head, staring at the ceiling, when at last the telephone rang.

"Mr. Arloff?" It was one of the hotel switchboard operators. "There is a call for you, from France."

"From *where?*" Good Lord, was that where they had taken Emily?

"Oh. A moment, please." She laughed. "I make a mistake. It is from United States."

"Okay. I'm ready."

"Hello, Daddy?" The voice was faint. The line was weak. But it was her, all right, and she could talk normally. She must be physically pretty much all right.

"Hello, sweetie. How are you?"

"Daddy, it's not very nice here. I want you to come and get me."

He wanted desperately to ask her where she was, what they were doing with her. But he thought that if he asked, her captors would almost certainly cut the line. And if she said anything indicating where she was being held, they might well simply move her, quickly and perhaps roughly, to another location.

"But, darling, you know Daddy's busy. I hope you're having a nice time with Nanny."

"No, Daddy. Nanny can't talk to me. Nanny's sick. Please come and get me."

"Okay, sweetie, you just do whatever the man says to do and Daddy will come and get you soon. You just be a good girl. You be a big, brave girl for Daddy, okay?"

"Okay, Daddy." The voice was so small, so disappointed, that Harry's heart melted.

"Do you feel okay, sweetie? Do you hurt anywhere?"

There was a pause, which lengthened into silence. Harry waited for a few seconds. He did not want to risk cutting the line by jiggling on the telephone. Finally he decided there was nothing else he could do. He signaled for the operator.

"Yes?" It was a different voice.

"Operator, I was talking to the United States, but now I can't hear my party. Could you do something, please?"

"Yes, sir. A pleasure." The Bristol telephone operators were fabulously polite.

"Thanks."

More seconds went by. The operator came back on the line. "Sir, is this a call you placed to the United States?"

"No, they were calling me."

"Aha. A moment, please."

More seconds.

"Sir, the international operator says your party must have hung up. Now it is finished."

"Operator, could you do me a favor, could you ask the international operator to tell you where that call came from in the U.S.?"

More seconds.

"Sir, I'm sorry, they say they do not record such information for incoming calls. They say they regret it, but they have no time."

Harry rubbed his forehead. "Okay, thank you very much indeed. Could you possibly get the supervisor of the international operators for me? I'd just like to—"

"Sir, I am sorry, that was the supervisor I talked to just now. Now, I've got to go, we are so busy." The operator hung up.

Harry lay back on the bed. His first instinct was to get the bottle of scotch out of his locked attaché case and take a big, anesthetic nip. But instead he lit a cigarette and had a sip of cold coffee from the cup beside the bed. He had to think fast. He could call Hobie Stiles and ask him discreetly whether the CIA monitored that sort of call, or whether the Iranian intelligence did. But the chances were that no intelligence agency in the world would keep records on a brief and innocent-sounding long-distance conversation between a father and a daughter. And to have the slightest involvement with any intelligence agency now would be to risk disaster: if Gumbert learned that Harry had been in touch with any security officials, God knows what he might order Emily's captors to do to her. No, Harry couldn't call anybody now.

He lay back on his bed and gave way to self-pity. If only he had had sense enough to stick with Mrs. Naghi at the ambassador's dinner dance. He might be on his way to being thousands of dollars richer now. He might be flying back to Rome, his nearest pickup point, to get a consignment of jewels for her and her chums to look over. He might be, at this moment, drinking brandy sodas with her in her flashy living room. Or even, in the line of duty, in her boudoir.

He rubbed his temples and thought about what to do next. Obviously, the first thing he had to try to do was to figure out where Emily was being kept and how she could be freed. But how could he do that? He took another sip of the coffee and grimaced. In the park behind the Bristol, a dog began to howl.

In Marcel's long and checkered career, he had been in several other banks at times when alarms went off—times that were rather more delicate than now. So he had no trouble remaining calm while the alarm—actually a kind of siren—went *beep-beep-beep* in deafening tones. Marcel thanked his stars that he had no gun with him, that he had not even brought with him the small two-edged blade, known as a palm knife, that he sometimes secreted between his belt and the waistband of his trousers.

But the guards were not searching anyone. They stood watchfully while the inner gate closed automatically, having been set in motion by the alarm. Marcel assumed that, out in the vestibule, gates were also closing automatically, but they were out of his line of vision. Then two uniformed guards and two men in civilian clothes—apparently plainclothesmen—strode through the vault. They stopped at a case that contained what looked, from some yards away, like heaps of spaghetti overflowing from a big brass box. Marcel knew the box was actually wood overlaid with enameled gold, and that what looked like spaghetti was hundreds and hundreds of strands of the finest-quality natural pearls, many of them taken from the Persian Gulf and some of them brought from as far away as Venezuela.

The guards inspected the case carefully and stared at the visitors who were standing nearest to it, among them a blond-headed boy. One of the guards smiled and patted him on the head. The alarm abruptly stopped, and the guide began to talk again:

*"Relax, ladies and gentlemen; nothing has been stolen. It looks like the alarm went off because someone touched that case back there, the one with the pearls. The slightest shaking of any of these cases releases the alarm system. It also flashes a signal to a control room that indicates which case has been touched. All the cases are locked, of course, and made of bulletproof glass. Now the guards have inspected the pearl case and found it hasn't been broken into. It looks to me as though that little boy tripped against the case or something. So there was no wrongdoing. As a matter of fact, no one has tried to steal any of the crown jewels in the two decades since they first went on show here. Now kindly follow me."*

As the group moved ahead, the inner vault door began to swing open again. Marcel peered around the room, trying to estimate how many plainclothes security men were on hand. There was actually no telling, but he counted more than a dozen athletic-looking Iranian men, some wearing raincoats loose enough to hide compact submachine guns. These men paid particular attention to what the visitors were doing with their hands, and the men's heads swiveled toward any excited burst of laughter or chatter in the vault.

*"Now if you will stop a moment, ladies and gentlemen. Yes, here, please. Kindly do not get too close to the cases. Now, as is well known, this enormous collection of precious things dates largely from the time of the Safavid dynasty, which ruled over what was then called Persia from the sixteenth century to the eighteenth. The origins of the Safavids are mysterious; their roots were probably Kurdish. But their rule was crucially important in Persian history: some say that it enabled Persia to survive as a unified nation into modern times. The greatest of the Safavid rulers was Shah Abbas. He was a passionate collector of jewels—jewels for his royal person, for his treasury, even to decorate the royal horses. In time the Safavids grew weak,*

*and in 1722 an Afghan ruler named Mahmud invaded Iran;
there was a period of chaos, and many of the crown jewels
disappeared as plunder. But before long, a tough Turkmen
tribesman named Nader formed an army which expelled the
Afghans from Iran. In due course he made himself Nader Shah,
but even afterward he kept on mounting military campaigns to
expand his power. The most glorious of these was his victory
over the Moghul emperor of India. He conquered Delhi, the
Indian capital, and brought vast booty back to Iran—including
much of the present-day Iranian crown jewels. Now kindly
follow."*

Marcel followed, taking an inconspicuous place in the middle of the group. He was amused, as always, to see that the
display cases bore humble signs that said, in Farsi and English,
"Please do not touch." His amusement made him feel good; he
lit a Gauloise and took a contented drag. The group gathered
around a case full of shiny red stones that looked like so many
oversized cherry cough drops.

*"Now, ladies and gentlemen, here are some of the rubies
and red spinels in the collection. A spinel is a gemstone which
comes in several colors. Red spinels are very similar to rubies,
and in this and other collections around the world, famous red
stones which were long thought to be rubies have proven, on
recent scientific analysis, to be spinels. You see that big stone in
the tray there. That is a Burmese ruby of perhaps one hundred
carats, one of the largest in the world. All told, there are thousands of loose rubies, red spinels and emeralds in the collection.
Many of them were part of the spoils that Nader Shah took back
from Delhi. Please follow."*

Marcel wondered how much the big ruby would fetch from
a fence. That depended on the quality, he supposed. He was
gazing back at it respectfully when a muscular young Iranian
in civilian clothes tugged at his sleeve. Marcel stood stock-still.
The other members of the group went ahead, following the
guide. The muscular young man's face was expressionless. He

made a flourish with his left hand, indicating that Marcel should move toward a corner of the vault.

Marcel took a deep drag on his Gauloise and considered his alternatives. The young man was obviously a guard. There was not telling why the man was harassing him. But the situation might be grave. Marcel could slug the man and try to slip out through the gates. But the chances of his making it out to the street were tiny. Alternatively, he could start right now to bluster and complain, to wave his Belgian passport, to say this sort of harassment was bad for the tourist trade. But with twenty billion dollars a year in oil revenues, Iran didn't really need a tourist trade. So Marcel kept his mouth shut and strolled over to the corner, trying to look inconspicuous.

*"Now here we come to the items worn by the present Shah and his family. That crown there, topped with the white egret plume, is the one the Shah wore for his coronation in 1967. His father, Shah Reza the Great, had worn it for his own coronation forty years before. It contains three thousand three hundred and eighty diamonds, including a sixty-carat, pale-yellow brilliant there in the center of the front. What did you say, madam? ... Why yes, the large brilliant does rather look like a headlight. Please note the crown's exotic design, worked in platinum bands set with diamonds and pearls. The form is modeled after crowns worn by Persian kings of the Sassanian dynasty, which ended in the seventh century.*

*"At his coronation, the present Shah also wore that gold belt there, with the huge emerald set in the buckle. The stone is two inches across and weighs a hundred and seventy-five carats. No one knows why it has that faint groove across its face. Some historians think this is the same huge emerald that the seventeenth-century Indian emperor Jahangir was known to wear in his turban. They think the stone must have been part of the loot that Nader Shah carried back from Delhi.*

*"That crown there, with the emeralds and the large pearls, was put together from loose jewels in the collection so that the*

*Empress could wear it at the coronation. And that tiara there, with the platinum and the seven emeralds, was made by Harry Winston, the New York jeweler, for the empress's wedding in 1959. It seems to be one of her favorite pieces of jewelry; she has worn it many times. That other tiara was also made by Winston for the Empress's wedding ceremonies. The main stone is called the Nur al-Ain, the Light of the Eye. It weighs sixty carats, which makes it the largest known rose-pink brilliant diamond in the world. It, and the other stones for the tiaras, also came from the collection."*

The muscular young man strolled over to the corner with Marcel. He nudged Marcel's arm and pointed at something: a receptacle for cigarette ashes, like the ones placed beside the elevator doors in American department stores.

"No smoking," the young man said. "Please put your cigarette there."

Marcel did so, with record speed, and asked, "Is that all?"

"Yes, sir," the muscular young man said. "Please enjoy your stay in Iran."

"Oh, I will, I will," Marcel said, and he slipped back to rejoin the group. No one had noticed his absence; the other visitors were staring as if hypnotized at the sweep of yellow glitter in the case before them.

*"Now we come to the truly large diamonds. Those big yellow stones are South African Cape diamonds which another Shah, Nasser-ed-din, bought on a trip to Europe in 1889. I especially like that squarish one there; it is more than an inch and a quarter wide and weighs a hundred and thirty-five carats, which makes it the tenth largest cut diamond in the world whose whereabouts is known. It is known as Iranian B. There's a bigger one, there: that one weighs a hundred and fifty-two carats and is known as Iranian A—it's the seventh largest. And three of the other ones, as you can see, are only slightly smaller.*

*"And here, here, is the historic pink diamond known as the Darya-i-Nur, the Sea of Light. Stunning, isn't it? Please remem-*

*ber not to touch the case. It's the sixth largest cut diamond
whose whereabouts is known, and it weighs a hundred and
eighty-five carats. What makes it fascinating and valuable is
not so much its size or its pink color or its rectangular cut, or
even the fact that it is utterly flawless and of an extraordinary
clarity. This stone is one of the world's great historic jewels. It
is thought to be part of the even larger 'Great Table' diamond,
which was seen by a Western gem expert in Golconda, India,
in 1642. The Darya-i-Nur was carried off from India by Nader
Shah, and after he was murdered in 1747, it passed to his grandson, Shah Rukh. Later it came into the hands of Lutf Ali Khan,
the last ruler of the Zand dynasty, and after he was killed in
1794, it passed to the Qajar dynasty, which was overthrown by
the present shah's father. So it is very precious to our nation.*

*What's that, sir? . . . The five largest known diamonds? The
very biggest are the Cullinan I and II, which were cut from a
single, fist-sized diamond that·was discovered in 1905 in South
Africa. They are now among the British crown jewels. The third
largest belonged to the Nizam of Hyderabad at last report. The
fourth was in a private collection in Paris, as of 1971, and the
sixth is in the Soviet diamond treasury in Moscow. Actually,
some of the world's largest diamonds are widely scattered. Some
are in India, some are in New York, one was sold to a Japanese
businessman in 1972. But fully one-third of the world's very
largest known cut diamonds are among the Iranian crown jewels—seven out of the top twenty-one. Now, if you'd like to step
over here, we have some jeweled sabers . . ."*

Marcel turned away and headed for the exit. He wanted
another cigarette. And he had found out what Gumbert had
asked him to find out: the mysterious death of Pegano, an adventurer known to be interested in gemstones, had not
prompted the Iranian authorities to make an increase in the
security precautions surrounding the crown jewels. Specifically,
the authorities had not installed metal detection devices to
determine whether visitors were carrying weapons. And they

had not ordered the guards to begin frisking visitors for arms. They were evidently convinced that the alarm system, the guards and the double steel doorways constituted ample protection. In consequence, Marcel concluded, the operation could go ahead as planned.

# 7

THE DAY WORE ON IN TEHERAN, A TYPICAL IRANIAN DAY: THE
radio reported a minor earth tremor near the Persian Gulf
coast; a few dozen tribesmen were killed; relief supplies were
airlifted to the survivors. An American aerospace firm with
dealings in Iran was accused, in the early edition of a Baltimore
newspaper, of having bribed Iranians to get an Iranian air force
contract. Teheran officials denied this heatedly, the radio said,
and they pointed out that the newspaper had failed to learn just
where the money had gone. The Queen Mother of England was
visiting Iran, which is an important trade partner for Britain.
She used the afternoon to award British decorations to a hand-
ful of deserving Iranians. One recipient was a London-trained
lawyer, whose roly-poly wife had bought a diamond brooch
from Harry two years before—ten months, as it happened, before the birth of her first son. She was a good-hearted soul, and
this happy sequence of events had led her to invite Harry to her
parties, or at least to her larger ones.

And so, late that afternoon, Harry took her latest invitation
from the vanity table in his hotel room, told the hall porter that
he would be gone for two hours, and took a taxi to her villa,
where hundreds of people were already milling decorously on
the lawns, crowding the long bar tables that had been set up to
celebrate the lawyer's being made a member of the Order of
the British Empire. Harry went partly out of longstanding professional habit, partly to keep himself from going stir-crazy in

the Bristol, and partly out of a gambler's hope that Something Would Come Up—that his luck would in some way change for the better.

All Teheran was at the garden party, which is to say, many of the same people who had been at the U.S. ambassador's the night before. The lawyer wore his M.B.E. medal hanging from his lapel; the minister of the Iranian royal court was being photographed shaking his hand. Ambassador Fraser, after a lifetime of Middle East garden parties, was cautiously eyeing the tables of hors d'oeuvres.

And Hobie Stiles was observing the scene, this time with a champagne glass in his hand. "The British gave that man the medal for spying for them; everybody knows that," he told Harry jovially.

"What do you mean, he's only a lawyer; he doesn't even represent the British embassy. He—"

"Dear boy, don't be naïve."

Harry said nothing. He wondered whether the CIA had asked Hobie to spread that particular rumor, and for what reason. He felt an impulse to spill his guts to Hobie, to tell him about Emily's kidnapping and the crown-jewels plot. But he did not want to run the slightest risk that the kidnappers might harm Emily; he let the impulse pass. He was about to start kidding Hobie about the man's rumor-mongering when a slim young Iranian, obviously drunk, stoned on drugs or both, lurched past them across the lawn.

Gail was with him, holding him by one elbow as he weaved his way toward the gate leading out to the street and the guests' parked cars. He staggered forward, and she moved quickly to keep up. She seemed unfazed; she was evidently accustomed to this kind of situation.

"Dear Hossein," Hobie said. "Always drunk as a lord. Not a credit to his ministry." He raised his glass to Harry and wandered off toward the table with the caviar.

Harry waited a few moments and then followed Gail, walking slowly so as not to draw attention to himself and to his limp. He felt mixed emotions: he wanted to shout at her, to kick her tail, for helping to get him into all this trouble, even though it was in good part his own fault. But he was also pleasantly aware of the body, now not unfamiliar, under her dress. He was thankful to her for not going along with Marcel's rape frame-up plan, and he nourished a grain of hope that she somehow might help him more.

He met her at the gate; she had obviously put Hossein into a taxi and was returning to the party now, moving with a good, firm stride—neither a bar girl's saunter, he saw, nor an American debutante's stiff-legged walk.

"Hi," he said, "want to take a stroll?"

She looked pleased to see him. She nodded and took his arm, and they ambled away from the gate, which was guarded by a brace of policemen. As soon as she and Harry were out of their hearing, she said, "I heard you were supposed to get a call from your daughter; is she okay?"

"Yes. They have her, all right, but she's okay so far."

Gail squeezed his arm. "I'm real glad to hear that. Believe me, I didn't have anything to do with kidnapping her. Those bastards. I hear you gave them a rough time before they broke you down." She looked up at him. The china-blue eyes seemed darker and more direct than they had the night before. The June Allyson smile was gone. The whole face had a dead look, like an actor's between acts.

"What do you mean, 'bastards'?" he said guardedly. He looked around; they had arrived at the edge of a heart-shaped lily pond, and no one else was near.

"Relax, there's nothing wrong with you and me being seen together. We make a nice couple. Gumbert and his boys, if they hear that we were together here, they'll think I was just keeping an eye on you."

"You're on their side, aren't you?" he said softly, trying to sound her out.

"Yes, I am," she said. Her voice was flat and defensive-sounding. "It'll make Gumbert feel good when I tell him I saw you here, and that you were behaving yourself. But look, I'm trapped in this, too."

"What do you mean? You came out here on your own hook, didn't you? You're over twenty-one."

She was quiet for a moment, thinking, and then, obviously deciding she owed him an explanation, she began talking quickly: "Sure, I came out here on my own all right, but I'm trapped now, just like I was when I got started on all this . . . all this making a living off men."

"How so?"

"You heard me say I was a cocktail hostess, right?"

Harry grinned ruefully. "Sure, you said it back in the room with Marcel. I bet you were a good one."

"I tried to be, even though I'm sort of lazy by nature. It was back in Buffalo, and my parents were dead, and I was trying to save up money from my tips, so maybe I could go to beautician's school or something."

"And?"

"And a cool, gorgeous young guy came into the place one night—very rich-looking and Old Buffalo. He had on one of those expensive French neckties, like the one you were wearing at the ambassador's party, and he laughed a lot. After that it was all kind of sudden: I fell for him, and he started coming to see me a lot in the little studio apartment I had. Pretty soon I was having fantasies that we were going to get married, only then I found out I was pregnant, and he said he was scared his folks would find out about it and cut off his money. He gave me a big check written on a Citibank account and signed by some guy with a Polish name that he said was his accountant. And he said I should go up to Toronto fast and get myself an abortion. I didn't have any vacation coming, so I quit my job and went to Toronto and checked into a hotel and went out to cash the check. Only the cashier at the Citibank office checked with the computer and said no such guy had an account with Citibank. I called my boyfriend in Buffalo, but he just hung up."

"So you were trapped."

"I sure was. I went to the hotel bar and got smashed. There was this French Canadian bartender with gray sideburns and a real soft voice, and I wound up telling him my troubles. Finally he said, 'Never mind, let me help you earn some money.' I was at the end of my rope, and I was pretty drunk and I was crying, and I said, 'Okay, only I never did that before, and I don't know if I can; I might freak out.' So at first he just sent old guys up to my room, Canadian gentlemen they were, sort of fuddy-duddy. A couple of them really only wanted to talk. After three days, he said, 'Hey, you're a good kid, here's a phone number for a doctor and here's the money to pay him. Go get yourself fixed up and after that you can pay me the balance you owe me.' So I went to the doctor, and the bartender fixed it so I could stay at the hotel resting up a few days and then I said okay and he started sending business my way again—only this time it was more regular guys, if you know what I mean, and I found out I could handle them okay.

"Well, pretty soon I realized three things: First, it wasn't so awful, doing that work; while it was going on I'd just send my mind off to someplace else, walking in the woods or something. Second, I was making good money, better money than I'd ever have made in a cocktail lounge in Buffalo. Much better than what my old man would have earned if he'd made foreman before he died—which he never did. And third, I had the feeling I was in control of my life; I didn't have much education, and God knows I didn't have any pull; what I had going for me was my body, and I was putting it to use, the same way a rich man invests the money he inherits. It got to be very important to me, the feeling that I was in control, that the money I was making would let me do about anything I wanted. After a while I thought, If I'm going to do this, I might as well do it in the big leagues, and I moved on, to New York."

"How did you happen to come out here?"

"What I wound up doing in New York was kind of hanging out, being a semi-pro, a party girl, picking up a few
bucks here, a fur coat there. Having a ball a lot of the time,
and just taking it easy when I felt like it. But things started
to get a little nasty, you know? Too much cocaine, a little
rough stuff here and there, and my girlfriends were saying,
'Look, you can't just operate with an answering service, you
gotta get with an organization, or at least with a pimp.
Pimp, they said. I didn't like that word. I'd gotten real used
to being my own boss, and I didn't want to give that up.
Well, I'd had a couple dates with Iranian fellas, and they
kept saying I should come out here, so I sold a bracelet that
I got from a sweet old geezer at the Pierre Hotel. And I
bought a plane ticket to here." The emotion of talking freely
about herself made her want a cigarette, and she began
going through her pseudo-Gucci purse, clumsily, like a
schoolgirl fumbling in a messy schoolbag; she was no longer
bothering to be a woman of the world.

"What did you do then?" Harry asked. He gave her a Parliament, which she lit herself, tossing the match out into the lily
pond, halfway out to a tiny island adorned with a fountain in the
shape of a urinating boy. The fountain was new, but it seemed
to be out of order already. Maintenance is a problem in the
Middle East.

"I sort of hung out some more," she said. "The pickings
were pretty fair: Iranians and foreigners, too. Believe you me,
if I wanted to I could lay every single American businessman
that's waiting around in the lobby of the Bristol Hotel. Except,
some of the architects are gay."

Harry grinned. "Your work wasn't so different from mine."

"Hey, that's right." She squeezed his arm. "We were both
peddling stuff to the richies. Except you got to keep your
clothes on."

"Not all the time."

She gave a low giggle, a more relaxed giggle than last night. Her face had come alive again.

"How did you get with Gumbert?" he asked.

The daylight was fading, and the surface of the lily pond was turning gray. Somewhere a dance band had begun to play.

"Gumbert gets around. He has that travel agency, and he's mixed up in lots of other stuff: bringing German girls out here, a little dope action, a little gunrunning down in the Gulf. So he fixed me up with some dates, and then he said to me one night, 'Look, I'm on to something big, a deal that ought to make me one of the richest men in the world. You want in?' We'd both been drinking some, I guess, and I said sure and he told me about it and he said I'd get a huge cut, enough so I could buy an estate"—she pronounced it "ee-state"—"and be a rich lady the rest of my life. So I got with the program. They said all I had to do was get close to a few guys for them, which was okay with me. But then I met Marcel, the bank robber, and he gave me the creeps. I mean, I think he's been in the jug a long time someplace—America maybe, because he speaks English so well —and he's kind of weird about women; I don't want to be alone with him. And then one of their other partners got blown up, and they called me quick at the ambassador's house and told me to, uh, get close to you. And it turned out they were building up this stockpile of nitro, nitro—"

"Nitroglycerin?"

"Yes, only they didn't get all they wanted, and now they have some different stuff, too. French stuff. And two of their Iranian buddies got shot by the police. So I got scared. I mean, I don't care if somebody snitches the Shah's goodies. He can afford it. But I knew their partner who got blown up. He was nice to me. He was about the only guy in this whole country who didn't keep looking at my breasts. I felt bad about him dying like that. And then I heard they grabbed your little daughter and they might hurt her, and it made me sick to my stomach. So I said, 'Look, I want out,' but by then they had my passport and they said it was either keep on working with them or they'd get Marcel to cut me. That was bad enough, but then they said they had all this film of me taking cocaine with some fellas. And loving it up with some guy they said was a Russian spy. And they started saying how they'd get me put in jail for life up by the Russian border, with Turkish dikes putting stuff up inside me. So I said 'Okay, I'll do anything you want.' They said 'Fine, you do that and you'll be a rich lady for sure.' Simple as that. So I'm still part of the organization. Same as you. Except when it's all over I'm supposed to get a lot more money than you, and right now I have to, uh, work more."

He put his arm around her shoulder. He had the feeling for the moment that she was only a child, although God knows she wasn't. "Like a drink?"

She shook her head. "Just keep your arm around me a minute." She fell silent. She had got a lot off her chest.

"Who's the man you were with tonight?" he said, after a bit. "The man who was tipsy."

"Drunk, you mean. He's a very unhappy guy. That's Hossein, the main man in this whole operation. Gumbert would kill me if he knew I let him go home alone. But I'm so bushed. I had to."

"How do you mean, 'main man'?"

She looked around. No one was near. Someone might have rigged a microphone that could pick up what they were saying, but that was highly unlikely. There were a lot of other people at the reception, not least Ambassador Fraser, whom the Iranian intelligence would be much more interested in bugging.

"Look at it this way," she said, "a job like this has to be an inside job, one way or another; otherwise there's no way a gang can get that stuff out of that bank without getting locked in by the gates and massacred by the guards and the police."

"That's for sure."

"Well, Hossein comes from a very wealthy family in the

south; they have a lot of land, and they're into shoe manufacturing and all kinds of stuff. But he hates the Shah, he hates him so much that it about makes him crazy."

"Why so?"

"When Hossein was a student here, he got mixed up in demonstrations against the Shah. One time he really got worked over by a couple of cops, or maybe it was intelligence men."

"What do you mean?"

"Worked over so now he can't have babies."

"Christ."

"Can't even try. Believe me, I know."

"The poor bastard."

Harry looked down at Gail; her eyes were wet. She rubbed them with the back of her hand.

"Hossein's father is a very big wheel," she went on. "He's in the Iranian senate, and the Shah has given him a couple of medals, and he's on some important committees, which is where we come in."

"How's that?" Harry found he was oddly happy standing there, feeling her body under his arm, watching the pond's color darken in the fading light. Listening to the hum of cocktail chatter behind him through the dance music. Hearing a burst of tenor laughter somewhere, which could only be Hobie's.

"This is how," she said. "You know the crown jewels are backing for the Iranian currency, right?"

"Sure," he said.

"If you want to get technical, the system is that part of the currency is backed by government notes, and those notes are partly secured by the jewels. The exact numbers change around from month to month. You follow me?"

"So far." He was impressed by her grasp of these complexities. Business was where she was at, all right.

"The system is supposed to be watched over by a fancy committee called the Note Reserve Control Board. It's got nine members: two members of the Iranian house of representatives, the attorney general, a man from the treasury, the chief government auditor, two senators, and a couple of other guys I forget. And guess what?"

"What?"

"Hossein's father, Senator Qazvin, is a member."

"The plot thickens."

"You bet it does. Hossein's the senator's only child, which means that now the senator can't have any grandchildren to inherit the lands and the shoe factory and the other stuff. Which means he's pretty mad at everything to do with the government."

"But if he hates the government, why do they let him serve on the committee?"

"Because the bosses of the men that messed up Hossein have kept the whole thing quiet. The Shah doesn't know about it, over at the bank they don't know about it, and the senator and Hossein aren't saying anything about it. Not in a country like this."

"No."

"Now, this committee does a lot of things, but it has one special job: there's a law that says at least four of the members have to be on hand any time the bank wants to open up the display cases that have the crown jewels inside them."

"Does that happen often?"

"Once a year, for cleaning, and a few other times. Like a couple of years ago when the Iranian government let some Canadian experts take the jewels out to study them. That means the senator knows in advance every time the jewel cases are opened up, because the bank has to make sure in advance that it's going to have the four members there."

"How long has he been on this committee?"

"For years and years, and all that time he could have tipped off jewel robbers anytime he knew the cases were going to be opened. But he didn't because he knew that if robbers got into

the bank when the cases were open and took the jewels, someone would sound the alarm fast and the robbers would be dead.
Well, now, this year, Hossein, through Gumbert and his buddies, has finally found a way to get around the alarm system. I
don't know what it is, but he's decided to go ahead and have a
robbery. So they got me to help them, and a man, a retired
American army colonel, to be like a commanding officer, and
they've been getting in other men, foreigners, to help them. I
guess they're afraid that if they had a lot of Iranians in their
gang, the Iranians would rat on them."

"But how are they going to get the jewels out of this country? As soon as the government learns the jewels are missing,
it'll seal off the borders. If the robbers try to fly the stuff out of
here, they'll get shot down."

The dark-blond head shook slowly. "I don't know."

"And once they get out of this country, where can they take
refuge? And how can they sell off a huge mass of jewels like
that? If they try to dump them all on the market, jewel prices
will fall and they'll lose a lot of money. And they'll get caught.
They'd need to have the services of a big, sophisticated organization of some kind."

"I just don't know. But they seem pretty sure that everything's going to work out all right. And soon."

"How soon?"

"Couple of days. That's what all the rush is about. An
American TV crew is coming here to make a documentary
about Iran, and the Shah is letting them film the crown jewels.
He wants to improve his image. To film the jewels right, you
have to take them out of the cases, which is what the bank is
going to do. Meantime, Gumbert and his friends have made all
kinds of preparations, like renting buildings under phony
names, and getting guns and disguises and vehicles and fake ID
cards and some kind of special drugs and I don't know what
else."

"Christ."

"They say they've thought of everything, and I guess they have. They're sure there's no way you'll turn against them, and risk having something awful happen to your daughter. And I won't try to rat on them because I don't want my face sliced open. And I don't want fifty years of Turkish dikes. But I'm shit-scared; I don't mind telling you. I'd turn these guys in in a minute if I thought I could get away with it."

"Have they told you what they're going to do with you after this is all over?"

"Not a word."

"They didn't say anything to me, either. Which makes me think they'll eventually kill us. We may still be useful to them for a while, but they won't want us hanging around to tell the cops about them once they've left the country. And I don't think they'd want the hassle of taking us with them wherever they're going. So we may wind up dead in a couple of days unless we think of something fast."

"Okay, but what?"

"I don't know, Gail, but I bet you and I could get hundreds of thousands of dollars in reward money if we helped Gumbert and his friends get caught."

"Lover boy, now you're talking my language. I know just what I'd do with all that money."

"What?"

"I'd buy an estate"—she pronounced it "ee-state" again—"in Virginia, in what they call the horse country, and I'd lie around all morning and eat Eggs Benedict, and then I'd go out riding in the afternoon."

"Not a bad idea, if you can afford it." He smiled at her.

"So what do we do?"

"Two things, to begin with. First, would you please try and figure out just why Hossein is doing all this? Why would an alcoholic dissident spend years trying to steal the crown jewels?"

"For the money, dummy."

"Maybe, but you said his family was already rich. I think he must have some other reason for doing this."

"To make the Shah look bad?"

"He could have done that in much easier ways long ago. Like putting a mild poison in the punch bowl at one of these big establishment parties. So why the obsession with the jewels? There must be some other reason. If you can find it out, we're bound to be able to use the information somehow."

"Okay. What's the other thing?"

Harry's face turned grim. "Find out where Emily is, and how I can get her away from them. That has to be the first step before I do anything else."

"I will," she said, and she gave him a kiss. Not a big, businesslike kiss, but a little light one on the cheek. "I got to go back to work," she said. "I'll check with you tomorrow. In your room."

"Can you get into my room without the house detectives making a fuss?"

"Relax," she said. "Leave it to me."

Harry had to smile again. Getting around hotel detectives was obviously one of the professional skills she had picked up in her career. The way he had learned how to work an ambassadorial dinner dance. Then she was gone, walking with that resolute stride across the lawn. Harry wandered back toward the bar table. He found Hobie, glass still in hand.

"You have the tiniest touch of lipstick on your cheek, dear boy," Hobie said. "I *told* you you'd find Miss Olsen interesting."

# 8

BUDDY BRABHAM WOKE WITH A HEADACHE AND A SWEET FEEL-
ing that for some reason he was happy. It was almost dawn; the
hotel-room window was an oblong of gray-blue sky. He felt a
small hand caress his forehead and run ever so slowly through
his hair, and he remembered why it was that he felt so good.

"Hi, there," Gail said. She was sitting up beside him. In the
faint light he could see the smile she gave him and the warm
shining of her eyes.

"Hi," he said simply, his usual P.J. Clarke's glibness with
women having long since faded away. He rolled over and put
his head in her lap. If he had thought about it, he would have
realized that at some point during the night she had got up and,
very sensibly, put her blouse back on to keep warm; the room
was cool. He did realize, out of longstanding sensitivity, that his
balding scalp was now right under her nose. It must be glaringly
obvious to her. But he felt so trusting, so content, that his bald-
ness, for once, seemed not to matter. He mumbled something.

"What is it, honey?"

He lifted his head. "I said, 'It was never like that before.'"

"Oh, Buddy, I'm *glad.*"

"You know what?"

"What, honey?"

"I didn't cheat much before. Sure, I been playing around
now and then, but you know what I mean: it never *meant* like
this before."

He felt a finger across his lips, and he began kissing it.

"Sssh, honey," she said, "go back to sleep. You got a lot of work to do, and you're going to need a lot of sleep; you didn't get much tonight."

Gee, she was thoughtful. He put his arms around her a little roughly, a little awkwardly. He wanted to bury his face in that bosom again. He wanted to do a lot of things with her body. But most of all, he wanted to prolong the wonderful feeling that when he was with her, he could let his guard down—his guard against Armbruster and other sharpies at the network, his guard against all the hypocrisies of his home life.

Gail slipped deftly out of his embrace and turned to the night table. Ice tinkled in the wine bucket as she lifted the champagne bottle. She poured two more glasses. Buddy raised himself on one arm to take the glass she brought carefully to his lips like a doting mother—although she was a good twenty years younger than he was.

"Chin-chin, honey," she said.

"Chin-chin." He drank the glass down and drowsily set it on the floor beside the bed. As he drifted off to sleep again he found himself thinking, I ordered that champagne, but when the room-service waiter brought it, she got out her own money and she gave him a big tip. She has class, he thought, and I love her.

At the appointed time, Harry left his hotel room and took the elevator down to the ground floor. The lobby was half full of non-Iranian businessmen whiling away the afternoon by reading newspapers in the hideously upholstered chairs. Several of them cast sharp looks at him as he strolled through to the bar. They were wondering, Harry knew, whether he had been at some late-night party beating them out for the contracts that their home offices were pressing them to win; whether he had been bowling with a prince, perhaps, at a palace bowling alley. Or whether he had been attending some superexclusive brunch for foreign businessmen more favored than they.

In the bar the mood was different: here were the American oilmen, a rougher lot, up from the oil fields in southern Iran. The room smelled nicely of beer and pistachio nuts, which Iranian bartenders serve instead of peanuts. There were loud bursts of laughter, and some of the men were unstable on their barstools, unfazed by the imperious stare of the Shah, whose portrait hung on the brocade-covered wall beside the bar. Under the picture sat an impassive figure drinking beer and reading a French newspaper. It was Marcel. Harry slipped into the chair beside him.

"You're four minutes late," Marcel said. He took a sip from his beer glass, then put it down abstractedly. He was looking at Gail, who had just strolled through the lobby, past the double doorway of the bar. He lit a Gauloise and pensively sucked the smoke in through his nostrils.

"You like that body, don't you?" Harry said, unable to resist a dig.

"Make the jokes later, Arloff. Now we're going."

"Let me say hello to her first."

"No, funny man."

"Come on, Marcel, just a minute."

"No. I said no." Marcel was holding a metal Cinzano ashtray in his hand. He sucked in breath oddly between his teeth —and Harry, looking down, saw that the man was slowly bending the ashtray between the fingers and thumb of his right hand. The enamel made a tiny cracking sound.

"Okay," Harry said. "We go."

They strolled to the hotel parking lot and climbed into the vehicle that Marcel had parked in a far corner: a blue Plymouth Voyager Maxiwagon. Harry knew that Maxiwagons and other multipassenger vans are useful for, among other things, carrying tourists over the long dusty distances that divide the various tourist attractions in Iran. A traveler encounters many such vehicles on the roads.

With Marcel at the wheel, they drove to a dowdy, pre-oil-boom quarter in the southeast of the city. Harry recognized the neighborhood: it was where Gail had taken him for the party with the red-wine punch. They turned into a blind alley. On one side was an abandoned brick building, four stories high, that must once have been a warehouse. It had a large truck-sized doorway, which was closed and locked. They parked outside, went in a narrow side door, along a hall and into a sparsely furnished office: it might once have served as a dispatchers' room for a trucking firm. In a canvas chair sat a barrel-chested man in his sixties with a grizzled crew cut and a military way of holding his chest and shoulders. Beside him was an elaborate medium and shortwave radio receiver with a long collapsible antenna. The radio was chattering softly with a British accent; it must be tuned to the BBC.

"Hello, Colonel Kates," Marcel said.

" 'Lo. Have a seat." The colonel snapped off the radio and gestured to Marcel and Harry to sit in two other canvas chairs that were drawn up to a white enameled table. He pulled his own chair up to the table. "Any sign that people in this neighborhood are interested in what we're up to?"

Marcel said, "No, we didn't see anybody looking at us from windows as we passed."

Kates nodded. He seemed relieved. "Now then," he said, looking at Harry. "We gather you're a gem expert." He had an American accent, mildly Southern—the way many American career officers speak.

"Only more or less," Harry said. "I've had a lot of practical experience."

"Right. Now we're goin' to give you a little test, to get to know each other better."

"Okay."

"Shall we proceed, then?"

"Okay, but—what if I fail?"

The colonel smiled affably. "Let's just say we couldn't

guarantee your safety. Now then, Harry, we're goin' to show you a little collection that was left by ah, by an old American friend of mine who has left Iran. He used to enjoy tellin' us about it."

Marcel went over to a chest standing at the side of the room. He rummaged past some blankets piled inside and produced a two-inch chunk of gray-blue rock. He tossed it onto the table. It made a small *clunk.*

"Think you could tell us what that is, Harry?" the colonel asked.

Harry took the stone in his hand, examined its rough surface and put it down.

"Unpolished lapis lazuli. That's a semiprecious stone."

"Right," Kates said. "Any idea how it came here?"

Harry thought a minute and concluded that the best thing for him to do was to show off what knowledge he had, to do his best to pass the test. If he flunked, he assumed that would mean Kates had decided his knowledge was too limited to be useful. And in that case, these men might want to lock him up someplace or even kill him to make sure he didn't tip off the Iranian government before they mounted their robbery.

Harry swallowed. "How this stone happened to be here?" he said. "It's pretty easy to make a theory, as a matter of fact. *Très facile.* It probably came from the lapis-lazuli deposits in the northeastern part of Afghanistan, where lapis has been mined for thousands of years. They say even the ancient Egyptians got lapis by caravan from there. You hear a lot about lapis smuggling, and I wouldn't be surprised if some hippie brought this here in his or her car, overland from Aghanistan. Or some real smuggler."

"You seem to know a lot about this area," Kates said. "Now, on to the next question." Marcel took a chamois bag from the chest and shook a sizable pearl out onto the table. It rolled around for a moment, then came to a stop.

"Real or fake?" Kates asked.

Harry took the pearl in his fingers, wiped it off on his shirt, hefted it, put it in his mouth and rubbed it across his teeth.

"Fake," he said.

"Okay, but why?"

"The luster looks wrong; you can see that right away. I'd say this is really made of glass with some pearly-colored substance inside it."

"Why'd you put it to your teeth?"

"To check the texture. It's smooth, not slightly granular, the way it should be. Therefore, *donc,* it's fake."

Kates looked impassively from Harry to Marcel and back; he seemed unimpressed. Now come the hard questions, Harry thought, squinting up at the fluorescent light.

"Okay, okay, we know you're at a disadvantage lookin' at gems in unfamiliar light," Kates said, and chuckled. "You don't need to be dramatic about it."

Marcel reached into the chest again and took out a blue box. He snapped open the lid and dropped a blue stone on the table. The gem glittered coldly.

"Real or fake?" Kates said.

"Sorry, I can't tell with the naked eye."

Marcel produced a jeweler's magnifying glass. Harry had one, but it was locked in his attaché case at the hotel. Harry put the glass to his eye and peered at the blue stone. He was having trouble concentrating. He found the stone swimming before his eyes.

" 'Real or fake' is the question," Kates said, his voice a shade louder now.

Harry looked awhile longer. Then he exhaled and said, "Real."

"That's right, good for you—but where from?"

Harry rubbed his eyes and sat back. "Well, a lot of sapphires come from Ceylon," he said. Kates's face darkened. Then Harry quickly added, "but this one comes from Burma."

"How can you be sure?"

"Because of what you see inside the stone. A special pattern of crisscross lines. Only Burmese sapphires have that look."

Kates nodded. Marcel tossed another jewel, a red one, onto the tabletop. This one was far larger than the other.

Kates opened his mouth to speak.

"I know, I know, real or fake?" Harry said. He peered at the stone through the glass. He looked for what seemed a long time. He could hear the breathing of the other two men and the ticking of a watch. Finally, he leaned back and said, "I can't tell. It looks all right to me, but to be sure, I'd have to have an ultraviolet lamp or a microscope."

Kates smiled. "Marcel, can you help us out?"

Marcel rummaged deep down in the chest. He came up with a small gooseneck lamp fitted with an odd, squarish bulb. He set it on the table and plugged it into a wall plug.

Harry's palms began to sweat. The truth was, he couldn't remember: was it synthetic rubies that are bright red under ultraviolet light and natural rubies that are dark red or a moderate red color? Or was it the other way around? He had known once, but now the knowledge had vanished from his mind.

"Marcel," he said, "could you turn off the ceiling light, please; it weakens the glow from the—"

The telephone rang. Kates answered. "Hi there, Charley," he said, and listened for a while. "So he wanted to buy her an antique dagger. The bald fellow? Ah, true love." He listened some more. "I know, I know, Charley, there's a lot to do. It's a matter of sortin' out the priorities, that's all. If I were you, I'd get crackin' on the arrangements for that, ah, for that theatrical equipment. Then—"Kates broke off and looked over at Marcel and Harry, who was sweating profusely now. "Gentlemen, I've got business to attend to here," he said. "You're both dismissed. Harry, you go back to the Bristol and wait. If you want to leave your room for more than an hour, leave word with the hall porter where you'll be." He resumed speaking into the telephone: "Now, our other friends . . ."

Marcel returned the things to the chest, and he and Harry went back out the hall.

"Did I pass?" Harry asked.

Marcel said nothing.

"Come on, Marcel, tell me. We're in this together."

Marcel shrugged. "You're alive, aren't you? That means you passed—so far."

# 9

EARLY IN THE AFTERNOON THE TELEPHONE IN HARRY'S ROOM
rang. It was Gail, calling from the lobby. Her voice was
tired-sounding but intense. She had a flask of Courvoisier,
she said. Would he care to split it with her? He would, indeed, and in minutes they were strolling out into the big
drab park that extended behind the hotel. It was a new
park, formed out of waste ground that had been fit for little
until the oil boom came, spawning a tide of new building
that surged beyond the old edges of the city. Now the park-
land was flanked by rows of buildings, all bristling with TV
aerials. They found an empty wooden bench and they sat
there, watching Iranian youths with gloriously scruffy beards
walking, talking and gesticulating along the paths. Here and
there other young people sat on benches and played Western popular music loud on portable radios. Gail had a radio
with her, too, the kind with a tape recorder built into the
case. But she did not turn the radio on. Instead, she reached
into her purse and passed Harry the fat silver flask, clearly a
memento of a boyfriend, perhaps of Hossein. Harry took a
healthy slug while she took a tape-recorder tape out of the
purse and slipped it into the recorder. She flipped the little
orange switch on the top of the radio and fiddled with the
volume knob. Voices began to seep out of the radio: a deep
American male voice, and voices that Harry recognized as
Gumbert's and the colonel's.

DEEP VOICE: . . . can help you fellows to pick up a little cash here or there.

GUMBERT: To say the least.

KATES: Chaz, the floor is yours.

DEEP VOICE (clearly CHAZ): Well, now, sir, I believe you have a pretty extensive technical background—

KATES: True enough, but no specialized trainin'. You'll have to keep your remarks general, I'm afraid.

CHAZ: It's pretty simple, all right, considering that what's involved is billions of dollars.

*Snap.* Gail flipped the switch. Harry looked up. A young Iranian couple was strolling arm in arm down a path intersecting their own twenty yards away. Harry could see why Gail had flipped the switch—now the radio was playing jazz—but the pair didn't look like intelligence agents with monitoring devices that could pick up a tape recording being played softly thirty yards away. Gail evidently agreed with him. *Snap,* she switched off the radio. *Snap,* she ran the tape backward an instant. Then *snap,* the tape began playing again.

CHAZ: . . . pretty simple, all right, considering that what's involved is billions of dollars.

KATES: Right. Proceed.

CHAZ: There's been a lot of advances in security systems lately. Back home, in the U.S. of A., there's all kinds of new gimmicks: sound systems that can hear a baby mouse walking, let alone a th— er, an intruder. Systems that tell you if anybody opens a single door inside a whole big museum during the hours it's closed down. Stuff like that. But what we have here, what we're going to be dealing with, is more a sort of strong-arm approach.

KATES: How do you mean?

GUMBERT: Ah, here's Ibrahim with the coffee.

There followed some rumbling sounds in the background, as though coffee was being handed around and the chairs moved. Harry looked around the park. The young Iranian couple had kept on walking; they were moving away now from where he and Gail were sitting. The young man was keeping one hand in the back pocket of the girl's gracefully convex jeans.

CHAZ: Naw, just black. Thanks. Well, what we have here is a classical alarm system. Its receptors are extremely sensitive: if you jiggle practically anything at all inside there, it'll trigger the alarm system.

GUMBERT: Tell us what happens then.

CHAZ: Two things can happen, matter of fact. Number one, the system activates what they call in the burglar-alarm business the "local annunciator."

KATES: What's that? Sounds like somethin' in the Bible.

CHAZ: Could be several things. Now, different technicians'll tell you different things, but basically there's five species of annunciators, the way the technology is now: bells, electronic sirens, mechanical sirens, what's called resonating horns, and light-beacons.

KATES. And what are we up against?

CHAZ: A resonating horn. Loud as hell. Scares the shit out of the tourists. That's because—

GUMBERT: Gentlemen, the whole point is that this local, um, local noisemaker can become academic—

CHAZ: Yeah. You're so right, Doc. What we can do now is just prevent the alarm signal from functioning.

KATES: How?

CHAZ: (gaining assurance): Let me explain.


"Look, Ingo, a problem has come up; you've got to do this for us. Please do it for us." Marcel was talking softly, urgently, to the wiry, fair-haired Finn who had joined the team earlier in the day. The two men were standing half hidden between two cars in the Central Hotel's crowded parking lot. Their voices mingled with the noise of the traffic in downtown Teheran and the distant blare of march music.

It was an old European march, "Prussia's Glory," being played to the beat of kettledrums.

Marcel took a drag on his Gauloise, threw it down and ground it into the gravel. "You know you like a little excitement now and then, Ingo. I'll tell you exactly what to do. You have to make it happen in the next hour, while they're still marching. It'll be over before you can say 'Paavo Nurmi.' "

"Shit. I just got into this country. I don't do it." Ingo spread his arms in a mock pleading gesture; there were long white scars on his forearms and hands. "I'm too young to die."

"You're not scared, are you?"

Ingo shook his head calmly, he was a man with no need to test his reactions to stress. "I do not fear danger. But I just got here. I don't know the odds yet. I don't go to work when I don't know the odds, that's all."

"No odds, Ingo, there's practically no danger to you; the stuff is wrapped in enough cotton batting to cover the Eiffel Tower."

"Then why don't the Indian do the job?"

"The Pakistani, you mean, Faiz Kiani. The smuggler. No guts, that's why. He drove the stuff down here from where it was stashed, up in the north. It's a long drive, and on the way his nerve gave out."

"I don't do it. I don't need this work which I don't know about. I can go back to circus work anytime. In Scandinavia, in Germany, where I like."

"Bullshit, Ingo. Not any more. Not with your record. In your business they know you're too crazy. Too mean. You kill too many big cats. Expensive cats. It makes the humane societies angry."

"Those were accidents, man. I got to protect myself. What's an old sick lion worth, anyhow? Nothing." Ingo spoke without conviction, repeating excuses he had recited many times.

The march music was growing louder.

"Come on. You know you'll get a kick out of it when you get started."

"How come you don't do it?"

"Because I've been here awhile. The cops may have my picture. And I have a lot to do on the big day. If I get picked up now, even for a traffic violation, the whole project may be screwed."

Ingo scowled. He did not quite accept Marcel's explanation. He folded his arms across his chest. With his left hand, he absent-mindedly rubbed the scars on his right forearm. "No," he said.

"Come on."

"No."

Marcel sighed. "Okay, we add a thousand U.S. dollars to your fee."

"Five." Ingo smiled a wolfish smile.

"Okay, two thousand five hundred. Here's the keys to the Fiat."

Ingo paused. He cocked an ear to the music. There was a glint now in his cold green eyes. Already he was beginning to get a little high on the risk-taking.

"Okay," Ingo said. "Now tell me what to do, say it very slowly. And, Marcel?"

"What?"

"I got my old whip with me up in the room. If you forget my two thousand five hundred, I'm going to whip you. Chastise you like you was a bad old lion."

Marcel was quiet now; his square jaw was set. He knew that some men were tough, some men were crazy, some men were both. Ingo was both, but he was *too* crazy, too much the sadist. Damn Gumbert for recruiting him. Better make sure Ingo was happy in his work. "Sure, Ingo. For you, we'll make it three thousand, because you talk so nice."

"You are all heart inside, Marcel. You only *look* like a professional bank robber. Now tell me what to do."

Without further comment, Marcel did so. He also gave Ingo a battered briefcase and a map of Teheran. Then Ingo climbed gingerly into the car and put the map and the briefcase on the seat beside him. He drove to the corner of an expanse of barren land near the northwestern edge of the city. The land had once belonged to the army, and there were plans now to use it for a new, multimillion-dollar city center. Ingo got out of the car and smoked a cigarette. If people had been watching, they would have thought that Ingo's actions were logical: a foreigner —an artisan or laborer by the look of him—was relaxing for a few minutes and taking a look at a site where vast construction projects might soon be under way.

Standing by the car's open door, Ingo stooped to tie a shoe. Then, before he straightened up again, he transferred the briefcase from the seat to the gutter beside the road. His movements were largely concealed by the bulk of the car; it was almost certain that no one had noticed what he had done. The nearest houses were scores of yards away, low villas nestling behind high walls. The nearest visible people were three small boys standing way down the street, waiting for the parade, which was to pass a quarter mile from where Ingo was standing.

Ingo peered past them into the distance. The marchers were still out of sight, but the march music was audible, and getting louder. The parade was on schedule, but the kettle-drumming was growing ragged. What a lousy band, Ingo thought. The band and the marchers were not from the Iranian army but from the Imperial Iranian Gendarmerie, a lesser force whose chief mission is to maintain law and order in the Iranian countryside. They were parading to commemorate the anniversary of the founding, in 1911, of the Gendarmerie.

Ingo got back in the car and headed back toward the Central Hotel. The marchers proceeded, led by an officer on horseback with an arch of flowers hung over his shoulders—a special Iranian touch. Behind him came lower-ranking officers, on foot, then two old sergeants, carrying a flower-bedecked portrait of the Shah. Then companies of tired-looking men. For an hour and a half they had been moving through the gasoline fumes of downtown Teheran. Now, at last, they were approaching the outskirts of the city, where they would disband.

As the marchers approached where the three small boys were standing, an old Teheran policeman, in uniform, got off his bicycle, set it down, and waited by the curb with a grin on his lined face. A few yards away stood a fat woman who had stopped hawking lottery tickets so that she could watch the parade. Next to her was a messenger boy carrying six glasses of tea on saucers on a tin tray. He was letting the tea grow cold while he waited to see the marchers go by.

Then, *boom!* The simple pocket-watch detonator in the briefcase set off the minute vial of nitroglycerin, one of the most powerful explosives known . It was a sample taken from the shipment that Faiz had brought down from Rezaiyeh. The blast flung dirt, gravel and shreds of cotton batting for yards around and sent up a cloud of fine brown dust. But it caused no casualties.

The lottery-ticket woman screamed. The tea boy dropped his tray. A stray dog howled.

The commanding officer's horse might have bolted if the man hadn't yanked furiously on the reins. The marchers scattered. A lieutenant sensibly shouted an order to take cover, and they dashed southward, away from the blast. The commander yelled at them to stop, to charge toward the explosion site, but it was too late; the men kept running the other way. The old policeman, dazed, stooped stiffly to pick up his precious bicycle.

Within seconds, police sirens began sounding, first from two directions, then three, then four, as more and more squad cars responded to radio calls. From three precincts away, a squad car roared out of a station-house courtyard, siren sounding, and sped past the gates of the Central Hotel.

Upstairs, in the second-floor bar, Ingo and Marcel were sharing a big bottle of the good local beer and a plate of the matchless local pistachio nuts. Ingo, eyes still somewhat aglitter, had been complaining that the beer wasn't cold enough, that the bartender had been misled by British drinkers, who liked warm beer.

It was a matter of pride with Ingo and Marcel that they did not turn a hair when they heard the distant boom. After all, the noise might conceivably have been from blasting at a construction sight. But most of the customers in the bar rushed to the north windows, and Marcel and Ingo, not wishing to be conspicuous, ambled after them, carrying their beer glasses.

"I guess the stuff was okay," Marcel said softly.

"Was that in doubt?" Ingo asked.

"Somewhat. Pure nitroglycerin is colorless, and usually commercial grades of the stuff are slightly impure, which makes them pale yellow. When this consignment arrived, I thought it was a little *too* yellow, and so did Gumbert. We thought it might possibly have been diluted too much to be effective. Or that it might not even be nitroglycerin. We had to make sure it was okay. So now we know it is."

Ingo looked at his own wolfish grin reflected in the side of his glass. The beer was relaxing him. "How come you didn't tell me this beforehand?"

Marcel sensed Ingo's calmer mood and knew he could afford to chaff him a little. "Shit," he said, "if you had known there might be something wrong with the stuff, you would have held me up for too much money. I might have had to kill you."

"Bullshit," Ingo said amiably. "Not if I saw you first." He took a swallow. The Adam's apple in his scrawny throat worked up and down. "So now we can go ahead with the project, huh?"

"Oh yeah. That's the point. Now nothing can stop us."

Harry pricked up his ears; he thought he had heard the sound of a far-off explosion, but he could not be sure. He took another swallow from the flask, handed it back to Gail and leaned closer to the tape recorder.

CHAZ: The point is, sir, that almost all burglar alarms use ordinary telephone lines to transmit their alarm signals. As it happens, that's as true for this alarm system that we're going, uh, to interdict here as it is, say, for people's summer houses back home, places like Cape Cod and like that.

KATES: How do you know about the system we are addressing ourselves to here?

CHAZ: The reason is sort of complicated. You could say it was just one of those things: just one of thousands of things that are going slightly wrong, or worse, in this country now that the new oil money is changing everything around so fast. One big change is that Teheran has boomed. The population has doubled in a few years; it's over four million now, they think. So the city telephone system went all to hell. There were just too many people, not enough phones, not enough lines and like that. So the Shah's government hired foreign companies as contractors and subcontractors for fixing up communications around the country, not just in Teheran. And the work was supposed to get done in a hurry. Some of these foreign businessmen looked around real fast for personnel to put in here. Well now, the money is good here, but the country is, well it's difficult. The work here involves a lot of hassle and harassment. So it was natural that some pretty rough-and-ready boys got hired. Boys that knew the value of the dollar.

KATES: You mean, men that would do anythin' for money?

CHAZ: Well, sort of like that. Now me and some friends, we've been on a job down in central Teheran. And I happen to have access to the two-line circuit that this particular alarm system uses. It was installed about twenty years back, but it's still in good condition. Has to be, after all, that stuff it's guarding, that there is worth billions.

KATES: Three billion, if it's marketed right. Maybe more.

CHAZ: Okay, three. Now the stuff is in a big public showroom that's armor-plated, like a bank vault, under a big bank called the Bank Melli, that was founded by this Shah's father. But now the stuff is under the control of the Central Bank, the Bank Markazi, which occupies other buildings next door.

KATES: Yes, Chaz. We know.

CHAZ: Now, every tourist that's ever been into that vault knows that the cases with the jewels are attached to a burglar-alarm system that is set to be very sensitive.

GUMBERT: That's right; if you even nudge those cases the alarm system goes off.

KATES: What makes that alarm system so sensitive?

CHAZ: That's a big, dark secret. Far as I know, the Shah's government won't even say what foreign company put in the system; that must be so nobody can try to pay off the foreign alarm technicians to find out just how it works.

(There followed a clinking sound; Chaz's coffee cup was evidently being refilled by a silent retainer.)

CHAZ: But, uh, I've had something to do with burglar alarms over the years, and I figure what we have here is what they call "vibration contacts." That's a system that includes what they call a detector, usually a very thin bronze leaf. The leaf has a contact point, and this contact point—

GUMBERT: Thanks, Chaz, but you needn't go into, um, detail. It becomes academic, anyway, doesn't it?

CHAZ: Well, what it all boils down to is that hundreds of objects in that vault room are plugged into the alarm system. The display cases, the panes of glass on the cases, the vault doors, and like that, they're all obviously connected to this system. That way, if anybody nudges against a glass pane, or monkeys with a vault door, or tries to fiddle with the frame of one of those cases, that creates an electric signal that is passed along to this two-wire circuit. But that circuit isn't like a telephone line that you see a lineman putting up on a telephone pole. And it doesn't hook into the city phone system. What it does is tie into three points, what they call remote reporting points: one is the nearest precinct house of the Teheran municipal police. One is the wardroom of the Bank Markazi guard force—a separate organization—in a building nearby. And one is a utility room on the ground floor of the same Bank Markazi building.

That's where they have the mechanism that switches on the local annunciator, the sound the tourists hear. And the mechanism that automatically closes the steel gates that lead into the vault. So that anybody in the vault when the alarm goes off is trapped.

KATES: Can we just cut that double telephone line to knock the system out of action?

CHAZ: Better not. This special circuit is capable of transmitting at least two signals: one is what they call the "positive position"; that means a green light or something like that is turned on in the police precinct house, the wardroom and the utility room. The other signal is what they call "the alarm state" —that is, if somebody activates the system, say, by trying to pry open a case. The "alarm state" is indicated by a red light or something similar in the precinct, the wardroom and the utility room. But if we cut the circuit, the voltage through it would be lost, and that fact would show up some way at the three terminals. Usual thing is to have an amber light turn on. It's a sort of standard thing in the business. That brings us to the most important point: how to deactivate the system without anybody noticing. But before we get into that, I'd like to talk a little business.

KATES: What's that?

CHAZ: Now, I been to a lot of trouble and expense to collect all this info, and I've spent a lot of time briefing the good doctor here, Dr. uh—

GUMBERT (icily): Gumbert.

CHAZ: Yessir, Doctor, like I was saying, you gentlemen hired me to advise you on the telephone aspects of this situation. So, now I figure I've done that, plus I've thrown in a lot of extra information about burglar alarms and such. Now, the way I see it, the deal we made calls for me to show you the way to where that wiring is and explain what you should do. Now if you want me to give you on-the-spot help when the time comes, you gotta raise the ante a little more—

GUMBERT: That's nonsense, Chaz, and you know it. You expressly agreed, when we had our negotiating session—

CHAZ: Now, Doctor, I'm a reasonable man, but you got to admit three billion dollars is a lot of money.

KATES (casually): Chaz, we all can understand that the mention of all that money could color your judgment. I must say if I were in your position, I'd feel the same way—

CHAZ: Right you are.

KATES (more softly, evidently speaking to one side): Ibrahim, get ready.

IBRAHIM (a heavy, accented voice): Yes, sah.

(A loud thump and a cracking sound followed, as though someone, presumably Ibrahim, had smashed a chair.)

CHAZ: Hey, what'd he do that for? What's he gonna do with that chair leg?

(Silence.)

CHAZ: What's that with the knife? What's he carving that chairleg for, like he's sharpening it? Look, you guys, I've had it. Call off your freak!

KATES: Ibrahim is not a freak. He's a trusted colleague. What you see are only the symptoms of a glandular disorder he had as a teenager. He was brought up in a tiny village in the far east of Iran, what they call Baluchistan, without much medical care.

CHAZ (defiantly): Freaks is freaks.

KATES: Yes, well, his hands and feet *are* pretty big and powerful. Now, let's get to the point. We could easily find someone with your technical knowledge. You know that. But it would take several days and we're in a hurry. So you're goin' to stick to your side of the bargain. We'll make the agreed payment to you. But you're goin' to give us your fullest cooperation. And you *will* give us on-the-spot assistance when our project is getting under way. Is that understood?

(Silence.)

KATES (louder): Otherwise Ibrahim's goin' to work you over

with the big end of that chair leg until you can't move much, and then with the sharp end he's—

(Another loud sound followed. It was as though a man, presumably Chaz, had knocked over his own chair in an attempt to flee the room. Then there was a thump, as of someone being tackled or hurled to the ground.)

KATES: Shall I tell Ibrahim to go to work?

(Silence. Some panting. Then the sound of a punch, and, almost simultaneously, a grunt. Another punch. Another grunt. A pause. A deep-pitched mumble. It sounded like "Okay.")

KATES: What's that? Speak up, man. Loud and clear. Otherwise—

CHAZ (evidently in pain): Okay, I said okay. You win. I'll do it all. Like I said to the doc. Only get your freak out of here. Get him—aagh!

(More thumps, more bumping sounds, perhaps of furniture overturning on a carpet, perhaps of a man being knocked down.)

KATES: Ibrahim, my friend, now you can stop. Ibrahim, please! Ibrahim, for God's—

There followed a snapping sound on the tape, and the recording ended, although the tape was still running.

Harry looked sharply at Gail. Were those tears in the corn-blue eyes? "Jesus Christ," he said. "I assumed these people were vicious, but I didn't think they were *savages*. Isn't it dangerous for you to have that tape? How did you get hold of it?"

"Yeah, it *is* risky," she said softly. "I better try and sneak it back into Gumbert's office now. Then I got to go out driving with the TV guy." She sighed and took a deep swallow from the flask. Then she put it back in her purse, along with the tape. They stood up and began strolling toward the hotel. "I—I got it earlier today; I was sort of hanging out with Gumbert: I had to give him my report on Brabham, the TV guy."

Harry said nothing. He found that he did not want to know what she had been doing with the two men.

"Harry." Her voice was softer now, almost a whisper.
"What?"

"He told me what they've done with your daughter."

"Christ, why didn't you tell me before?" Harry said.

"I'm going to tell you all I know now," Gail said, "but first I wanted to play that tape for you to show you these guys are real dirty operators. I—I don't want you to get busted up with a sharpened chairleg. I wanted you to get it clear in your head that if you try funny stuff with them, and they catch you, there's no telling what they'll do to you."

"Thanks," he said curtly. After years of manipulating other people, he disliked being manipulated himself. "Where the hell is she?"

Gail reached into her neckline and plucked out a bit of pink paper: a cocktail napkin from the Bristol Bar. She had written four lines on it in a girlish scrawl:

347–2289
Ferris Road
Southport
name: Adair

"Southport, Connecticut?" he asked.

"Yes. Not too far from Greenwich. I don't know where Ferris Road is. I don't even know if those spellings are right. But the phone number is. I've heard him say it twice to the international operator, when he was trying to book calls."

"Did you hear him talking to Emily? To whoever it is who's holding her? How is she? What kind of a place is that?"

"I don't know how she is. He talked German to them, and he knows I can't understand it. He didn't tell me much, but it seems like they have her in a house. They've sublet it from this family named Adair. Gumbert says it's a big house and the Adairs had been having trouble trying to sublet it. That's how Gumbert's men could get it on short notice."

"Why did they pick a big place, I wonder?"

"He says because if it's big and fancy, the neighbors don't think it's suspicious if you move in there with a little girl and a dikey woman that looks like a governess. And if you have a couple of extra men around as a yardman and a chauffeur."

Harry walked much faster. He went to a phone booth in the hotel lobby, put in a two-rial piece, and dialed the U.S. embassy. The phone-booth line was less likely to be tapped by Iranian intelligence than the phone in his room. He got through right away to the ambassador's secretary, but she put him on hold. Harry looked at his watch. After forty-five seconds the ambassador came on.

"Prince Arloff! To what do I owe this pleasure?" On the phone the ambassador's voice sounded hoarse, old and surprisingly cool; the last time he had greeted Harry, at the dinner dance, he had joked and called him Harry.

"Mr. Ambassador, I have an urgent personal problem. I'd like to ask your help."

"Uh-oh. Sounds like a matter for the consulate—"

"My daughter has been kidnapped from our home in Connecticut and she's being held prisoner not far away."

"That's terrible news, terrible. But, ah, are you sure about this, ah, Harry? This isn't some sort of jet-set prank?"

"No, sir."

"Well, now, you know it's nighttime in Washington now."

"Yes, but you could send a cable to the State Department, and they could get on to the FBI right away. Let me give you the address where she's being kept. The FBI has to be careful; there are two or three men with her. They've also kidnapped her governess."

"Goodness. How have you learned all this?"

"I'm sorry, I'm not at liberty to say just now. But—"

"Harry, I'll be blunt with you, if you'll permit me. You and I know that you have a reputation out here for being a little— how shall I say—fast on your feet in your business dealings. My wife says you're a marvelous spinner of tales to these *nouveaux riches* Iranian ladies, but I'm afraid my consular people would need a little more in the way of, ah, hard facts before they decide to act—"

"Please. It's urgent. I was just going to say, if the FBI can just get her back, I'll be in a position to give you some important information—"

"Look, fella, this is getting a little too complicated for me to sort out just now." The ambassador clearly thought Harry was trying to hoodwink him somehow. "There are a couple of other calls coming in. Let me put you on hold for a moment and my secretary will switch you over to Joe Vizzini, my consul general. You've met Joe at parties, I'm sure. The one who does the Victor Borge imitations."

Harry's heart sank further. "Look, Mr. Ambassador, couldn't you just send an urgent message yourself, couldn't—"

"Let's do it my way for the time being, Harry. If you don't get results from Vizzini, come and see me in a day or two, will you, and I'll see what I can do."

There was a click. The ambassador had hung up. Harry knew the man was not callous; he had a couple of daughters himself—long-legged bachelor girls, who smiled out from silver-framed photographs on top of his grand piano. So if the ambassador was brushing him off, it was, pure and simple, because the man didn't trust him as far as he could throw him.

Harry decided not to wait for the oafish Vizzini to come on the line. He hung up, dialed the embassy again and said, "Mr. Karthian, please. Karth-i-an."

In a tight-knit diplomatic center like Teheran, the name of the chief CIA man in the U.S. embassy often becomes an open secret among people interested in his line of work; it becomes merely a matter of good form for his wife to assert to her dinner partners that she is married to the agricultural attaché, or whatever her husband's cover is. Harry wished now that he had been nicer to Mrs. Karthian at the dinner dance.

A male assistant to Karthian came on the phone. His voice sounded strangely faint; some sort of recording machine was evidently attached to the phone line.

Harry said, "My name is Harry Arloff. I'm an American citizen, regional sales manager for De Kirsch and Company, the jewelry firm. I'd like to speak urgently to Mr. Karthian."

"Well, sir—"

"I'm an old, old friend of Hobie Stiles."

"One moment."

There was a pause. Then Karthian's voice came on. He and Harry had never met, but the man spoke with the effortless informality that is sometimes, among other things, a useful interrogation tool: "Hi, there, Harry, how are you? The missus was telling me you were being a real gadabout at the dance the other night. And Hobie says you're quite a character. How *is* he? Behaving himself?"

Harry ignored that last remark; Karthian doubtless debriefed Hobie every few days.

"Mr. Karthian, do you have a pencil handy?"

"Of course." Karthian's voice was suddenly more business-like. After all, compiling information was his profession. "But is this something you'd rather talk about here in the office? We serve a pretty good cup of coffee."

"There's no time. And what I have to discuss is a federal crime that's been committed in the United States. It's something that wouldn't interest any Iranian security official who might be listening in now. If you can get the FBI to get back my little girl, I'd be happy to pay you back with an important piece of information."

"Okay, Harry. How can we help you?"

"My five-year-old daughter, Emily Arloff, was kidnapped from my house in Greenwich, Connecticut, at some time within the last two days. The kidnappers put her through to me on the telephone some hours ago. There's been no ransom demand, but the kidnapping is part of a complicated extortion plot."

"Of course." Karthian did not quibble, did not accuse Harry of being a shady character, did not ask whether Harry had spoken to the consulate. The man had spent his career dealing with shady characters, Harry reflected—and taking chances on the information such characters provided.

Forcing himself to speak slowly and clearly, Harry gave Karthian the details about the house in Southport, then asked softly, "Can you help?"

"Glad to. I'll call Washington now, and they'll get on to the FBI. There may be some red tape about dealing with the Connecticut state police, but I'm sure it can be cleared up fast. I hope to have some progress to report to you within a few hours. You're at the Bristol, aren't you? My wife told me. If you haven't heard from me by ten o'clock tonight, call me at home. I'll leave word with the embassy switchboard to put you through to my house. Okay?"

"Okay, Mr. Karthian."

"Call me Leo. Glad to help a fellow American." And always glad to get information from a new informant, Harry thought to himself.

"Okay, Leo."

"But look, Harry, do me a favor?"

"What's that?" Relay to him the latest rumors from the business community? Report gossip about the East German ambassador?

"Next one of those parties, would you dance a couple dances with my wife?"

Harry said yes and good-bye and hung up. It was hot in the phone booth, and he was sweating. He opened the door with some relief, wanting to tell Gail what had happened. But she was gone. He went to the concierge's desk to see if she had left a message. On his way he felt a soft hand on his arm: it was Gumbert.

"The countdown has begun, my friend," the man said. "We have a little, um, preliminary chore for you; we're short-handed. Be at the southwest corner of Elizabeth II Boulevard and Los Angeles Street in exactly two hours. Without fail." The last words had a menacing emphasis. Harry barely had time to say okay before Cumbert turned away and ambled out the hotel's main entrance, pausing only to glance at the glass case displaying cans of Iranian caviar.

# 10

"THIS IS THE PLACE, HONEY," GAIL SAID. "LOOK OVER THERE."
She pointed out the car window with her right hand, keeping
her left hand on Buddy Brabham's thigh.

Buddy looked. He had had a lot of Beaujolais at lunch, and
he was feeling happy. He shrugged. "The Riviera it's not," he
said amiably. Nothing could spoil his mood, not even the view:
the dump lay in the middle of an expanse of flatland that was
scarred here and there with tumble-down brick walls and abandoned huts. Pieces of broken glass glinted in the dirt. In the
middle distance a plume of greasy-looking smoke rose from
inside the dump and wobbled into the sky.

"What's to see?" Umberto the cameraman snapped. He
had flown into Teheran from New York early that morning, and
he was grouchy from jet lag and lack of sleep. He jammed on
the hand brake and turned to pick up his camera, which was
lying on the empty front seat beside him.

"Watch, Umberto," Gail said soothingly. "Watch and you'll
see something you'll want to film real bad."

Two men in work clothes were clambering around the
edge of the dump. They wore rubber boots. One was smoking
a cigarette, perhaps to ward off the general stench. One had a
piece of cloth, like a bandanna, wrapped around his face. A
large gray panel truck was parked near them.

"Jee-zis," Umberto said scornfully. He was also grumpy
because Gail and Buddy had sat in the back seat during the

drive out here, making him sit alone up front like a chauffeur, driving the rented Volvo sedan. Then Umberto's mood shifted suddenly. His face took on an intent look. He slipped out of the car, clamped the camera on one shoulder and began to stride across the bare ground toward the two workmen, filming as he walked.

What Umberto was filming so avidly was one of the workmen, the one with the cigarette. The man had climbed into the truck and was now bundling dog carcasses out through the rear doors. The corpses were landing in a wheelbarrow held by the other workman.

"Is it okay if Umberto shoots that, honey?" Buddy asked. "That's good stuff he's getting, but we don't want to queer the interview with the Shah."

"Don't worry, it's okay. They don't guard this place; there's nobody else around now; there's nothing worth stealing here."

Buddy and Gail followed Umberto across the waste ground. Here and there bits of glass and old metal clinked under their feet. The feeble breeze that tugged at the rising smoke also disturbed the arrangement of the hairs across Buddy's scalp. He put them more or less back into place with absent-minded pats; his mind was on what Umberto was doing.

"He's getting damn good footage," Buddy said. "Man, I can just hear the voice-over now." His voice deepened: " 'In the capital of the Shah's authoritarian state, stray dogs are not supposed to wander at will. Employees of the Teheran municipality hunt them down with the latest in poison dart guns, bought with his huge oil revenues, and—' "

"Look, it's not as bad as that," Gail said. "The point is that those dogs could spread disease if they kept on running around loose."

"Maybe—but this is a good way to show in visual terms that this is a mighty tough regime we have here."

"Okay, honey." She put her hand through his arm.

Now, at this moment, he thought to himself, he was just

about as happy as he could possibly be. His happiness was complete because Gail was at his side—and Umberto was getting good film. Buddy could already hear the appreciative murmurs when this footage was screened back at network headquarters. Dogs were always good stuff. Unless maybe what Umberto was shooting now was too graphic, too disgusting. Then maybe the film wouldn't be aired. Buddy thought of trotting up and telling Umberto to watch it, to shoot some footage far away from the dogs, so it wouldn't show them too clearly. But he decided to hell with it. He would lay back, with Gail's arm in his and Gail's soft hair flying a little in the breeze, enjoying his happiness.

Buddy and Gail watched as the man with the cloth over his face trundled the wheelbarrow toward the six-foot earthen cliff that formed the edge of the dump. The man emptied the wheelbarrow over the side. Umberto filmed away.

"Who are those men, anyhow?" Buddy asked. Now there was an edge of suspicion in his voice. "You say one of those businessmen at the ambassador's party tipped you off about all this?"

"Right. But I don't know who they are. Teheran has got to have a garbage department, like anyplace else; they must be Teheran garbage men."

"Okay, but why does the man working the wheelbarrow have fair hair? He doesn't look like an Iranian to me."

"Ah, honey, relax. Maybe he's a Turk from the north; they're not as dark as the real Iranians. Maybe he's a whatchummacallit, a Kurd."

"Yeah. Maybe. But that's not so good visually, you know. 'Shah's blond garbage man.' "

"How come you're all business all of a sudden." She tickled his stomach over his belt, where the flesh bulged. But he would not be distracted. He strode more quickly now, toward Umberto.

"Let's see if they speak some English. They don't seem to mind us filming them, so maybe they'll talk." Buddy came within thirty feet of the truck. The other workman was lighting another cigarette.

"Hey, something's definitely weird," Buddy said. "Look at that blue cigarette pack. Those are Gauloises—French cigarettes. Whoever heard of an Iranian garbage man smoking French cigarettes?"

The man looked at them; his square face lit up with a smile. He was wearing gray pants and a gray windbreaker. He had a flat belly and stood solidly on the balls of his feet. He put the pack of Gauloises into a pocket of the windbreaker. He reached under the windbreaker and pulled out a .38-caliber revolver with a silencer. The gun looked well cared for.

"You, Baldy, get in the back of the truck," he said in English with a slight foreign accent, French perhaps. "You, photographer, take your camera and get in the truck, too. And keep quiet."

Buddy gasped. "Jesus H. Christ" is what he wanted to say, but his throat was suddenly dry.

"Buddy," Gail whispered. "For God's sake, don't leave me. I don't want to get raped."

But Buddy was already moving, very slowly, toward the truck. He did not want to get shot. Umberto got in after him, setting the camera down on the truck floor.

"You, Blondie," the gunman said loudly, "you start walking that way, west. Don't move fast and don't move slow. Just keep moving and you're gonna be all right. If you make a peep, you're dead."

Buddy peeked through the truck's back doors to see what the gunman was doing. But then a *pow* sounded and a tin can at one side of the truck scooted back five yards. The gunman had put a bullet through it.

"Move back inside the truck, Baldy," the gunman said.

Buddy did so. He began to sweat. He knew the sweat would make his hairs curl, would show the bald spot. What a crazy thing to think of now, when he might be dead in five minutes.

He wished he had had children. He wished he and his wife had been happier. He was awfully glad that he had had this happy time with Gail. Gail—it looked like they were just going to let her go. Surely she'd give the alarm. But, Jesus, that might mean a shoot-out with the police. Buddy shifted his footing—and stumbled on something soft. It was the corpse of a dog. He shrank back. He glanced at Umberto. The man's eyes were closed. He was praying.

The preliminary chore that Gumbert had spoken of began as the gray Teheran afternoon wore on toward dusk. The gray clouds had a brownish tinge from the dust off the arid plains. The usual traffic jams strangled the avenues, with the usual sullen drivers honking and poking their heads out of car doors. Harry amused himself, as he stood at the corner of Elizabeth II Boulevard and Los Angeles Street, by watching to see if fistfights broke out, as they not infrequently did.

He had not seen any in the ten minutes he had waited when a pale-blue Fiat sedan stopped in front of him. The driver honked lightly. The Fiat's door bore a stenciled trademark in Farsi: a circle of Farsi characters around a lightning bolt. It was clearly some sort of electrical contractor. Gumbert was smiling from the rear seat. Harry climbed into the front seat, beside the driver, a lanky American. The man had wrinkles in the skin around his mouth, as though he kept his lips permanently pursed. He looked selfish, disappointed with life, angry with the world.

"This is Chaz," Gumbert said, by way of explanation. Chaz looked glumly ahead and drove.

This was obviously the Chaz who had spoken on the tape recording that Gail had played for Harry, the Chaz who had tried to get the plotters to pay him more money and had evidently been badly beaten for his pains. Harry gave the man's face a sharp look. Sure enough, one corner of his mouth was cut, and there was a large bruise on his throat. It was as though

Ibrahim the coffee server had gripped him there for a while with an oversized hand.

"Pleased to meet you," Harry said. The man merely nodded.

"Chaz has not been, um, much for small talk lately," Dr. Gumbert said jovially. He patted Chaz's bony shoulder. "When you get your compensation for your chores, Chaz, you'll cheer up, I promise you—you'll realize that you're being handsomely rewarded. And I shouldn't be surprised if there was a bonus for you, too."

"Thanks," Chaz said. "I could sure use one. I'm gonna have to have a lot of dental work when all this is over." Chaz's gaunt right cheek was briefly distended by the probing of his tongue among his teeth.

They drove down Ferdowsi and turned off on Naderi Avenue, two blocks north of the bank building where the jewels were. Then they turned southward into a side street lined with high-walled villas and minor office buildings.

Chaz parked the car, and they all got out. Chaz was flexing his fingers like a pianist about to perform. Gumbert put on a pair of dark glasses and a fedora. Chaz unlocked the luggage compartment of the car and took out a two-foot-long metal toolbox with a handle on the top and a plastic hard hat bearing the lightning-bolt trademark. He put the hat on. "Carry the case, please," he said to Harry, who did as he was told.

They walked for five minutes down the narrow sidewalk until they came to one of the older, European-style restaurants in central Teheran that date from the pre-oil-boom days. This one, Nikolai's, featured Russian cuisine. It had been founded by White Russian expatriates decades ago and was known for its chicken Kiev and its senile White Russian waiters. It was located on the western side of the parking lot that extended westward from the building where the jewels were, but it was separated from the parking lot by a high brick wall. The restaurant was housed in a converted brick villa, which faced westward onto a quiet north-south side street. The street was paved with asphalt. Ten yards south of the restaurant the street was partly blocked by three sawhorse-type wooden barriers, hung with unlit lanterns. The sawhorses formed a triangle enclosing a six-foot-square sheet of iron, dark gray in color, which lay on the asphalt. A watchman in Kurdish pantaloons was standing nearby. He greeted the three foreigners in Farsi. Chaz said "Hi."

With Chaz giving instructions in English and sign language, Harry and the Kurd helped him to drag the iron sheet out of the way. It was lighter than it looked because it was thin. Removing the sheet revealed a round, three-foot-wide, metal-ringed hole in the street—the kind of cavity that would normally be covered by a manhole cover. Moving with practiced ease, Chaz let himself down through the hole; it led to a small underground chamber. Harry handed down the toolbox to him and then, more cautiously, clambered down through the hole.

Gumbert remained on the street, standing with his hands clasped behind his back. He looked like a slightly fuddy-duddy old electrical engineer, but he was, of course, standing guard and at the same time keeping an eye on the Kurd.

Down below, Harry studied the small chamber. It had rough brick walls and a concrete ceiling that was only five feet high, which meant they had to stoop. The floor, also concrete, was an irregular octagon roughly six feet wide.

"This little room is what telephone engineers call a vault," Chaz said. He unsnapped a key ring that hung from his thick, hand-tooled belt. He used one of the keys to unlock the toolbox and then folded back the lid. He removed a tray of small tools and parts and took out from under it a small electric lantern, which he set on the floor and switched on.

The lamp's beam cast a circle of light against one corner of the vault, illuminating part of a rectangular object studded with dials and knobs, which was set against one wall.

"That thing is a transformer," Chaz said. "It's not important to us."

The beam also lit several fat cables, which came out of holes in one wall, ran across the lamplit wall and disappeared into holes in the next adjoining wall. They must be telephone cables or possibly power cables, Harry thought. They were sheathed with a substance that glowed dully in the lamplight. It could be either lead or rubber, Harry thought, but he decided not to touch it to test it. Among the fat cables was one thin cable, also insulated, which looked newer than the others.

Chaz took from the toolbox a dark-green plastic box. Its front side was set with four dials, which looked to Harry like the altitude dials on airplane control panels. The box was also set with four small switches—toggle switches, Harry thought they were called. And like a squid trailing tentacles, it trailed wires that had alligator clips—little clips with jagged jaws—at their ends.

"Okay, now comes the hard part," Chaz said.

"What do you mean?"

"As you can see, nobody has been messing with the vault. The Kurd upstairs is cooperative. I got my equipment here all ready to install. So far, so good. Now I want you to go back up topside and go over to Gumbert nice and casual-like. Don't shout at him and don't do anything else that might make people notice us. Tell him everything's okay, and I'm ready to install the equipment. Then he'll go back to the car and he'll start it and have it ready in case we have to skip out fast. Then you wait next to the manhole. If something goes wrong down here and I need you, I'll whistle soft and you can hop back down. Meanwhile, you listen very hard. If you hear police sirens and they sound like they're coming to that bank building across the wall, tell me quick. And tell me quick if you see any other funny police activity. So I can get out of here. You got all that?"

"Sure. But what are you going to do now?"

"I'm going to fool the crown-jewels burglar-alarm system,

that's what," Chaz said, with a note of pride. "This here device in the green case is a combination of two pieces of equipment called a multimeter and a potentiometer. That skinny cable there belongs to the alarm system. When I attach those alligator clips to the skinny cable, if I do it right, this device will make sure there's an even flow of current, no matter what. That means it'll make the alarm system indicate that everything's okay—even if somebody jolts one of the cases in the crown-jewels vault or does something else in the vault that would normally turn on the alarm. You follow me?"

"Sort of. And what happens if you don't do it right?"

"Then all hell breaks loose. The alarm starts to sound in the crown-jewels vault. The cops and the guards will check their equipment and they'll figure out that there's some sort of interference in the wiring somewhere. If they're smart, they've got a map somewhere that shows that this spot is one of the only places that gives access to the wiring. They'll come here on the double." Chaz flexed his fingers again; the gesture was in part a nervous habit. "Man, I'll be glad when the next hour is over. Then I'm all finished."

"What are you going to do after that?"

"I'm taking the early flight tomorrow to Paris. Bye-bye, Teheran."

"Then what?"

"Then I'm going to retire. Gumbert is going to make me a down payment tonight, and when the project is all over, I get a cut on the proceeds. I might go to Brazil, someplace like that, buy me a cattle spread. Brazil. I like those skinny bathing suits the women wear down there."

Chaz gave Harry a boost, and Harry clambered out through the manhole. He looked back down and saw the man bending down to get to work.

"Hand over your wallets," Marcel said to Buddy and Umberto the cameraman. Pistol in hand, he was standing at the rear doors of the truck now, with the fair-haired man—Ingo—in a backup position behind him. Buddy sighed. Maybe this was just a stickup. He and Umberto handed over their wallets. Marcel took them with his free hand and passed them back to Ingo, who riffled through them. From each wallet he took a fresh-looking white identification card.

"These them?" he asked, showing them to Marcel.

Marcel glanced at the cards. "Yeah, that's them. Let's go."

The doors were slammed shut and locked from the outside. The truck rumbled over the bumpy ground. Umberto squatted down on the truck's filthy floor, but Buddy struggled to keep his balance standing. He tried to make a joke. "Hey, Umberto, least this way you don't have to drive."

Umberto was not amused. He shrugged his shoulders and flashed Buddy a look of scorn. "Hey," he said softly, "what was that they took out of our wallets? Could you see?"

"Yes," Buddy whispered. "It was those ID cards the information ministry gave us. The ones that say we're foreign journalists, and government officials should give us all reasonable cooperation."

Umberto shook his head slowly. "I bet they can't get much for those cards on the black market. Shit. These guys are maniacs. Either that or they want my camera. Eight thousand dollars it's worth. Shit."

The truck stopped. In a moment the rear doors opened. Marcel gestured to the two captives to get out. The truck had stopped, Buddy could now see, next to a tumble-down brick wall. Built onto the wall was a small brick outbuilding, probably meant as a storage shed. One side was stenciled with a picture of a soda-pop bottle and an advertising message in faded red Farsi script.

The door of the hut was open. Marcel motioned at Buddy and Umberto to go in. Ingo came in behind them, carrying two coils of rope.

Marcel said, "Look, that rope stretches very little. So if my friend ties you up too tight, you're going to be uncomfortable. If he ties you up very tight, you'll be in pain. If he ties you up very, very tight, you might strangle to death. So don't make trouble while he ties you."

Buddy nodded. Umberto glared. Ingo set to work with the rope. He made a half-hitch and a loop, which he put around Buddy's throat. Then he went to work making the other knots around Buddy's body. Buddy began to retch when Ingo stuffed a handkerchief in his mouth and taped his lips shut.

"C'mon, Ingo," Marcel burst out. "Don't be so rough. These aren't animals. If that guy vomits in that gag, he'll choke to death."

"Okay, okay," Ingo said, smiling. He was clearly enjoying his work.

In minutes it was finished. The two television men lay trussed and gagged on the dirt floor of the hut. Ingo and Marcel stepped outside and closed the door. Then Buddy and Umberto, to their horror, heard the door being nailed shut with a hammer. Umberto flopped back and forth on the floor. He began to moan loudly into his gag.

Then two bangs exploded in the hut. Jerking his head around, Buddy saw sunlight through two bullet holes in the door. Umberto fell still.

"You, in there," Marcel said, his mouth against the door. "You shut up or we'll fire more rounds through this door. Maybe we'll kill you." He paused, listening for further sounds from inside. There were none.

Marcel and Ingo clambered back into the truck. They drove back and picked up Gail, who was sitting on the ground beside a heap of broken bricks. Ingo got into the TV-men's rented Volvo. Both vehicles drove off.

"Jesus, I hope you guys didn't beat them up," Gail said to Marcel, after they had driven in silence for ten minutes and her nose had grown used to the stench in the truck. Marcel patted her leg, not deigning to say anything. She hitched herself away from him on the front seat.

"You didn't beat them up, did you?" she said.

Silence.

"Tell me? Goddammit."

Silence. Then Marcel said, "Put your hand out and signal to Ingo that we're turning right soon. We're going to the Bristol, and we've got no time to lose."

Harry helped Chaz out of the manhole when the man was finished. No police sirens had interrupted his labors. Then Gumbert and Chaz drove off, and Harry, on instructions from Gumbert, killed time for an hour in the restaurant; he had a jigger of Iranian vodka and a bowl of borscht and read an old *Herald Tribune*. When he came out, he waved good-bye to the Kurdish watchman; the man smiled back. Harry caught a cab, told the driver to go to the Bristol Hotel, and leaned back in his seat—so far, so good; nothing had gone wrong.

But twenty minutes later, as they approached the Bristol, the cab got bogged down in an enormous traffic jam that tied up Cyrus Boulevard for half a mile. A wild chorus of honking rose from the four jammed traffic lanes. Curious drivers climbed out of their cars and peered ahead. In the distance the lights of police cars were flashing at the Bristol's main entrance. Harry got out, tossed the driver seven hundred rials—about ten dollars—and hurried on foot toward the hotel. As he approached he saw scores of people standing in front of the entrance, many of them staring up at the roof eighteen stories above their heads. Two ambulance attendants were leaning over a stretcher, buckling straps over blankets that covered a body. The blankets had been carefully drawn over the head; the person was dead. Two police officers were standing beside the ambulance, chatting imperturbably—probably about their pensions, Harry thought. Several lower-ranking policemen were holding the crowd back from the stretcher, and two others had evidently been ordered to look for clues: they were searching the ground around the entrance like schoolboys looking for shells on a beach. As Harry watched, one of them picked up something small, perhaps a button. The other stopped to wipe off one of his shoes on the hotel lawn. He had accidentally stepped in a three-foot smear of light-colored blood that scarred the sidewalk.

Harry, feeling a premonition of trouble, hurried into the hotel lobby and picked up his room key from the hall porter.

"Who died?" he asked. "It was someone who fell from the roof, wasn't it?"

"It was an American, Prince Arloff, a thin man named Charles Truitt. An electrical engineer."

Harry turned pale. That must be Chaz. He must have been killed by Gumbert's men, to keep him from telling anyone about the plot. Harry's fist tightened around the room key. "What was he doing on the roof of the hotel? How did he come to die?"

"Awfully sorry, sir, I don't know and I can't say more. The manager has forbidden us to speak about the case; this sort of thing upsets the guests."

Harry nodded. Half dazed with horror, he turned away—and found Marcel waiting for him by the elevator bank.

"Go up and get some clean clothes and a razor," the man said briskly. "Then you're coming with me. You're going to spend the night in a nice villa with some nice folks. We want to make sure you get a good night's sleep and don't do anything that might upset you—or us. Tomorrow is the big day."


"Ain't no answer from Arloff's room at the Bristol, sir," Lopez, Karthian's aide, said over the office intercom. Karthian, in his many-times-bugproofed inner office, said, "Shit, Lopez. When the FBI does something right for once, we can't get through to the man to tell him the good news. God*damn!* Give me the marine guards' office. I'm gonna send one of them over to the Bristol Hotel in civilian clothes, and he's going to plumb sit there in the lobby until this Arloff shows up."

Lopez began looking up the marine guards' extension in the embassy directory.

Karthian leaned back in his chair and began to whistle through his teeth, a nervous habit he had acquired in tense moments along the Berlin Wall ten years before. As a human being and as a family man—however unhappy his marriage was —he was delighted that the FBI had got the Arloff girl back, plus the governess, without a scratch. And it sounded as though the FBI had open-and-shut convictions on its hands, even though none of the arrested kidnappers had divulged even the tiniest scrap of information in hours of interrogation. Perhaps in time they would crack. But now, with Arloff out of touch at this crucial time, Karthian's intuition began telling him that bad trouble was brewing. Without realizing it, he began to whistle louder.

# 11

IT WAS WELL BEFORE DAWN WHEN THE LARGE GRAY PANEL truck appeared on the empty streets of central Teheran, cautiously stopping at every red light. Four men were sitting on the front seat: Ingo was driving, Marcel and Harry were in the middle, and Hossein was next to the right-hand window. Harry was uncomfortable. It was not that the seat was slightly too narrow for four men, not that Marcel's thick shoulder was jammed into his own, not that Hossein smelled faintly of whiskey. It was that the false mustache which Gumbert had made him wear was making his upper lip itch; Gail had evidently applied too much spirit gum.

Yet in a way Harry welcomed the itch; for a while it drew his attention away from the nervousness in the pit of his stomach—nervousness that had been fueled by too many cups of coffee at the villa and diluted only slightly by one of Hossein's Valium pills. He tried to concentrate on a pleasant thought: on the possibility that if he got through the robbery with his skin intact, and if he could figure a way to betray the robbers, he might be richer by thousands of dollars of reward money within a few days. He tried to imagine himself sauntering into Maxim's in Paris—with Gail, perhaps—and talking about wines with the sommelier . . . But inevitably he began to worry about what was happening to Emily—he had picked up no information about her during the night at the villa—about what might go wrong during the robbery, and about what would happen afterward:

Gumbert and his associates had told him nothing about their escape plans, and Harry had had no opportunity to talk to Gail alone during the night. Instead, he had been put to work hosing down the truck, which had smelled like a dog pound. Then he had been given an hour to study reference books about the crown jewels—which had not been necessary, really, since anyone in the jewel business who frequents the Middle East knows the principal jewels, crowns, necklaces and whatnot the way an American schoolboy knows the baseball stars.

Later Gumbert had introduced him to Hossein and had given him a limited briefing: about which of the Note Reserve Control Board members were going to be on hand this morning when the display cases in the crown-jewels vault were opened for their annual cleaning. He showed Harry photographs of them. About how the information ministry had informed the bank authorities that an American television crew, with the blessing of the Shah, was going to take advantage of the opportunity to film the jewels. About how the cleaning and the filming were to be finished before daybreak so that the vault could be open to tourists during the usual hours. About how the TV crew would arrive with Iranian press cards (the two taken from Buddy and Umberto and a third one, for Harry, hastily copied from the others by Faiz Kiani) and an Iranian official escort—Hossein—bearing the proper credentials and a letter from the palace.

Then Harry had slept for a few hours in a servants' bedroom. He had shared it with Ingo, who had smoked a cigar in bed and then gone to sleep, snoring intermittently. After too few hours Gumbert woke them up for a breakfast of white cheese, flat Iranian bread and Nescafé. While they ate, Gumbert showed them a plan of the crown-jewels vault—which Harry had visited now and then over the years—and repeated over and over the roles that each of the four men would play during the robbery. Without emphasizing the fact, Gumbert had said that Harry would be unarmed—which showed that, despite all the trouble Gumbert had gone to arrange Emily's kidnapping, he still did not trust Harry entirely.

Then Ingo and Marcel put on curly wigs that changed their appearances somewhat, and Harry acquired his uncomfortable mustache. Hossein made no attempt to conceal his identity; the credentials that he was going to show to the bank guards were, after all, his own.

Now Hossein was drumming anxiously with his fingers on the right-side door. Harry was sure the man had a flask of liquor on him somewhere, and that the drumming fingers were itching to grab it and put it to his lips. And yet, despite the enormity of what the four men were about to do, Hossein refrained from taking a drink. His eyes were closed, Harry saw. He wondered what the man was thinking or dreaming about with such fierce concentration after so many years of waiting for this day. The eyelids flickered, and the hand on the door drummed on.

On Harry's left, Marcel was relaxed and impassive, an experienced professional on his way to do another job. He lit a Gauloise and let it hang from his lips the way, say, a steam-shovel operator mouths a cigarette absent-mindedly while he concentrates on the business at hand.

In the driver's seat, Ingo betrayed his excitement by riding the clutch and manhandling the gearshift; he was obviously keyed up. He had put on low paratrooper's boots, Harry saw; as a lion tamer, he must be accustomed to performing in boots.

Ingo slowed the truck as he turned south down Ferdowsi Avenue. The show windows of the carpet stores were still lit up on both sides of the street. He slowed down further as the truck drew up to the bank building that housed the crown-jewels vault. He brought it to a gentle stop in front of the wide iron gates, which at this hour sealed off the private alley running along the building's north wall.

A guard was standing at one side of the gate, which was lit by a single lofty streetlight. In violation of the bank guards' rules he was smoking, but after the truck arrived he dropped the cigarette. That's a good sign, Harry thought; he thinks we're VIP's.

Hossein said good morning to the guard and added something quick and emphatic in Farsi. He handed the man an identity card and the palace letter, which was in a gold-embossed envelope. The guard squinted first at the card and then at the letter, which he slipped cautiously, almost reverentially, out of the envelope. The light was surely too weak to read by, Harry thought, but that did not matter: the guard gave both papers a quick glance—he had obviously seen many such cards, many such letters—and handed them back to Hossein. Then he saluted and shouted something over his shoulder. Another guard, inside the gate, opened it by hand.

Ingo drove the truck slowly into the alley and toward the inconspicuous doorway that led to the jewels. But then the second guard abruptly gestured at him to halt. The man's face, sallow in the lamplight, was unsmiling; his hand was up like a stop sign. He said something in Farsi.

"What's this?" Ingo growled. "Do we kill him? We can still back out and get away."

"No, no, relax," Hossein whispered. "Don't think so much about killing. He only wants to look in the back of the truck."

Hossein hopped out of the front seat, gesturing at Harry to follow him. Hossein opened the truck's rear doors for the guard. Harry smiled at the man, trying to look harmless and hoping his mustache would stay in place. The guard climbed into the back of the truck and jabbed with a stubby index finger at one of the many aluminum suitcases that were stacked neatly on the floor. They bore labels that announced, in various languages, that they were network property and contained TV equipment.

Harry obediently opened the case. The guard scowled at the collapsible TV camera tripod it contained. He made another gesture; Harry shut the case. He saw that the guard had two stripes on his sleeve; it was bad luck, he reflected, that they had happened to encounter a guard of the type that liked to throw his weight around. The guard made more gestures; Harry opened more cases. Harry even lugged one out of the truck and opened it on the sidewalk; it contained a batch of old work clothes; this was because there had not been enough TV equipment to fill all the suitcases, and so Gumbert and his men had simply stuffed a couple of them with secondhand clothing. At last the two-stripe guard was satisfied. He waved Hossein and his companions on, and the truck rolled on toward the unpretentious side door. Ingo carefully backed the truck up to the bank building with the truck's rear doors close to the doorway so that movement between the truck and the doorway would be as inconspicuous as possible.

As Gumbert had predicted, there was no guard on duty outside the doorway at this hour. The door was ajar, emitting a slice of light. Inside stood a young guard; he opened the door wide to let the party in. Hossein showed him the papers, and the man made a little bow; it was clear that he had been informed that a television crew was coming at this hour.

Ingo took Harry's arm and pushed him forward, hissing in his ear, "You first." Harry had not been told in advance that he was to enter first, and he knew why he had been chosen: if shooting broke out, the first man through the door was the likeliest to be cut down by the bullets. Harry noted with strange detachment that the thought did not make him more nervous; he was tense enough as it was. He moved ahead.

But then came another surprise: in a departure from the bank's established procedures, the guard began to frisk Harry for weapons.

"Christ," Harry heard Ingo say behind him. "Frisking, even when we have a letter from the palace. This is a fucking police state." Ingo's voice had an odd exultant ring to it; he was getting high on the danger.

The guard ran his hands over Harry's sides, chest, back, thighs and rear end and found nothing worth looking at. He nodded, and Harry moved on into the hallway.

Then it was Ingo's turn, and Harry, knowing that Ingo was carrying at least a blackjack, looked around for cover. But there was none. All he could do if fighting broke out was to bolt into the hallway; he hoped his bad leg would hold up.

But, inexplicably, Ingo's frisking passed quickly and uneventfully, except that the guard took a long and envious look at his gold ballpoint pen. Ingo moved on into the hallway, smiling triumphantly at Harry, who was left wondering why the guard had failed to find the blackjack.

Then the guard beckoned to Hossein, who, Harry knew, was carrying a small .22-caliber pistol. Hossein, stalling for time, not knowing what to do, pretended not to understand that the guard wanted to frisk him. The guard rumbled an order in Farsi. Hossein, his face pale, stepped forward. He pulled out a flask and showed it to the guard with a nervous smile. Then the guard ran his hands swiftly over the sides of Hossein's jacket, over its back and down to Hossein's waist. When he got to the waist, he stopped and frowned. He had felt something suspicious. He gestured to Hossein to pull his jacket back.

It was at that point, a moment before the guard was certain to discover Hossein's pistol, that Ingo, in a terribly quick and efficient series of motions, reached into the top of his right paratrooper's boot, yanked out the clear-plastic blackjack concealed in the boot top, and hit the guard on the right side of his skull. That blow had all Ingo's weight behind it, Harry saw; it was a killer's blow, harder than would have been necessary to knock the man out.

The guard slumped. Ingo caught him and lowered him gently to the carpeted floor so that there would be no unseemly thud. Marcel, bringing up the rear, glanced out through the doorway; no one had seen them. Ingo and Harry dragged the guard's body to one side of the hall. Then all four men, moving quickly, wrestled the aluminum suitcases off the truck and through the doorway.

From there, they began lugging some of the suitcases onward, past the postcard desk—which was now unlit and unmanned—along the hall that led to the outer steel gates. On the way, they were met by another guard. He had evidently heard their footsteps and had come forward to greet them. Hossein gave him a good morning in Farsi. This guard made no searches, no friskings. He even smiled, bearing out Harry's theory, first formed in the days when he had been skulking around Swiss luxury hotels, that the further you penetrate into an inner sanctum—any inner sanctum—the more lax the security becomes. This guard was a sergeant, older than the others, evidently nearing retirement: the kind of man who, in any organization, gets the soft jobs. He was really too old for security duty, Harry reflected, too complacent, too courteous. But this, too, was predictable: Harry's long years in the Middle East had taught him that elite guards inevitably grow soft, the reason being that ceremonial and representational duties distract them from their basic security role.

This guard showed his courtesy by trying to help carry one of the suitcases, but Harry smilingly refused to let him. He indicated with a gesture that the man should lead the way to the vault; Harry did not want Ingo to have any excuse to smash another skull.

Harry and the others lugged the first of the suitcases onward, past the anteroom with the handsome chandelier and through the outer and inner steel doorways, which were now unguarded; as Hossein had predicted, only a skeleton guard force was on duty at this hour. The sergeant led the way into the vault.

"Good morning," Harry said as he entered, although for an instant he could not make out the men who were already there; his eyes were dazzled by the bright light. He set down the two suitcases he had been carrying. He heard Ingo, Marcel and Hossein enter the vault behind him and set down other suitcases, making metallic clinking noises on the marble floor.

The vault, which was kept partly darkened during the tourist visiting hours, was now brightly lit to help the jewel cleaners spot even the tiniest bits of dust. The result was that the glitter of the jewels leaped at the eye more strongly than ever. It was like shiny green water, like sunlit ice, like fire. Harry caught his breath, oblivious for a moment to the "good mornings" from the jewel cleaners and their supervisors. In the jumble of emotions he was feeling—the fear for Emily, the worry about what Ingo and the others would do next, and about what the guards' reaction would be—one feeling came to the fore: sadness about all this beauty, all this tangible history, all this heritage of an entire people which was about to fall into alien hands.

Behind him, Marcel said softly, "Holy shit."

At the air force base outside the south Iranian city of Shiraz, not far from the famous ruins of Persepolis, a truck moved toward the main gate. It was an ordinary, U.S.-made, two-and-a-half-ton truck from the base motor pool, but there were two slightly unusual things about it: first, it listed somewhat to the right—a fact that might have suggested to a suspiciously minded observer that it had been hastily, perhaps surreptitiously, loaded with heavy objects of limited size. Secondly, a clean-cut, intelligent-looking young Iranian lieutenant was sitting in the cab of the truck, next to the driver. A suspicious onlooker might have noted that this was an unusual sight in Iranian military life; Iranian officers, particularly intellectual-looking officers of the staff-aide type, do not gladly sit beside truck drivers who go out driving well before dawn.

But there were no suspicious onlookers. The corporal on guard duty at the gate gave the lieutenant a sleepy salute and waved the driver on. He did not notice the truck's tilt—or the fact that as the truck passed the life-sized lantern-lit photograph of the Shah that was posted outside the gate, the officer leaned out of the cab window and spat into the dust at the Shah's feet.

The truck rumbled off down the highway, heading toward Persepolis. The driver seemed in no hurry.

In the scene in the vault Harry immediately noticed three details that were favorable to the robbers, although not essential to their undertaking. For one thing, all the main jewelry display cases had already been opened in preparation for cleaning and filming; Gumbert had expected that only a few would be open when the robbers arrived, and that consequently the guards would have to be forced to open the others. For another thing, the sergeant and the two other guards who were already in the vault all had their holsters snapped shut, which would slow them down a second should they try to draw their revolvers. And for yet another thing, the sergeant was shuffling over to the diamond case where all the other men in the room were standing. This bunched them all together, making them a convenient target if—Harry's palms sweated at the thought—the robbers should start shooting.

Grouped around the case now were the sergeant and the two other guards—one a sharp-looking captain and one a nondescript constable—two jewelry cleaners—grizzled workmen in gray smocks—and the four members of the Note Reserve Control Board. Harry recognized the board members from the pictures that Gumbert had shown him at the villa. The fat man was Senator Qazvin himself; the one with the white hair was a member of the Iranian house of representatives who was also a doctor; the thin man with the haughty bearing was the chief government auditor; and the one with the gold-rimmed glasses was the attorney general.

Marcel, cool as a cucumber, took the initiative. "Just a minute, folks, it'll take a while to unload our equipment," he said. He was a good actor; he had contrived a fine, rough-hewn TV producer's tone. Ingo leaned over and opened a suitcase which, like the others, was lined with foam rubber. He pulled out two collapsible light stands and laid them on the floor. Then Hossein and Ingo crowded around Marcel as he opened a suitcase that had a double bottom. First Marcel removed Umberto's $8,000 camera. Then all three men snapped around, pointing silencer-equipped Colt.45 pistols at the guards, the jewel cleaners and the board members.

"Keep absolutely silent; hands up over your heads," Marcel said. Hossein barked words which Harry took to be the same commands in Farsi. All the hands went up: the guards did not try to reach for their revolvers. But the captain, feigning clumsiness, jolted the diamond display-case with one arm. The auditor gasped. Each of the thirteen men in the room stood stock-still. Each of them knew that the shock to the case had been more than sharp enough to set the alarm system in action. In seconds, under normal conditions, the local alarm-annunciator would begin its hideous and deafening sound; the lights would start flashing at the local police headquarters and at the Bank Markazi building nearby—in the utility room and the guards' wardroom.

Yet nothing happened. The silence continued. It was broken only when Hossein, giving way to nervousness, began to snicker.

"I'm glad you bumped into that case, Captain," Marcel said. "Now every man here knows that the alarm system is out of action. Nobody's going to come and help you."

Ingo leaned over one of the suitcases and brought out three hypodermic needles: two contained a light-yellow liquid, and one contained a colorless liquid. He handed them to Marcel.

"Okay, Doctor, come here and take these needles," Marcel said. "You and my friend here"—he gestured toward Hossein —"are going to go and give an intravenous shot of ten cubic centimeters of the yellow fluid—sodium pentothal—to the guard you'll find lying just inside the entrance door; he's unconscious. Then come and give the same shot to each of the bank employees, the guards and your fellow committee members. That will put them to sleep for ten or fifteen minutes. Then go back and give a shot of five cubic centimeters of the clear fluid —Seconal—to each of the men. That will keep them asleep for three or four hours. And then our friend here"—he gestured at Hossein—"will do the same for you. You know these injections will harm nobody. If you tell us one of the needles is broken, we will give you another. If you say the same thing twice, we will shoot you. And we will shoot your friends."

The doctor's mouth worked a moment before words came out: "I will do what you say."

The doctor did as he was ordered, after telling the other victims in the vault to lie down. Senator Qazvin took his inoculations meekly, giving no sign that he was responsible for the robbery—or that he had been waiting for this moment for years. Afterward the doctor himself lay down, and Hossein gave him his shot of sodium pentothal followed a few moments later by his Seconal.

When the doctor's eyes were firmly shut, Marcel said, "Let's go." Harry, Ingo and Hossein put on gloves so that they would leave no fingerprints. Then the four men quickly emptied the suitcases—a procedure they had rehearsed at the villa. And then, without fanfare, without anyone's saying that this was the largest jewelry robbery in human history, without anyone's saying that they were despoiling a nation's treasures, they simply dragged the suitcases around the vault, filling them with jewels and jewelry.

Harry slipped his jeweler's eyeglass out of one of the suitcases and inspected some of the pieces; they were the real thing, all right. Even with all the distractions around him—with the unconscious Iranians sprawled out on the floor, with his fellow bandits dumping crowns, pearls, rubies, bejeweled mirrors and jewel-encrusted antique firearms into the aluminum cases—he felt a thrill of excitement when he held the great Darya-i-Nur in his palm, marveling at its heft and beauty. To keep it from harm he began to wrap it in his handkerchief, but Marcel knocked it out of his hand.

"Nobody puts any stuff in their pockets," he barked. "No embezzling."

Harry said nothing. He obeyed. He picked up the Darya-i-Nur and saw it was unharmed. He laid it in one of the suitcases, on a pile of pearls.

The work was soon finished. The suitcases provided enough room to take the great crowns and tiaras, all the main pieces of jewelry, many precious objets d'art, and all the loose pearls and jewels, except for a few platefuls of turquoises and some other minor stones that were inadvertently spilled on the floor. The things that were left behind, by plan, were mostly objects whose value was low in relation to their volume or weight, or both. The pearl-and-gem-studded coronation robes were left untouched, for example, along with the pieces of sumptuous enamelware, which contained few, if any, gems.

Then the robbers, their pistols concealed and their gloves removed, lugged the suitcases past the drugged men's inert bodies, out through the two steel doorways, past the chandelier and the postcard stand, through the corridor and out the unimposing door. Briskly, but not too briskly, they loaded them on the truck. In a parting gesture, Hossein scattered leaflets in the entrance hall and dropped a crumpled bit of paper among them. The two bank guards at the street gates watched as the four men climbed back into the truck, but the two did nothing; it was the other guards, now all unconscious, who were responsible for watching over the entrance hall and the vault.

The four men took their original places on board the truck. Ingo drove up to the street gates. He waved at the obliging first guard, who swung them open. The second guard, the sallow-faced two-striper, stepped forward. Hossein said something jovial-sounding in Farsi to him. Ingo noisily put the truck in gear, ready to roar out into the avenue.

But the second guard put his hand up.

"He wants to look at the suitcases *again*," Hossein whispered.

Ingo spat: "Kill him, Marcel, and I'll drive into the avenue; it's as simple as that."

But Harry whispered, "Wait before you open fire. If you can stall him for half a minute, and then bring him around to the rear door, I bet I can get us out of this without any shooting."

Hossein got out and began to harangue the guard in Farsi. Harry slipped past Hossein—heedless of the twinge of pain in his bad leg—and around into the rear of the truck.

Seconds later the guard looked in through the truck's rear doors. Hossein and Marcel were behind him. Even Harry could see that Marcel's pistol made a slight bulge under his jacket, but the guard didn't notice: he was too eager to exert his authority, to have another look at the suitcases, even though it was well known that the alarm system in the vault made robbery unimaginable.

Harry looked into the man's face from close up. It was hard and glum, a real Iranian cop's face. Yet there was a soft look around the eyes: the look of a man with rent to pay, daughters to marry off, boyhood dreams unfulfilled.

Abruptly Harry reached out and shook hands with the man. The glum cop's face registered puzzlement, then guile, as he felt something in Harry's grip. Then the man took his hand away, looked down in his palm and saw two fat rubies, which Harry had hastily slipped out of a suitcase. The man's eyes grew wide. He hesitated for an instant, and Harry knew why: a splinter from one of those stones would sell for enough money to change the man's life. Yet in accepting the gems he would be turning against everything his job stood for. In a way it was crazy for him to take them. How was he going to hide them? Where was he going to sell them? How would he conceal his sudden wealth?

But this was Iran, with its age-old traditions of splendor, squalor, palace intrigue, corruption. As Harry, an expert about the impact of jewels, had calculated, the man closed his square hand over the rubies. He waved the truck on. Harry, Hossein and Marcel climbed back on board, and it roared out into Ferdowsi Avenue. Harry thought, Emily, your daddy may be a bank robber, but at least today he saved a person's life.

PART

# 12

THE TRAFFIC WAS STILL SPARSE. ONLY THE FAINTEST DAWN light showed in the sky. Ingo swung the truck leftward, across Ferdowsi Avenue and along the dark and narrow side street, Berlin Alley, that bordered the West German embassy. Then he wrestled the truck through a maze of streets further to the south and east, where the buildings were older. Harry knew the quarter: it was where Gail and he had had the red-wine punch on that first night and where he had passed the jewel-appraisal test in the abandoned warehouse. Ingo made more twists and turns around the neighborhood, apparently to see whether they were being followed—which they were not; there were no sirens and no other signs that anyone at the bank had yet given the alarm. Finally, Ingo pulled into the blind alley that led to the warehouse. The big truck-sized doorway opened as they arrived, and they drove into the cavernous interior, a truck-loading room that smelled faintly of tea leaves.

Gumbert was on the loading platform, sitting in a camp chair with a sheaf of Iranian road maps on his lap. He gestured to Harry to get into a rear seat of the blue Plymouth Maxiwagon that was parked in one corner, near two other vehicles. Harry did so, and found himself sitting beside Gail.

"Don't move," she said as she peeled off his mustache. Then they sat back and waited while Gumbert directed the other men in what was evidently another well-rehearsed routine.

The men unloaded the aluminum suitcases from the truck and transferred the glittering contents into a row of well-scuffed cloth and leather suitcases that had been laid in a row, open and waiting, along one garage wall. They closed these suitcases and loaded them into three vehicles: the blue Maxi-wagon; the sage-green Maxiwagon that Faiz Kiani had driven down from Rezaiyeh; and a Jeep Wagoneer—a truck–station wagon that is also useful for carrying groups of tourists and other passengers over long distances.

"I see what they're doing," Harry whispered. "Their TV crew act is over, and now they're trying to look like tourists and tourist guides."

Gail raised her eyebrows and looked glum.

Harry continued: "That must be one reason why they want you along, to make the group look innocent. And they put me next to you so you can keep an eye on me. I can see the logic behind all this: the easiest way to explain why a bunch of foreigners is traveling here is to say they're tourists—"

Gail put her hand on Harry's mouth to make him shut up, but he went on anyway; "This is still terribly risky, though, they can't really want to try to escape in a bunch of tourist vehicles." His voice trailed off.

Marcel and Ingo tore off their wigs and tossed them on the loading-room floor. Then Marcel wiped off the aluminum suit-cases to rid them of fingerprints, and Ingo began dashing around the warehouse, wiping down doorknobs, light switches and other spots where fingerprints might have lodged. Then Gumbert and Hossein got into the front seat of the blue Maxi-wagon, and Marcel and Faiz got into the Jeep Wagoneer. Harry wanted to ask where they were going and what had happened to Colonel Kates, but he prudently held his tongue. They all waited while Ingo wiped off parts of the gray panel truck, drove it back out into the alley and parked it. With gloved hands, Ingo lugged two of the aluminum suitcases, now empty, out into the alley and dumped them beside the truck.

Now Gumbert was looking a trifle anxiously at his watch.

At last Ingo climbed behind the wheel of the green Maxiwagon. The three vehicles, with the blue Maxiwagon in the lead, drove down the alley and westward through the capital. A gray dawn was breaking; Hossein was kneading the bridge of his nose with a slender hand; his face was gray with fatigue and, Harry supposed, hangover.

No one in the lead vehicle said anything, but Harry could keep silent no longer. "Where the hell are we going?" he said.

"Shut up," Gail snapped, her voice at its most metallic. She was clearly under orders to keep him quiet. But her small, hard hand crept into his. Her palm was damp with fear.

The baggage pickup room of Shiraz Airport was crowded with strapping Baluchi tribesmen, breadwinners back from lucrative jobs in Dubai or Abudhabi or other oil-rich Arabian states across the Persian Gulf. The men were busy claiming their luggage: string-lashed old suitcases and piles of new tin-covered footlockers, bought across the Gulf with their earnings. They were too busy to notice the barrel-chested foreigner with the grizzled crew cut who stopped to pick up his Samsonite two-suiter and was escorted to the parking lot by an intellectual-looking young Iranian friend. The foreigner was Kates.

Outside, the two men ignored the few scoundrelly-looking taxi drivers who were waiting for business at this hour. They strolled to the far side of the parking lot, where the lighting was dim, and clambered into the cab of a big, old British-made Bedford truck. It was painted red, its wooden body was decorated with primitive little paintings of roses, mosques and lions, and it had a pronounced tilt to the left. They drove away from the airport and took the highway heading northeast.

"Truck handles pretty well, Sirooz," Kates said after they had gone a stretch. "But it sure is loaded crooked."

"I am very sorry; as you know, it was loaded in a terrible hurry; we had to get the military truck back to the base motor pool before it was missed."

"What else are you carrying?"

"You will smile when you hear, I think. Tuna fish. Hundreds of cans of Persian Gulf tuna fish. Very tasty. With that alone, we could survive for years."

Kates smiled stiffly. "Never mind. In five years we'll all be on easy street. You'll probably be regional commissar for Shiraz. Somethin' like that."

Dreams of the future were what sustained Sirooz; they were a serious matter with him. He said nothing. He gunned the truck onward, into the countryside.

The gray dawn light showed an early-rising mullah—an Islamic cleric—in black robe and white turban, walking beside the highway with long strides. Sirooz did not offer him a lift. Further on they passed a dusty gas station. Its pump was painted green, white and red, the Iranian national colors.

"Got enough gas?" Kates asked.

"Absolutely. Especially because we do not have very far to go, and we will not be doing much driving when we get there."

"True enough."

"Conceivably, I could have loaded on extra tins of petrol, but I wanted to avoid any risks of accidents involving the payload."

"Good idea."

The highway began to run slightly uphill, twisting through arid hillsides striped with rock outcroppings. The smell of dust grew stronger. They passed a road sign that said PERSEPOLIS 52 KM.

"Nobody here but us tourists," Kates said.

Gumbert was driving neither too fast nor too slow, Harry observed; he was driving like an organizer of international tours who was proceeding toward a rendezvous somewhere with his customers, some of whose luggage he was obligingly bringing along. In a few minutes the three vehicles were moving westward on Aryamehr Boulevard, past the headquarters of the Shah's political party.

Hossein was slumped against the front right door, brooding. "We should be hearing something by now," he said to Gumbert.

"Relax, my friend. I do not wish to be impolite, but in this part of the world the fuse materials are often a bit, um, irregular."

"It's four minutes behind schedule already."

"Your watch could be wrong."

Hossein merely grunted. He fumbled in a side pocket of his jacket and produced the flask. He took a deep draft, without offering any to his fellow travelers. He exhaled. Harry could smell whiskey fumes.

Gumbert said, "Please, my friend, do not overindulge. Not now, after all these years that you have been preparing for this day. Not after—"

From some distance behind them, from the direction they had just come from, came the boom of a large explosion. It had an oddly muffled sound. Harry looked over his shoulder, but he saw no flames on the skyline, not even a glow.

"That was the nitroglycerin, wasn't it?" he asked.

Gumbert said, "Yes, um, it was. And a bit of *plastique*."

"You don't seem to mind, so it must have been part of the plan."

"Hope so." Gumbert drove faster now. They passed the huge Shahyad monument on the western outskirts of the city and sped on westward along a main road leading to Teheran Airport. Harry could see why Gumbert had chosen that route: there were other vehicles on the highway at this hour, many of them carrying Iranian and foreign travelers to catch the early-morning flights to Europe.

Hossein, soothed by the whiskey, smiled back at Harry across the back of the front seat. "It's all right, old chap, never mind. We have blown up that old warehouse; most of the aluminum suitcases are crushed in heaps of brick rubble; it will take the Teheran city fathers hours to get all the brick dug out."

"But that is what they will probably want to do, um, most urgently," Gumbert said. "Because that wrinkled scrap of paper that Marcel so carefully left in the bank contains jottings in Farsi which hint, though they do not say clearly, that the jewels were to be hidden temporarily in the warehouse. And it's logical to expect that if professional bank robbers were involved they might have had explosives with them that went off by accident."

"Happens all the time," Hossein said. Thanks to the whiskey, he sounded practically debonair.

Gumbert said, "Our hope is that the authorities may be distracted for some hours by the belief that the jewels are buried in the rubble, and that this will keep them from putting up roadblocks. They will be anxious to avoid, if possible, any measure that indicates there has been yet another major act of terrorism or an important crime. And they will certainly not announce that the jewels are missing, if they can possibly avoid it; to do so would entail an enormous loss of face for the Shah; it would be an admission that he has proven unable to do what his father and other recent shahs were able to do: to keep the jewels safe."

"But sooner or later there are bound to be roadblocks," Harry said. "What will you do when we meet them?"

Gumbert said, "That is where our friend, Hossein, will once again prove his value, if he stays sufficiently sober."

Hossein said nothing; the flask was at his lips.

The Bedford truck sailed along toward Persepolis. At this early hour the highway was almost deserted; to the left and right, the country families were asleep in their brick farmsteads; the walled orchards were still.

"Christ, what's that?" Kates said, as an orange glow materialized on the skyline.

"That is only the local oil refinery," Sirooz said. "The glow comes from the unused gas that is being burned."

"Any change in the security precautions there? More guards? Heavier arms?"

"No. As far as we know, there are still only a few watchmen, with revolvers and shotguns. The usual."

They passed a small Islamic shrine, an expanse of wheat fields, a brace of camels cropping on wasteland. They crossed a small river on a modern bridge that had been built companionably next to a much older span, wrought handsomely of stone. On the north side a dirt road led off eastward along the river bank; Sirooz drove along it for two hundred yards and came to a stop in a stand of poplars. He jammed on the hand brake and opened the side door. "I'll tell the men it's all right to get out," he said to Kates.

"Right. After I've said hello, I'm goin' to go down to that creek and shave; it's light enough for that. Then maybe a little later, when it's lighter, we could all look over the equipment."

"You mean you want to have an inspection?"

"Right, if that's okay with you, Lieutenant." Kates smiled when he used Sirooz's military title.

"Absolutely. The men will be happy to show off their toys."

Gumbert drove on in silence for a few minutes before the first hurdle arose. Gail was looking out the window. The light of day was upon them now, illuminating the landscape beside the road: the usual brick and mud-brick country walls, and behind them, here and there, villas or small new industrial plants. They turned off on a road that headed south.

"The Shah wants to make a sort of industrial center out here," Hossein said. "A foolish idea—"

"Hey," Gail said. "Look up ahead."

Gumbert said, "Roadblock. That's quick work by the police. Well, Hossein, this is the magic moment."

"Okey-dokey," Hossein said. His English had become more colloquial and more slurred.

Two police cars were parked on the road, narrowing the

space available for southbound cars to pass. As the blue Maxi-wagon approached, Gumbert slowly applied the brake. He pulled to a stop behind a pickup truck laden with goats. The police were checking the driver's papers. They waved him on and turned to the Maxiwagon.

Hossein sat up straight in the front seat and made a gesture through the window, like a diner summoning a waiter. He held out another identity card and intoned a few words of Farsi to the nearest cop. The man, another sergeant, took it, read it, but not too carefully, saluted, and waved the three vehicles through.

Gumbert drove on, again in silence. Then he began to whistle "The Blue Danube" exultantly.

"What did you tell him, for God's sake?" Harry asked Hossein.

"It's elementary, really—I have this little card; it says I am an aide to the minister of tourism. I simply told him that I was escorting these three vehicles and their passengers to rendezvous with a group of VIP foreign travelers in Qom, the shrine city south of here."

"How come he didn't search the vehicles or ask for our papers?"

"First, one doesn't harass vehicles escorted by a minister's aide—not in an absolute monarchy, at least, and this one is rather absolute. And second, I had the impression that the police have not been told that billions of dollars' worth of Iran's national heritage is missing. They have probably been told merely to check the papers of travelers, and to look out for anything suspicious."

"How did you get that fancy ID card?"

Hossein smiled. "I *am* an aide to the minister of tourism."

Gumbert stopped whistling. "Our friend has, um, been preparing for this day for years."

Hossein gave a slightly crazed-sounding cackle. "And now, for the first time, I'm beginning to get the feeling that we may very well get out of here alive, *if* we can just make it through the next few hours."

They drove on southward.

It was hours later when the Bedford truck took to the highway again, barreling, more quickly now, toward the northeast. The men were riding in back again, with the payload; Sirooz and Kates were in the cab, as before. They had changed into fashionable bush suits, which were made of finely cut cotton but had a generic resemblance to combat fatigues. Over them they wore raincoats.

Now, in the fullness of the day, the flat countryside was busy. Black scavenger birds cruised over the fields, hunting vermin and carrion. Women in odd, flaring skirts strolled beside the road: Kates recognized them as Qashqai tribeswomen, members of a nomadic people, which is divided into about fifteen major tribes. Their menfolk were selling lamb carcasses to passing travelers. The turnpike was dotted with motorcycles, buses and trucks, many of them carrying cargo from Persian Gulf ports.

Gradually the route became more splendid. Lines of well-tended pine trees ran along both sides. The buildings by the road seemed better maintained, and so did the road itself. Its freshly painted white center stripe led straight as a lance now to where huge, ancient columns loomed up above the treetops: Persepolis. The truck stopped momentarily in the parking lot in front of the ruins. Kates got out, along with the two men who had been in the back of the truck. One of them, Chandler, was American. The other, Rumi, was Iranian. But they were much alike: wiry, muscular men with springy movements. They were obviously in peak physical condition. They, too, wore raincoats, although the sky was clear. They paused and drank in the sight before them.

# 13

ALL THE GRANDEUR OF ANCIENT PERSIA FINDS EXPRESSION IN the colossal stones of Persepolis. From the pyramids of Egypt to Angkor Wat in Cambodia, there is no more awesome relic of the past. In its heyday two millennia ago, Persepolis was not a mere stronghold, not a workaday administrative center, but the spiritual capital of the greatest empire the world had ever known. The Persian empire lasted only two centuries—from 559 to 330 B.C.—but its power extended from Libya all the way to what is now Pakistan.

The great sixth-century Persian emperor Darius began the construction of Persepolis, at the foot of the stony Kuh-e-Rahmat—Mountain of Mercy—which overlooks fertile flatlands stretching in the direction of modern Shiraz. Workmen were brought from the remote corners of the empire to help embellish the site. They worked so well that the huge carved stones of Persepolis still awe the traveler with something of the sacramental grandeur of Chartres and something of the pyramids' invincible agelessness. Ancient Persepolis was essentially a stone platform encrusted with splendid halls, portals, palaces and even harem quarters, which were used by Darius and his son Xerxes, the conqueror of Athens. The construction at Persepolis ranged from the weird to the gigantic to the humbly practical. It was adorned with carvings of bulls and other creatures—many of which have survived to the present day. Other strange carvings showed the emperors' subjects from exotic lands coming to Persepolis with tribute. The great limestone structure called the Apadana had a central hall, which measured two hundred feet on each side and could accommodate thousands of people. A wide cistern was dug deep into the bare bedrock at the mountain's foot, and a sophisticated system of underground tunnels was laid out to carry off the water from the torrential winter rains.

The grandeur of Persepolis was largely destroyed in a great fire that broke out in 330 B.C., after the arrival of an invading army led by Alexander the Great. Some scholars have deduced that the mysterious blaze was set on the conqueror's orders for political reasons; others speculate that it may have broken out accidentally during one of the wild orgies that Alexander occasionally staged.

In time Alexander withdrew, but the palaces, it is said, were never again used by Persian rulers; earth and sand gradually covered the ruins as the centuries passed, and travelers carved their names in the enduring stone. In the 1930s excavations were begun by the great German archaeologist Ernst Herzfeld on behalf of the University of Chicago's Oriental Institute. Work at the site has continued over the years, but still is incomplete: the tunnels have not been completely traced, for instance, and the great cistern, which became partly clogged over the centuries, has never been plumbed to its bottom.

The present Shah, wanting to underline the glories of monarchy in Persia and Iran, has once again made Persepolis a focal point: in 1971 it was the scene of the sumptuous celebrations of the 2,500th anniversary of Persian monarchic rule. In addition, the Shah's government has embarked on a multimillion-dollar program to rebuild ancient Persian ruins, including some of the Apadana's sixty-foot fluted columns, only four of which have remained continuously standing through the centuries.

Kates ambled off between two parked, empty tourist buses and discreetly urinated. He looked at his watch. Time to get things under way. He felt some pre-combat jitters, to be sure, but he kept them under control, telling himself that this was just another military operation. He had been through many others in World War II and Korea. This one was going to be particularly easy, he told himself, because he had the advantage of surprise: he and Gumbert had been right in choosing Persepolis as the site for this operation: it was a place where able-bodied foreigners could loiter—and be sure that their loitering would not attract attention.

Kates nodded at Chandler and Rumi, and the three men began to walk up the right-hand side of the great double staircase leading to the surface of the terrace, which is walled with huge limestone blocks. Kates looked with admiration at the irregular joinings of the blocks; they had been masterfully executed without mortar by the ancient masons. He could hear the sound of traffic on the highway and the rumble of the Bedford truck that Sirooz was driving off toward the southern end of the site, where recently constructed ramps and grading made it possible for trucks to drive up onto the terrace.

In the sky overhead he noticed unfamiliar, gray-bodied gulls wheeling in the sky, wanderers up from the Gulf. In the far distance he could see mountains shouldering up toward the clouds.

"Chandler," he said.

"What?"

"We are fuckin'—far from the U.S. of A., boy."

"That we are, Colonel," Chandler said without emotion. He was here because Kates had promised to pay him a very large sum of money; he was not given to abstract thought.

The three men in raincoats paused a moment beside the two dilapidated stone bull figures near the top of the staircase. A plump guard was standing next to one of the bulls, near where a nineteenth-century American traveler had carved into the stone the legend "Stanley, New York Herald 1870."

"Guard doesn't look so tough, does he?" Chandler muttered to Kates as they walked southward across the great terrace. The three men had a normal look—they could have been aviation technicians, for instance, down from Teheran on holiday; the only slight oddities about their appearance were the raincoats and the fact that Kates was continually looking at his wristwatch.

"Watch it! We have to be careful about talking," he whispered. "Voices carry well up here."

They moved onward across a Daliesque landscape of battered stones. The standing columns towered over them, looming against the sky. Dotting the terrace were sections of columns, carved column pediments and strange stone doorways—rebuilt by archaeologists but left without doors—which stared out across the flatlands like eyes.

Sounds did carry well across the ruins: the men could hear the voices of the groups of tourists scattered around the terrace, talking variously in Farsi, Swedish and French. The tourists were middle-aged people for the most part. There was little chance, Kates reflected happily, that they would do anything rash to defend the ruins. All told, three guards were visible, all of them unheroic-looking. Kates estimated that there were fewer than a dozen others stationed nearby.

The three men approached the remnants of the palace of Darius, near the southwest corner of the terrace, entering a fifty-foot roofless passageway formed by old stones on the left and a modern five-foot mud-brick wall on the right. They paused. Kates looked at his wristwatch once again and unbuttoned his raincoat; the other two men unbuttoned theirs.

Across the stones they heard the rumble of the Bedford truck again, and, seconds later, the motors of other, smaller vehicles.

"Okay, friends," Kates said. He slipped a slender submachine gun from inside his raincoat. Chandler and Rumi did the same. All three weapons were of the type known as the Carl Gustaf, or the Swedish K: a lightweight weapon, made in Sweden, and long employed by various armed forces in the Middle East and elsewhere. Swedish manufacturers, years ago, began providing the users of the Carl Gustaf with a special high-velocity bullet, which, some specialists have determined, has greater penetrating power than any other submachine-gun bullet in the world.

Kates was one of those specialists. He squeezed off a burst of bullets into the stone wall of the passage ahead of him. The slugs ricocheted but left a fine deep pattern of parallel scars—like claw marks.

From somewhere nearby came answering bursts of submachine-gun fire: Gumbert and the others had arrived. Kates and his men sprinted out of the passageway. As they had expected, the tourists were fleeing the terrace, screaming as they poured down the great stairs. Kates saw four guards loping across the terrace after them.

"Looks like there's no resistance," Chandler said.

Kates said, "Right. Let's move on to the harem."

The three men sprinted toward a low-lying structure with an odd, crenelated roof line: the modern reconstruction of Darius's harem, which is used as a museum. They could see the vehicles—the Bedford, the Maxiwagon, the Jeep Wagoneer—parked behind it, near where the mountain slope began to rear up along the terrace's eastern side.

They fired more bursts into the air, snapping out their used cartridge magazines and replacing them with the first of the spare magazines they carried in easy extraction cases hung at their belts. An old Iranian woman limped past in frantic haste, her face contorted with fear. Rumi brought his submachine gun forward to fire another burst over her bowed head, then took pity on her and did not. Instead, he shouted after her in Farsi: "Death to the Shah; Persepolis to the people."

The three men sprinted across the forecourt of the harem building, past the half-dozen pines planted in a semicircle, past the big modern pottery water pot, which Chandler demolished with a short burst, past the drinking fountain, which they sensibly left intact—they might well need the water in the hours ahead. They sprinted on between the wooden columns at the entrance, and through the tall doorway into the museum.

"Death to the Shah!" Rumi cried again, spraying the interior with another burst, fired high, which smashed a tall drab case of pottery fragments and peppered the walls with bullet holes.

"Cease fire," Kates called.

The three men stood at the doorway, their submachine guns lowered.

"Looks like there's nobody left," Chandler said.

"Rumi, guard the door; Chandler, let's you and I check the sound-and-light room."

They moved through the museum's main hall, on to the small back office full of electronic equipment, from where the nightly sound-and-light shows were put on.

"Goddammit to hell," Chandler said. "What do we do now?"

The room was almost intact. The tape-recorder players were all right, and ready to be switched on; the machinery that controlled the multicolored spotlights was untouched. But the shiny microphone that stood on the operator's desk, ready to broadcast special announcements, had been torn out of the wall and bent beyond repair.

"Shit," Kates said. "Somebody figured that anybody who wanted to take over the terrace and the museum might want to use that mike. Somebody was real smart."

There was a burst of shouting from the main hall. Kates and Rumi raced out of the sound-and-light office—and found Gumbert, submachine gun in hand. With him was Hossein, also carrying a submachine gun, and Gail and Harry, who were unarmed.

"Hi, friend," Kates said to Gumbert.

"Greetings. All visitors and guards have evacuated the terrace; we have men out at the prearranged guard points. The unloading of the vehicles into the tunnels is, um, proceeding. We are ready to give the government our demands. We have one—"

"Rudi, there's a fuckin' hitch."

"What's that?"

"Some bastard must have sabotaged the mike system when he heard us shooting."

Gumbert gestured with the muzzle of his submachine gun. "As I was going to say, we have one prisoner; he must have done it. Didn't you, Doctor?"

Leaning against the bullet-pocked wall, face to the wall, his hands over his head, was a wiry Iranian in a British-looking brown tweed jacket. He said nothing. Kates walked over to him and used his submachine-gun butt to club him in the small of the back. He fell down, and stayed down.

Kates looked at him. "You're Dr. Hiar, the conservator of the Persepolis ruins, aren't you?"

"I am." Slowly the man sat up. His eyes glittered with hatred.

"Your office is in this building?"

"It is. It has been for thirteen years."

Gumbert said, "We found him standing outside the east entrance to the museum."

Kates smiled at Hiar. "Well now, Doctor, why did you smash your own mike in your own museum?"

"Because I assumed this was some terrorist stunt," Hiar said in impeccable English. "I was doing my duty to hinder it."

Kates stopped smiling. "Okay, Doctor, we're goin' to give you a chance to make up for that little act of vandalism. To save your own life, matter of fact. We have a list here. It's the demands we are makin' to your government. We want you to run real quick across the terrace and down the big stairs. There must be guards and cops down there by now. You give them this list and tell them to relay it to the governor of Shiraz by radio before he does anything rash, like order a counterattack. 'Cause if there is a counterattack, we just may wreck half the ruins on the terrace. Maybe all of them."

"What do you mean?"

"Read the list." Kates thrust it into Hiar's hands.

Hiar read it. He read it again, turning pale. The edges of the paper shook ever so slightly: his hands had acquired a tremor. "Good Lord," he said.

Kates smiled.

Hiar said, "You have thermite bombs in that truck? You can substantially destroy the ruins for a radius of three hundred yards?"

"Sure can," Kates said. "We can do a better job of wreckin' than Alexander the Great, matter of fact."

"I don't believe you."

Gumbert said, "If our demands are not fulfilled, we shall blow up not only Persepolis, but the crown jewels. They will be reduced to a pile of ash, molten metal and splinters."

"I certainly don't believe *that.*"

Gumbert fished something out of his pocket. "Here is proof, Doctor."

Hiar looked hard at the glittering object in Gumbert's hand. "Oh my God," he said, "the Darya-i-Nur."

Kates smiled. "Dr. Hiar, as to the thermite bombs, you're an intelligent man. You know your government has been acquiring such bombs and stockpilin' them around the country, although you may not know that part of the stockpile is at the Shiraz air force base. But you don't need to believe us; we can take you over to the big truck and show you. Then you better skedaddle out of here and deliver our demands."

"No," Hiar said.

"What do you mean, 'no'?"

"No, I will not. I have spent my life studying these reliefs, these stones; my life is here. I remained here until your men found me, and I will remain here, to die if I must."

"Don't be silly, Doctor," Gumbert said, cajolingly now.

Hiar sat there. He said nothing more.

Kates smiled yet again. "Never mind, leave him alone, we'll take care of him later," he said. "There's another, very easy way to get our message out, and real fast."

"What's that?" Hossein asked. He looked weary, bleary-eyed and elated all at once.

"By telephone. There must be telephones in this museum; let's look."

Beyond the *son et lumière* room, Kates and Hossein found the director's office, which had a telephone. Hossein looked through the telephone book and found a number. Kates dialed swiftly.

"United States consulate in Shiraz?" he asked. "This is Colonel Walter E. Kates, formerly a member of the U.S. military mission in Iran. Please put me through immediately to the consul. This is an emergency." There was a pause. "Hello, Mr. Myers? This is Colonel Kates. No, I don't believe I've had the pleasure, but I knew your predecessor, Halenko. Look, Mr. Myers, I suggest you put your secretary on the line now and have her get ready to take notes in shorthand. I have a friend there who has a complicated and important message for the Iranian government. I and a group of patriotic Iranians have stolen the crown jewels and seized the ruins of Persepolis." Another pause. "Yes, I'm feelin' fine. We will destroy the jewels and the ruins unless the Shah fully meets the list of demands which my friend will dictate over the phone. Please get through immediately on your radio-telephone to the governor of Shiraz and Ambassador Fraser in Teheran. Tell them that if there is any attempt to retake Persepolis before these demands are met, the ruins and the jewels will be destroyed." Pause. "How? They will be blown up in a massive explosion of the six thermite bombs taken this mornin' from the Shiraz air force base. They are conventional weapons, but they are enormously powerful. The Iranian government will, of course, order the bomb stocks

checked at the base and will find that the bombs are missin'.
That will confirm our veracity." Pause. "What's that? You'll get
through to the governor now, and then the ambassador? Good,
thanks a lot. You do that, and my friend will start dictatin' the
demands, first in Farsi, then in English. Yes, yes, I won't do
anythin' rash. Give my compliments to the ambassador." Pause.
"Hello, who's this? Mrs. Azeri? How do you do. You ready to
take a little dictation? Okay, just a moment, please."

Six box-shaped M-113 armored personnel carriers rumbled through the flag-bedecked gates of the small Iranian
army cantonment outside the town of Marvdasht, fifteen
miles southwest of Persepolis. They sped down a side road
and turned right onto the main highway leading toward Persepolis. After three minutes they were overtaken by two police cars, which provided an escort for them, sounding their
sirens at full volume. But the sirens were not really necessary: civilian drivers immediately pulled over onto the shoulder of the road when they saw the armored vehicles hur-
tling along the turnpike.

Hossein took the telephone receiver from Kates and began
speaking while with his free hand he unfolded his typewritten
declaration.
"Mrs. Azeri? How do you do?" he said in Farsi. "I shall read
the following communiqué in Farsi and then in English. Actually, if it is possible, I suggest that you have a second stenogra-
pher ready to take the English version, because Mr. Myers will
doubtless want you to relay the Farsi version to the authorities
as quickly as possible. Are you ready? Right, then:
"'To Whom It May Concern,'" he read in Farsi, " 'We the
progressive membership of the Nightingale Brigade, Iranians
and non-Iranians united, declare that we have this day taken
possession, in the name of the Iranian people, of the crown
jewels of Iran, which were formerly under the control of the

fascist Shah Mohammed Reza Pahlavi and his corrupt police state.

" 'Accordingly, we call upon the Shah and his government to take the following measures within the next twenty-four hours.

" '1. To release five hundred political prisoners.

" '2. To dismiss the hated director general of the national intelligence service, which is in reality a fascist secret police, to make sweeping changes in its structure in order to make it more liberal and democratic, and to criticize it publicly for the cruel and dictatorial methods it has used in the past.

" '3. To rescind the longstanding ban on the Iranian Communist party, otherwise known as the Tudeh party, and to appoint three members of the Tudeh party to cabinet posts, to wit, the ministerships of defense, of foreign affairs and of petroleum.

" '4. To conclude immediately, on terms acceptable to the Soviet Union, the current negotiations toward a thirty-year agreement for the delivery of Iranian oil and natural gas to the Soviet Union.

" 'When these four measures are taken, the Iranian authorities are to so inform us by loudspeaker at our Persepolis headquarters. It would be futile for the authorities to lie concerning these measures, since we will be receiving independent information as to whether or not they are being implemented. At that point, the Iranian authorities must permit an unarmed helicopter from a neighboring country to land at the Shiraz air force base to pick up an observer, to wit, Dr. Shepehri, the head of the crown-jewels office in the Bank Markazi. The helicopter pilot will be unarmed. The Iranian authorities must then permit the helicopter and its passenger to land on the terrace at Persepolis. There we shall load onto the helicopter only the loose, unmarked, unnamed gems from the crown-jewels collection. These jewels are to be used later to further the cause of democracy and progress in Iran. Dr. Shepehri will be permitted to observe the loading of the jewels and to confirm, using the helicopter's shortwave radio, that only the loose, unmarked, unnamed gems, which have relatively little historical value, have been loaded onto the helicopter. The Iranian authorities must then permit the helicopter to travel across, and to depart freely from, Iranian air space.

" 'If all the demands and conditions of this communiqué are not fulfilled within twenty-four hours, it will be our sad duty to destroy the jewels and/or the greater part of the ruins of Persepolis. This we shall do by detonating one or more of the six one-hundred-and-fifty-pound thermite heat bombs which the Nightingale Brigade confiscated yesterday from the Shiraz air force base. As is well known, the heat of the bombs is sufficient to melt, burn or otherwise destroy the precious metals, the pearls and many of the jewels. It may not destroy the diamonds in their entirety, but those which are not entirely consumed will be split and shattered beyond recognition. Thus the crown jewels of Iran, which were unjustly withheld by the shahs from the Iranian people, will for all practical purposes cease to exist.

" 'In addition, all or part of the jewels and the ruins of Persepolis will be destroyed by us, at our discretion, if any hostile measures of any kind are taken toward us, or, indeed, if any persons set foot on the terrace without authorization from us.

" 'In conclusion, kindly note that we shall take one or more of the thermite bombs with us on board the helicopter when we depart. We shall arrange to detonate this bomb or bombs, and the bombs left at Persepolis, at our discretion should the helicopter's departure be interfered with.

" 'In the name of peace, progress and democracy,

" '(signed) the Presidium of the Nightingale Brigade.' "

Hossein's voice was slightly hoarse when he finished reading the communiqué in Farsi. While he waited for the second secretary to come on the line to take the text in English, he leaned back in the director's chair, his face glowing with satisfaction and joy. His eyes filled with tears.

"Take it easy, Hossein," Kates said, "We've got a lot of work ahead of us."

"I can't help it; I have been dreaming of this moment for so long." Hossein's voice broke with emotion; he gave a sob. His right hand, moving as though it had a will of its own, dropped the telephone receiver and fished the flask out of his jacket pocket. He took a long, slow pull on the flask, put it down on the desk a minute and let the feel of the whiskey move through him. Then he put the flask to his lips and began to drink yet again.

# 14

KARTHIAN SPRINTED UP THE EMBASSY STAIRS AND INTO THE communications room. He bent over the teleprinter machine, where a covering message from Myers and the first paragraphs of the Farsi text of the Nightingale Brigade's demands, relayed by radio-teletype from Shiraz, were being typed out on a roll of paper automatically, as though by an unseen hand.

"Goddamn that fucker Kates," he said, half to himself and half to Lopez, who was standing beside him, panting from the dash upstairs. "I knew that bastard was going to get us into trouble. He's stolen the crown jewels and he's holed up in Persepolis. This embassy has got to help the Shah get them back or the Shah's going to be mad as hell, and that's not going to do the oil prices any good." Karthian turned to the communications technician on duty. "Hey, Riley, is the ambassador getting a copy of this stuff from Shiraz?"

"Yessir, Mr. Karthian, he's in his office right now reading the first pages."

Reading them and figuring out how he can use this crisis to help his career and how he can keep from taking responsibility, Karthian thought to himself. As usual, he felt a mixture of admiration and scorn for the ambassador. Admiration, because Fraser was a professional; he almost always kept his cool. Scorn, because the ambassador, with his Ivy League manner, his skill at entertaining, his fashionable wife, had effortlessly floated to the top in the U.S. foreign service while he, Leo Karthian, second-generation Armenian-American, had had to push his way up through the CIA by taking chances and using his head. Soon, Karthian knew, the ambassador would be calling for him, asking what should be done. Karthian began to whistle between his teeth; he was thinking hard.

"Hey, Lopez," Karthian said, "I'd bet you dollars to doughnuts that these jewel thieves are mixed up with Harry Arloff, the guy with the kidnapped daughter that the FBI picked up. The guy that's missing from his room at the Bristol."

"God almighty," Lopez said.

"Look, the chances are that these robbers took Arloff with them; maybe we can figure out a way to use him. I want you to get a cable off to Washington requesting information about him. On an urgent basis. His service record, stuff like that. Get cracking!"

Karthian turned back to the teleprinter. His Farsi was adequate, but somewhat rudimentary. He moved his lips as he read on.

Harry and Gail found themselves momentarily alone in the harem's main hall; Kates and Gumbert evidently had no fear that they would try to flee: Harry would have to stay with them or risk harm being done to his daughter; Gail would have to stay with them because as things stood now, if she tried to flee, the Iranian government would surely regard her as one of the robbers. And anyway, if either of them tried to run for it across the terrace, to sprint over the old stones and down the great staircase, the odds were prohibitively high that one of the men would cut them down with his Swedish submachine-gun bullets.

Gail was about to say something, but Harry raised a finger. They both listened; they could hear Kates haranguing the consul on the office telephone. Then Hossein began to dictate in Farsi. Harry decided what to do. He glanced around the main hall, did not see what he was looking for, and walked quickly but softly down the rear hall, peering into the side rooms. Then he smiled: he saw a telephone sitting on a small dusty desk, which was evidently used on a part-time basis, perhaps by visiting scholars. Very, very gently he picked up the receiver—and almost shouted for joy: as he had hoped, it was an extension line; he could hear Hossein droning away in Farsi to Mrs. Azeri.

After some minutes, Harry heard Hossein's voice, now grown slightly hoarse, stop dictating. He heard the telephone receiver being dropped on the desk top, and then he heard Kates and Gumbert in the background. Their words were not distinct, but they were obviously trying to get Hossein to put his flask away. Their voices rose as he evidently kept on drinking.

Then Consul Myers's voice came back on the line: "Sorry, but it'll be a minute before the English-language secretary comes on the line."

Harry whispered: "Myers."

"Yes? Who's this now?" Myers sounded nervous.

"My name is Harry Arloff. I'm an American and I'm being held prisoner by the robbers. I have an urgent message for Karthian at the embassy."

"What is it?"

"Just this: tell him that if my daughter is free, he's to make a big X sign somewhere where I can see it from the Persepolis terrace. Just tell him that. He'll know what it's about."

"Okay."

"Bye."

"Bye."

Harry kept his ear to the receiver. First he heard Kates, Gumbert and Hossein talking in the background. Then Hossein came back on the line.

"Anybody there? Hello, hello," Hossein said in English. His speech was less distinct than before.

There was no answer.

"HELLO!" Hossein yelled into the phone.

"Yes, *sir.* " A woman's voice came on the line. "Sorry for the delay. I had to run over from the other building. Do you have something more to dictate? I'm Mrs. Kronstad, ready anytime you are."

Hossein began to read the communiqué in English. Harry listened carefully. Hossein was almost finished when, *bam!*, a blow to the back of Harry's head sent him reeling out of the chair. He looked up from the floor and saw Kates standing over him, the submachine gun dangling from one hand. Fearing another blow, Harry scrambled to his feet, heedless of the twinge in his bad leg. But Kates merely leaned over and picked up the telephone receiver.

"Lady, you tell Myers we're goin' to cut this line now," he said. "When you or the embassy or the Iranian government have an answer for us, give it to us by bullhorn. Bye-bye."

Kates yanked the phone out of the wall. He strode back into Hiar's office. Harry could hear him tell Gumbert that "that shit Arloff" had been eavesdropping, that it was necessary to cut off telephone communications so that nobody could make unauthorized use of the phone. Then Kates and Gumbert began to discuss logistics: how the shifts for the lookouts were to be arranged, where bedrolls were to be placed, and so on.

Harry rubbed the bruise on his head and thought hard. Well, he had had one good break: Kates and Gumbert had evidently not realized that he had spoken to Myers on the phone. And now, he reflected ruefully, it was clear that Hossein had, indeed, had another motive for arranging the jewel robbery: he wanted to wring big concessions out of the Shah. He had evidently thought out the demands very carefully; if the Shah responded to all of them, there were bound to be sweeping changes in Iran's political life—changes that would delight Iranian leftists and their covert supporters, the Russians. But Harry wondered whether Hossein might not have overplayed his hand—whether those demands might be asking so much that the Shah would decide he could not accept them, even if it meant losing the crown jewels *and* Persepolis.

"Oh, Harry, take *care* of yourself." It was Gail, standing in the room's doorway, looking at him with horror. "Did he hit you hard? I heard you fall."

Harry mustered a grin. "No, I'm okay; let's both take care of ourselves," he said. "If we keep our wits about us there still ought to be some way to get out of here alive—and rich."

"That'd be okay by me," she said, managing to grin back. "But how?"

Hunched in the lead armored personnel carrier, Captain Saza, the Iranian officer in command of the contingent, could not believe his ears: the lead vehicle's shortwave radio set had crackled out a message from the commanding officer back in Marvdasht: the APC's were to stop immediately and await further orders. The captain instantly asked for a repeat of the message; it was absurd for Marvdasht to countermand the original order he had received only minutes ago, which was to proceed at full speed to Persepolis, where a terrorist attack had taken place. The second order was duly repeated, but the captain still did not give the APC's the order to halt; he knew that a terrorist attack in Persepolis was a matter of the utmost importance, something His Majesty the Shah himself would take an active part in putting down. He knew that for the Marvdasht radio operator to order him to halt now, at this crucial moment, was madness. He, the captain, had no intention of taking the responsibility for such an insane action on his own shoulders. Clearly, his patriotic duty lay in continuing the charge on Persepolis, across the historic soil where Persian troops had long ago clashed with the army of Alexander the Great. He radioed that he insisted on having the order in writing, and that in the meantime his APC's were proceeding as originally planned. The APC's rumbled on. The lead police car fell back; the lieutenant in the front seat gesticulated frantically at the captain's APC; there was no response.

After a few moments, two F-5 fighter-bombers from the

Shiraz air force base streaked across the sky, flying directly over the highway. They whooshed low enough so that the noise was deafening in the captain's APC. Then they banked off toward the east, forming a huge loop over the flatlands, carefully flying nowhere near Persepolis. The captain had thought at first that the F-5's were on their way to mount an air strike on the terrorists, despite the danger to the ancient stones, but now he saw the planes were coming back toward *him*, again flying low. It dawned on him that they were in fact signaling him. That he had better stop or risk, for some unknown and unfathomable reason, the possibility that he, the officer in command of what would be the first armored contingent to reach beleaguered Persepolis, would find himself under aerial attack from Iranian warplanes.

The APC's came to a sudden halt.

"Get those radios placed right," Kates rasped at Ingo. The man lugged in two big portable shortwave-mediumwave radio receivers and set them on Hiar's desk. Gumbert fiddled with the dials on the left-hand set until he found Radio Moscow, broadcasting in English: a bass voice was talking about crops. Then Gumbert tuned the right-hand set to the Teheran English-language station. It was playing a medley of Cole Porter tunes. He sat back in Hiar's chair and unbuttoned his vest. "Gentlemen," he said, "we are now open for business."

"Be sure you listen every minute," Kates said. "The Shah is bound to react goddamn fast. Shit, he's reactin' already; look over there." He pointed out the window, toward the west.

Just beyond and below the terrace was a grove of young trees. They had been planted to dress up the site for the 1971 celebrations. Beyond them was the gaudy form of the Hafiz Hotel. The architects had tarted up its functional, angular silhouette with arabesque arches and domes.

At that moment an Iranian military helicopter was landing

on the hotel roof. Another was hovering overhead, like a hummingbird. As Kates and Gumbert watched, two more helicopters materialized in the sky off to the southwest; they were approaching fast.

"They must be making the hotel their field headquarters for, um, dealing with us," Gumbert said. "Smart move."

"It is, it is," Kates said. "But, shit, if they're concentratin' their field commanders only a few hundred yards from us, that means they're probably goin' to concentrate troops and armor not far away."

"Relax," Gumbert said. "Let them draw up the entire Iranian army out there if they want to; that doesn't affect our plans. Remember, we have stolen something that no one else has managed to steal from the Shah; the fact that he is moving in officers over there doesn't mean he's going to get his jewels back any more quickly; it only, um, indicates how badly he wants them back."

Kates was pacing the room. "Right you are, Rudi, but it means we have to be on our toes." He saw Gail, Harry and Hiar standing together in the main hall of the harem. They, too, heard the helicopters; they moved toward a window to try to catch sight of them.

Kates said, "I don't want those people eavesdropping on us. Hossein, please clear all three of them out of here. Tell them to get out and to stay at least fifty yards from this buildin'. Tell them we'll shoot them if they come too close. And the lookouts will shoot them if they try to move off the terrace. We want them where we can lay hands on them; we're bound to be needin' them before we're through."

"Yes, Your Majesty, yes, sir," Ambassador Fraser said. He was speaking into the receiver of the radio-telephone in the little room adjoining his office in the U.S. embassy in Teheran. The Shah's tone was more imperious today than ever, it seemed; Fraser almost felt he had to stand at attention to hear the rush of imperial complaints, the thunder of the imperial wrath.

"Yes, Your Majesty, of *course* we recognize that the United States is indirectly to blame for the fact that this Colonel Kates was able to engage in large-scale corruption here. Yes, of course. Yes, we do recognize that your government had put a stop to it and when the colonel disappeared inside Iran, you put out an order for his arrest. I need hardly remind you that he had long since been asked to leave the U.S. military mission's staff, long since retired from active duty with our army . . .

"What's that? Do I think he was a Communist? No, sir, I think he had become simply a soldier of fortune. When he was here in his, ah, official capacity, he realized that he could make enormous profits through unethical business dealings. Now, I feel sure, he is simply putting all his poker chips—What's that? . . . Oh, yes, excuse my slang. I meant he's simply wagering all he has on this attempt to get half your jewels out of the country. After all, the man is in his sixties now; he has evidently decided that it's worth risking prison for the rest of his life, or the possibility of being killed, for the chance of becoming one of the richest men in the world . . . No, no, your Majesty, I do not for a minute believe that those loose jewels would actually be used to finance some movement against you, as the wording of the communiqué suggests. That's just hogwash; what must have happened is that this man has joined forces with opponents of your regime in a sort of mutual-interest pact: he and his men stand to become terribly rich while these, ah, these terrorists hope to achieve these extraordinary demands.

"What's that? What do I think the Soviets' role is in this? Well, the chief problem for Kates, in helping to plan this crime, must have been to find a way to get the jewels out of your country. And to arrange a safe haven in some foreign country for the rest of his life so he could enjoy his ill-gotten gains. This he has evidently arranged with the Soviets. They stand to gain enormously if you should accede to these demands. Yes, yes, I

know it will cost you billions of dollars in lost oil and gas revenues if you accept the Soviet demands in negotiating this deal
. . . Yes, I know." The ambassador sighed and ran his hands
nervously through his hair. "Yes, Your Majesty, it *would* be
humiliating to have to legalize the Tudeh party."

There followed a considerable pause while the Shah unbur-
dened himself further. Fraser's face began to look dazed; he was
realizing that if he managed to please the Shah by helping to
recover the jewels, it would be an enormous plus for his career;
for his next post the Secretary of State might give him a real
plum—Tokyo, say, or even—dare he hope?—Rome; Fraser
knew his wife would be blissfully happy in Rome. But it also
dawned on him that if he failed to please the Shah, U.S.-Iranian
relations would get an awful jolting in the next couple of days.
In that event, Fraser knew the Shah might come to hate him;
if *that* happened, Fraser would be lucky to get posted even to
Baghdad after this; and if he had to go to Baghdad, his wife
would simply pack up and move back to the U.S.A. Fraser ran
his hands through his hair again. "Yes, Your Majesty, I'd be glad
to hop down to Persepolis and see what I can do; who knows,
maybe Kates will lose his nerve. Well, that's very kind of you;
I'll be waiting in ten minutes with two or three of my men; the
palace helicopter can land right on the embassy's front lawn
. . . What's that? Oh, yes, sir, I'm sure we'll find the Hafiz Hotel
*most* comfortable."

KARTHIAN'S CORDOVANS MADE A CLUMPING SOUND AS HE HUR-
ried along the corridor toward the royal suite of the Hafiz Hotel.
He, Ambassador Fraser and Feeney had come down from Teheran on emergency transportation provided by the Shah: helicopter from the embassy to the military part of Teheran Airport, Iranian air force jet to Shiraz air force base, another
helicopter to the hotel. The ambassador had rushed to attend
a strategy meeting that was to be held by the local Iranian
commanders. Feeney was establishing a field office of sorts in a
suite on another floor. Karthian had stopped in the switchboard
room of the hotel to make certain arrangements; now he was
belatedly catching up with Fraser.

Karthian turned a corner and found himself in front of a fat
Iranian in civilian clothes, who sat, impassive, in a gilded chair.
On the carpet beside the man was a new machine gun, smelling
of grease. Its barrel was mounted on a bipod. Karthian recognized the weapon as a West German–designed machine gun,
the MG-1A1, manufactured in Iran under license from a West
German firm.

"Good afternoon, sir," the fat man said. God knew which
of Iran's several security agencies he worked for, or whether he
was only a police plainclothesman.

"Hi, there," Karthian said cheerily, conscious that the fat
man could cut him in half with a burst from the machine gun,
provided he could operate it. It was, of course, the wrong sort

of weapon for a guard on duty inside a hotel. But what could you do; this was the Middle East.

Karthian moved on and eased open a teakwood door covered with arabesque carving. He found himself in a sumptuous chamber, which had evidently been designed to serve as a private banquet room for occupants of the royal suite. The damask curtains were drawn for security's sake, and two sinuous Venetian glass chandeliers lit the scene. The banquet table was covered with a white linen tablecloth, which someone had already spotted with spilled coffee.

At the head of the table, Karthian saw, was General Karavi, commander of the military region that included Persepolis. He was a solemn, slim man in his forties, skilled at service politics, a favorite of the Shah. At the foot was Fraser, unruffled-seeming despite the hasty journey and the gravity of the situation. A fabulous front man, Karthian thought to himself as he took the chair to Fraser's left.

In the minutes that followed, the other seats were taken by a dozen harassed-looking Iranian officers and officials. Senior among them was the minister of the imperial court, who had flown down with the Americans. He was plump and soft-looking, the son and grandson of high-ranking palace officials—a man totally loyal to the Shah. Karthian also recognized old General Jaddad, the iron-fisted local provincial governor; Major Avali, the fox-faced intelligence officer, also down from Teheran; and a certain Major Tatrak, General Karavi's aide. The mood in the room was somber: the Iranians were aware that their careers were on the line; if they failed to recover the jewels intact, the Shah would be furious. These men might find themselves fired, demoted, even jailed.

Coffee was served. General Karavi waited until all the cups were filled and then motioned brusquely to the waiter to quit the room. The general cracked his knuckles and took a deep breath.

"Gentlemen, I need hardly tell you that the situation is

grave," he said, speaking English for the Americans' benefit. His voice was shaking with emotion. "We find ourselves in a terrible dilemma. You are all doubtless familiar by now with the demands of this gang of bandits. We do not know yet exactly what His Majesty's response will be. We do not know what the Russians will do. In the meantime, we have sealed off the area. We are bringing up army troops and armored vehicles, but we are holding them well back from Persepolis itself so as not to anger the bandits. Similarly, General Jaddad, who, as governor, commands the Gendarmerie units in this province, has moved gendarmes into this area, but is keeping them out of sight of the bandits.

"We have also told the air force to keep combat planes well away from Persepolis, and we have made sure that our helicopters have not approached too close to the ruins. By so doing, we have hoped not to increase the tension, and we have helped to keep this entire crisis secret from the populace and the world at large. The blast that the bandits set off in Teheran early this morning to distract the police has been reported by the Teheran afternoon papers as a boiler explosion. Similarly, the radio will soon report that an outbreak of cholera has been discovered and traced to the Hafiz Hotel, and that in consequence this entire area has been declared off-limits to civilian traffic."

General Karavi took a sip of his coffee. Karthian noticed that the man's hand shook ever so slightly.

"In the past hour, we have moved a couple of radio-equipped army reconnaissance experts up the back of the Mountain of Mercy to its ridge line," the general went on. "From them and from the crews of the helicopters that have been hovering around this hotel, we have acquired some information about the bandits' deployment. There are at least seven persons—six men and a woman—outdoors on the terrace. Most of them are evidently serving as lookouts; most are equipped with submachine guns and walkie-talkie radios, which they have not yet used. They evidently fear, correctly, that we are monitoring the airwaves. One of these men is evidently drunk; he has been seen staggering and falling down. We have not seen the bandit Kates; we assume that he and an undetermined number of other persons are in the building known as 'the harem' and/or in the truck parked near the harem building. Three smaller vehicles are parked near the truck; we assume that the jewels and the bombs are still on board these vehicles, although we do not know for sure.

"In light of all this, we have decided that for the moment we cannot risk a frontal assault on the bandits; the odds are too high that they would make good their threat and destroy the national treasure known as the crown jewels."

Karavi looked around the room. The court minister was avoiding his eye, gazing down at his pudgy hands. General Jaddad was looking sullen. Fraser was skillfully keeping his face devoid of expression. No one wanted to volunteer advice.

Karavi took another deep breath. "Now, gentlemen, I have to report to you that there has been another grave development."

Kates and Gumbert, alone in the harem, sat listening to the two radios. Now and then they went to a window to watch a helicopter come or go from the hotel roof.

"At least the Shah hasn't sent any warplanes here," Kates said. "That shows he takes our threats seriously. That—"

Suddenly Gumbert gestured at him to be quiet, to listen to the radio that was tuned to Radio Moscow. Gumbert bent over the radio that was tuned to Teheran's English-language station and turned up the volume; the hourly newscast was beginning. The familiar Australian announcer's voice filled the room. There was an Arab League meeting in Cairo, a political scandal in Pakistan, a decree by the Teheran municipal government providing penalties for speculative hoarding of building supplies. Then, without changing his tone or giving any sign that he was reporting something unusually important, the announcer said: "His Imperial Majesty the Shah today pardoned five hundred prisoners who had been convicted by military courts for sedition against the Iranian nation and various similar charges. The imperial decree implementing the pardons is effective immediately. Her Imperial Majesty Empress Farah today called for the speeding up of moves to establish a training center for midwives. Her Majesty's statement came during an inspection tour of the—"

Gumbert's beard was distended by a huge grin. He turned to Kates and made a V-for-victory sign with two pudgy fingers. "Did you hear that?"

"Sure did, Rudi. That's great news; shows how fast the Shah can act when somethin' important is at stake."

Gumbert nodded. "So far so good. One demand fulfilled and three to go. You didn't, um, by any chance, hear a signal for us from Moscow radio while I was listening to Teheran?"

"Nope." Kates shook his head. He began to nibble nervously on his lower lip.

Another helicopter hung over the hotel roof, preparing to land.

General Karavi sighed. "Major, read the message."

Major Tatrak began to read in English from a blue sheet, which was evidently the decoded version of a secret cable.

"Soviet fishing trawler *Timoshenko,* bound southeast from the Iraqi port of Umqasr toward the Strait of Hormuz, changed course about four hours ago. It veered off to port, that is, due eastward, across the Persian Gulf, and is now thirty miles off the Iranian port of Bushehr. That is, a hundred and sixty-five miles from where we are sitting. This vessel has a large afterdeck, which could serve as a landing and takeoff platform for a helicopter. No helicopters are on deck. It is not known whether the *Timoshenko* is carrying a helicopter or helicopters below-decks."

Fraser raised a long finger. "Would you mind clarifying for us, General, what it is that you consider so grave in this development?" Karthian glanced sidelong at Fraser with a kind of admiration: the man was being a good bureaucrat, keeping his head, making sure that there were no misunderstandings, even when, any minute now, Persepolis might be blown to bits.

General Karavi leaned forward across the mottled tablecloth. He almost began to crack his knuckles again, but remembered his manners and did not. "Ambassador, it is extremely unusual for a Soviet fishing vessel to venture so close to Bushehr, where we have important naval facilities. We feel the bandits may plan to make use of this vessel to effect their escape by helicopter. The question now arises: What can be done?"

"This fishing vessel isn't in your territorial waters, is it?" Fraser asked.

A typical Fraser bureaucratic observation, Karthian said to himself.

"No, as a matter of fact, it is not," Karavi said. "As you know, we claim that our territorial waters extend twelve miles from our shores."

From a divan in the rear of the room, old General Jaddad mumbled something in Farsi.

"My colleague thinks we should consider a preemptive strike against this vessel," General Karavi said to Fraser. "But we should have to think very, very carefully before we took such a step."

"It would precipitate a crisis in our relations with the Soviet Union," the court minister said. "God knows where that might lead; we want, at all costs, to avoid war with the Russians."

"So do we," Fraser said quietly. He sipped his cup of coffee and tried to hide a grimace; the brew was too strong for him. "Also, if you will forgive my being pessimistic: if you were, say, to sink this vessel, it is possible that the robbers might immediately react in some unfavorable way. They might consider the sinking an act of bad faith; they might damage the jewels or even Persepolis."

The court minister examined his hands. "Yes, Ambassador, we have thought of that," he said softly. "Yet if we fail to act now, we may regret it. His Majesty the Shah may regret it."

"Have you done anything already?" Fraser asked. A little silence followed. Karthian raised his eyebrows; he knew that the pause meant the Iranians had been doing something that made them feel embarrassed. Something that they perhaps should have checked first with the U.S. about.

*"Oui, monsieur,"* old General Jaddad said, rumbling now in French, the Western language that was taught to Iranian military cadets in his youth. "Our national honor is at stake, our imperial traditions, the very center of our national soul. The crown jewels and the Persepolis monuments—without them Iran would not be Iran." He leaned forward, his dark eyes flashing. "Mr. Fraser, we have begun shadowing this vessel on its strange course with two of our Tang-class submarines; if the Soviet Union considers this provocative, let them."

"I'm afraid that *is* a provocative act, General," Fraser said. "When our government sold you the submarines, it was with some misgivings. There was fear in Washington that the mere fact that you had them in your arsenal might increase the odds of some sort of flare-up in the Persian Gulf—"

Old General Jaddad rumbled some objection, but Fraser, pursuing his argument, did not stop to listen. He rushed ahead, hoping to convince Karavi and the court minister.

"Look, gentlemen, the situation is extremely delicate. On the plane flying down here we were informed that His Majesty had decided to grant one of the robbers' demands; he has released the political prisoners. But we have had no sign of what he will do about the other demands—or what the Soviets' response will be. Do you *really* want to inject more tension into this already agonized situation by trailing  that fishing vessel with subs? What if the Soviets lose patience with the whole undertaking? What if they send a message to the bandits telling them the situation is hopeless, saying there is no choice but to detonate the bombs?"

"All right, Mr. Fraser, all right," General Karavi said, his temper clearly wearing thin. "Have you any better course of action to suggest? I need hardly remind you that our government considers the United States partly responsible for this crisis, since the bandit Kates, a former U.S. officer, is one of the ringleaders. And since, I am sorry to report, two other American citizens are with the bandits now."

There was a stir of surprise in the room. Fraser stiffened. "Who do you mean?" he asked.

Karavi fished a scrap of notepaper out of a uniform pocket. "A certain Prince Mikhail Arloff, whom you yourself have entertained in your home. And a Miss Olsen, who has also been your guest."

"I, ah—how do you know they're there?" Fraser asked, his poise fading. Karthian knew the man was worried now about what the State Department would say when it heard this.

"Two of our helicopters have been taking photographs of the persons on the Persepolis terrace with Telephoto lenses. Our intelligence personnel have made the identifications using photographs from their files. This couple has been strolling among the ruins, along with a Dr. Hiar, the chief archaeologist at the site, who is evidently a prisoner. We cannot be sure of the status of Miss Olsen and this Arloff."

Fraser fiddled with the handle of his coffee cup. The room had become deathly still. General Jaddad cleared his throat and spat noisily into a gilded wastebasket.

"We suspected that Arloff might be accompanying the jewel robbers," Fraser said softly. "My colleague, Mr. Karthian, here, has received information suggesting that Arloff was the victim of an extortion plan mounted by them."

General Karavi looked skeptical. *"Very* interesting," he said, his voice now loaded with sarcasm. "And since you are in possession of this information, are you in a position to suggest any alternative action? Or are you merely telling us that our use of our submarines is rash?"

Fraser took a deep breath. "I have no sure-fire suggestion to make to you, General," he said. "But as you know, my colleague, Mr. Karthian, has considerable experience in unconventional, ah, tactical situations. He has some suggestions that he has drawn up about what action might be taken; you may find them interesting."

That bastard, that dirty, cookie-pushing bastard, Karthian thought to himself; he doesn't want to take any responsibility for me and my ideas. Karthian realized that all eyes in the room were on him.

"Well? What is it, Mr. Karthian?" Karavi snapped.

Karthian set his shoes squarely on the banquet-room parquetry and leaned back a bit in his chair. For a moment he let his mind flicker again over the complicated tactical problem at hand. It was like the old days in West Berlin, deciding whom it was important to smuggle out of East Berlin and how to go about it without starting an international incident. Only, now the stakes were infinitely higher. Also, then he had been young, with his life before him. Now he was middle-aged, he had failed to make his wife happy, he wasn't even trusted by his ambassador. He had nothing going for him but his wits.

"Hello, gentlemen," Karthian said, speaking more elegantly than usual. "Two Iranian experts have very kindly taken the time to help me in some thinking about this situation. You probably have heard of them both. One is Dr. Mehdri, the chief archaeologist on the staff of the Empress Farah. The Iranian air force has very efficiently flown him down here today. The other is Dr. Shepehri of the Bank Markazi department that oversees the crown jewels. As you doubtless know, the robbers have demanded that Dr. Shepehri act as a kind of observer if and when you let them leave Persepolis. Both these gentlemen are in the hotel if you should want to speak to them later.

"Now, in addition to the information they have provided, our own Pentagon has been helpful. We have already checked the service record of this man Arloff, who was drafted into our army during the 1960s. As you know, he is a resourceful character. By means which are not clear, he managed to spend most of his service time as a clerk-typist in Fort Dix, New Jersey, which is conveniently close to the bright lights of New York. But before that he was given advanced infantry training, which means that he knows—in theory at least—how to fight. And he should be able to handle a submachine gun. I understand from Major Tatrak that the Iranian army could lend us a couple of submachine guns if it saw fit."

"We would lend you a hundred if it would help," General Karavi burst out. "But, frankly, I do not think that mere fire power will help us now. Or at least it will not help of itself. We need new approaches to many aspects of the problem. Communications, for instance. How—"

Karthian smiled. "Well, now," he said, forgetting his manners, happy to be interrupting a full general. "Well, now, General. Funny you should mention that . . ."

# 16

THE DAY WORE ON. HARRY AND GAIL SAT ON OLD STONE SLABS
well away from the harem, waiting. The Parliament butts pro-
liferated at Harry's feet. He was lighting yet another cigarette
when it dawned on him that he was hearing the faint drone of
an airplane engine. It was getting nearer. Gail had been nodding sleepily, but her head soon snapped upright; she had heard
the sound, too.

Within moments, two black dots appeared low in the sky
to the northwest. They grew rapidly larger. Kates stepped out
into the forecourt of the harem and studied them with field
glasses.

"Unarmed Iranian army spotter planes; Piper L-eight-
eens," he said over his shoulder to Gumbert. "Must be on a
photo-reconnaissance flight; well, let 'em come."

The planes droned closer and closer until Harry could
make out the Iranian markings with the naked eye. They were
flying low and slowly, at a speed considerably under a hundred
miles an hour.

"Hey," Kates barked suddenly. "Gas!"

Billowing white smoke began trailing from the two aircraft,
but in seconds it became obvious that it was only skywriting
smoke. The two planes veered apart, then converged at slightly
different altitudes, their paths crossing, before taking parallel
courses toward the southwest. Their little maneuver had
formed an X in the sky.

Harry gasped upward, his lips forming the words "Praise

be." There was no chance that two Iranian army planes had come all the way to Persepolis and marked an X in the sky by coincidence; their mission had obviously been to inform him that Emily was now safe and well. He took a deep breath. An enormous weight was lifted from him. He felt like opening a champagne bottle, tap-dancing, shouting for joy—except that he was still a captive, still standing here among these ancient stones, with Kates pacing the courtyard, his submachine gun slung over one shoulder.

In the distance the planes banked, gained altitude and turned back toward Persepolis. The droning grew louder as they approached again.

"Look at that," Gail cried. "They must be drawing some-thing."

They were: the lead plane made a sharp turn, then another; its smoke trail was making an odd, irregular shape in the sky. The second plane, off to the west of Persepolis, was drawing a different, more complicated shape. They droned on until each had drawn an enclosed form, a kind of box, in the sky. The lead plane's box was five-sided:

The number two plane's box was a kind of hexagon:

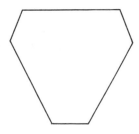

Then the planes flew off, flying wing-and-wing toward the northwest. Wind over Persepolis soon tore at the two boxes, tugging them out of shape.

Gail came up to Harry and took his arm. "What the hell does all that mean?"

Harry felt an urge to share his joy with her, to tell her that the FBI must have successfully raided the Adair house in Southport, must have had the advantage of surprise. Must even now be giving Emily lollipops in some local FBI head-quarters, in Bridgeport perhaps. He hoped poor old Miss Mac-Donald was all right, too—and free. But he decided to tell Gail nothing. She was a tough cookie, all right, but there was al-ways the chance that Kates and Gumbert might torture her, or threaten to torture her, if they thought it would gain them something. And Harry wanted there to be absolutely no chance that she would tell them that Emily was free, that Harry could now take action against his captors—and that if he did so he stood a good chance of earning a fat reward from a grateful Shah.

"It's a code message, and it's at least partly for me," he said. "I know what the X meant, but I'll be darned if I know what the pentagon and the hexagon are supposed to signify. What do you think?"

"No idea."

"They may have chosen some system of symbols that they thought would have a special meaning for me. But what could it be? What—"

Harry stopped talking. His jaw snapped shut. He glanced around. Kates was back in the harem now. On the terrace the lookouts were standing quietly at their posts.

"Where's Hiar?" he asked Gail.

"Last time I saw him he was wandering around over there, beyond that big stone arch. Why?"

"Look, Gail, I'm going to go and find Hiar, and then he and I are probably going to do some more wandering around the terrace; now I think I've figured out what that skywriting meant, and only Hiar can help me apply the message. Who knows, we may get out of this in one piece, after all."

"Can I help?"

"*Ah, chérie,* you sure can. Would you please try to distract the guards? And Kates and Gumbert, too, if you can? Any way you can. Without getting yourself hurt."

"I'll see what I can do," she said with a wry smile. She pulled out a pocket mirror and checked her appearance. "Good luck."

"Good luck to us both," he said, turning away. He was sorry to leave her.

Inside the harem, Gumbert was crouched over the short-wave radio that was tuned to Teheran's English-language station, hoping that the music would stop, and that there would be news of another demand being fulfilled. Kates was standing behind a window curtain, peering out over the terrace, watching Gail saunter across it, racking his brain about the meaning of the signs in the sky.

"Rudi, what do you think—"

"Ssh." Gumbert cut him off.

"What is it? Something on the radio?"

"No, something outside on the terrace. A falsetto cry. It sounds like a woman laughing, or screaming, perhaps."

"I hear it now. It can't be Gail. I can see her from here. She's looking around, too, to hear where the noise came from. What the—"

A single shot rang out. Then two shots, quick-fire. Then there was silence.

"Rudi, I'm going to break our walkie-talkie silence."

"By all means."

Kates took up a walkie-talkie and barked, "Nightingale One to all hands. What the hell was that?"

An answer crackled out of the set's speaker. "Nightingale One, Nightingale One. This is Nightingale Four."

"Go ahead, Nightingale Four." Nightingale Four was Faiz Kiani.

"Nightingale One. It's very odd. I saw two Qashqai tribal women running across the center of the terrace, among the great pillars. God knows how they got there. I waved at them to clear off, and I fired one warning shot, then two more. And then I lost sight of them. Now I'm searching the area where I saw them run, but they've disappeared. They must have jumped off the west edge of the terrace."

"I hope they broke their asses," Kates muttered. Then he barked into the walkie-talkie: "How do you know they were Qashqais?"

"Because they had those strange flaring skirts. They must have sneaked up onto the terrace to get something. Maybe they had stashed valuables there. Maybe—"

"That's enough, Nightingale Four. Resume radio silence. Over and out."

Kates put the walkie-talkie down and hit the desk with the flat of his hand. "Shit, Rudi, the Shah's men are tryin' to mount a war of nerves. First the Pipers with that weird skywritin'. And now Qashqai women. They must have figured our men wouldn't shoot to kill a woman. And they were right. Shit. Serves us right for hirin' Kiani. A fuckin' tourist guide, a two-bit smuggler."

Gumbert looked up from the radio. "What I would like to know is how, um, those women breached our security perimeter. We have daylight, good visibility, and they still managed to slip past our guards."

"You're right, it's problematical. But it's not the end of the world. The Shah and his generals would never risk tryin' to infiltrate fighting men onto the terrace, because they know that if they do we can blow up the jewels and the ruins."

Gumbert, his brows clenched in a worried scowl, nodded. He bent over the radio again.

Harry found Hiar leaning against an old block of stone and staring gloomily across the ruins of the treasury of Darius. His gaunt face had a bleak look.

"Hello," Harry said.

"Good afternoon." Hiar smiled. Harry had already told him that he had been blackmailed into joining the robbers.

"It must be harrowing to face the threat of having everything you've worked on for years blown up at the whim of a band of robbers."

"That it is." Hiar's voice was somber.

"I want to ask your help; I think the Iranian government has been taking steps to provide me with weapons to make a counterattack."

"How so? Surely the government would not risk a confrontation that could lead to the destruction of Persepolis and the jewels."

"You're right. But the government may well feel—as I do —that one chance of stymying the robbers' plot is for someone who they know is already here on the terrace to catch them by surprise from up close. Someone like me, who the robbers think is in their power through blackmail. Someone like you."

"But how can that be done?"

"Did you see the signs the two planes made in skywriting? Did they mean anything to you?"

"No. The X—that could be anything. I assumed the pentagon and the hexagon had some special meaning. I racked my brain and I could think of none."

"I think the signs were meant for me. I'm a jewelry salesman by trade, and I recognized the shapes."

"For God's sake, what are they?"

"They're the outlines of two standard ways a diamond can be cut. The names of the forms are derived from their shapes, more or less. The irregular pentagon is called the 'bullet cut.' The other is called the 'calf's head.' In conjunction the symbols must be intended to mean that bullets have been provided for me at or near a sign of a calf's head. Or, less literally, that weaponry is available for me at or near a symbol that is common at Persepolis: a bull's head."

Hair nodded. "An ingenious theory."

"So now I want to ask your help. Can you figure out what bull's head this message refers to? If you can, we may be able to lay our hands on guns. We may be able to save the jewels. And Persepolis."

Hiar chuckled grimly and spread his skinny, tweed-tailored arms. "There are many bulls and bulls' heads here, as you can see. I have no idea which one may be meant. I can only suggest that we look around and see if anything strikes our eye."

"Let's go," Harry said. "But we've got to walk slowly, casually, so the guards will only think we're killing time."

The music being broadcast by Teheran radio—the tune was "Rhinestone Cowboy"—came to a sudden stop. Gumbert snapped his fingers to get Kates's attention, then gestured for silence. The English-language newscaster with the Australian accent came on the air:

"We have a special bulletin. After long negotiations, the imperial government of Iran today concluded an epochal, long-term agreement to provide oil and gas to the Soviet Union. The announcement of the deal was made in a communiqué from the National Iranian Oil Company. Details about pricing and about the amount of oil to be delivered were not disclosed, but the communiqué said that Iran is to provide the Soviet Union with more than five hundred billion cubic meters of Iranian natural gas a year. The communiqué said the deal was by far the largest economic agreement ever concluded between Teheran and Moscow.

"We wish at this time to broadcast an announcement from

the ministry of health. Cases of cholera have been diagnosed in recent hours in the vicinity of Persepolis. A source of the infection has apparently been the Hafiz Hotel. Accordingly, the hotel has been closed down. The Persepolis area has been declared off-limits to the public. Roadblocks have been put up. Public health workers have been brought in by helicopter."

After a moment's silence, "Rhinestone Cowboy" came back on the air.

Gumbert turned to Kates, giving the thumbs-up sign. "That is three times the amount of natural gas the Iranian government had intended to provide to the Soviets. That shows that the Iranians must have made enormous concessions."

"Yes, but how *much* in the way of concessions?"

"We have no way of knowing. But we'll know they were acceptable if we hear Radio Moscow play our tune."

Kates nodded. He looked at his watch. His manner was worried. "That baloney on the radio about cholera, you know what that means, don't you?"

Gumbert shrugged. "It means that the Shah has definitely been moving troops into this area. And that he wants to keep this whole business secret from his subjects. All that was expectable. At least he's had the courtesy to keep his troops out of our sight. He doesn't, um, want to make us nervous."

"Hell," Kates said. "I'm nervous anyhow." He took a pistol out of a trousers pocket and checked the clip.

It took half an hour of peering at bulls' heads—bulls' heads at the top of columns, carved in relief, the heads of bull statues —before Hiar found what they were looking for.

"Stop right here," he said to Harry. "Look casual so that if anybody is watching us, they won't know we have discovered something."

"Okay." Harry lit a Parliament and tossed it on the pebbly ground. They were standing at the north end of the foundations of the ruined palace of Xerxes, in a sheltered cul-de-sac formed by the foundations and a battered ancient staircase. It was a secluded place, out of sight of the lookouts. To judge by the smell of urine, many tourists had taken advantage of the privacy to use it as an outhouse.

Hiar looked carefully around, made doubly sure that no lookouts were in sight and gestured with his head toward the foot of the staircase. "You see *that* bull's head, the small gray one?"

"Sure, it looks like a lot of the others—as though it had once been on the top of a column. Only this one is a little smaller. Made out of some kind of gray stone. What is it?"

Hiar's eyes flashed. "It wasn't there last week."

*"What?"*

"Believe me, I have spent years studying these stones. I have not seen that bull's head here before. And yet it seems oddly familiar. Let's investigate."

Harry moved partway up the ruined staircase so that he could warn Hiar if anyone approached.

Hiar crouched beside the bull's head and touched it with one hand. The head seemed to move ever so slightly. He pushed with his hand—and the head slid three inches across the pebbled ground. "It's made of papier-mâché or some similar substance," he said to Harry in a stage whisper. "It's obviously hollow." He began to chuckle.

"What's so funny?" Harry asked.

"Now I know why it seemed familiar. It was part of a display put up by the tourism ministry at the Hafiz Hotel." Using both hands, Hiar gently turned the bull's head over on its side.

*"Voilà,* Harry said.

Under the bull's head was a package wrapped in semitransparent plastic sheeting.

Harry could not contain his curiosity. He hopped down off the staircase and peered through the wrapping.

"Is it what I think it is?" Hiar asked.

Harry began to unwrap the fabric. "It's two submachine guns—the Israeli kind called Uzis, with four extra clips of cartridges—one revolver, a box of revolver cartridges, flashlights and"—he smiled— "a sheet of instructions for the Uzis. How the hell did this get put here?"

"Probably by those Qashqai tribal women."

"How so?" Harry asked. "How could they have crossed the perimeter without being seen by the lookouts?"

"I don't know for sure, but I would assume that they evaded the lookouts by entering the terrace from underground —using one of the old drainage tunnels that crisscross underneath the ruins."

"Hey. Could we go through one of the tunnels to get back to the harem—and surprise Gumbert and Kates?"

Hiar thought an instant. "We might just possibly be able to. There is an entrance to a complex tunnel system a few dozen yards from here, on the northeast side of the foundations of Darius's palace. If we don't get caught, and if we don't get lost, we could enter the tunnel there and come out at the south end of the Hall of a Hundred Columns, which is a few yards from the forecourt of the harem. We might be able to surprise them with some sort of ruse—"

"And take control of the jewels. In the excitement when we first arrived on the terrace, I didn't see what, if anything, they did with them. I thought I heard Gumbert tell Kates that vehicles were being unloaded 'into the tunnels,' so that's presumably where they are, now, somewhere underground. But God knows where the bombs are."

Hiar smiled ruefully. "It seems the odds of our succeeding are very small—"

"But there is nothing else we can do. Except first—"

"First what?"

"First I'd like to give one of these weapons to Gail. She may be able to use it."

"Ah. She is pretty. I think she is important to you."

"Sort of, Hiar."

"You could find her and arrange for her to take a weapon; but in doing so, you would risk having the lookouts discover our whole cache of arms."

Harry nodded. "You're right. We'd better get going. I'll go back up the stairs and signal to you if the coast is clear. Then you lead the way to the tunnel."

Hiar leaned over and took the cumbersome package in his arms.

# 17

IN THE COURSE OF A THIRTY-FIVE-YEAR CAREER SPENT LARGELY
in the Middle East, James Fraser had long ago picked up a
useful piece of wisdom: there are times when the shrewdest and
safest thing a career diplomat can do in the service of his country is—precisely nothing. This Fraser judged to be one of those
times. And so it was that the American ambassador, in vest and
shirt sleeves, was well into a chess game with Feeney when
Major Tatrak burst into their suite in the Hafiz Hotel. Karthian
was absent, having gone up on the roof with General Karavi to
watch for signs of action on the terrace.

"Important news, Your Excellency," Tatrak said. "As of
half an hour ago, we are told, crewmen of the Soviet trawler
*Timoshenko* had opened a large hatch on her afterdeck." Tatrak was breathing heavily; he must have been trotting through
the hotel corridors—which was a most un-Iranian thing to do.
"And a military helicopter had been hauled out onto the deck;
it was being prepared for flight."

"What model is this helicopter, Major?" the ambassador
asked. He had just taken one of Feeney's pawns, and he set it
neatly at the end of a row of Feeney's pieces that he had already
taken.

"It's Polish-made, Your Excellency, the model known as
Mi-two. Its NATO code name is Hoplite. A general-purpose
helicopter, a standard model. It is in the Soviet and Polish air
forces and in the air forces of many countries which obtain
armaments from the Soviet bloc."

"Is it armed?" The ambassador moved one of his knights closer to Feeney's king.

"We don't know for certain. We assume this one is unarmed, as specified in the bandits' original demands. So far our reconnaissance planes have observed no rockets or other large weaponry."

"Hmmm." It was unclear whether the ambassador was thinking about the chess game or the Hoplite. "Tell me, Major, can this helicopter fly as far as Persepolis and back?"

"Yes, absolutely."

"Can it make the flight and carry off several passengers and the loose stones, as Kates evidently plans?"

"Easily. It can accommodate a pilot, a dozen passengers, and almost a ton of freight. More, if the number of passengers is reduced."

"Your move," the ambassador said. A look of uneasiness crossed Major Tatrak's face, but then he realized that Fraser was speaking to Feeney. Feeney scowled at the board and moved a bishop so that it threatened the ambassador's knight.

"Could this helicopter carry *all* the loot and all Kates's men at the same time?" the ambassador asked.

"We don't know for certain. That might depend in part on what sort of containers the jewels were packed in. We still have no firm estimate of the weight of all the jewelry. This is because the official catalogue of the items lists the weight, or the estimated weight, of the largest jewels in each piece, but not the weight of the piece itself."

"But the helicopter could carry all Kates's men and the most valuable of the jewels, the crowns and that sort of thing?"

"Probably. But they might have to leave a couple of the men behind."

"Hmmm." The ambassador moved his knight out of danger. "Tell me, Major, what would your side do if you thought Kates was trying to get away with *all* your crown jewels?"

"But we would know; as you are aware, the idea is for the

helicopter to land near here and take on an official of the Bank Markazi to make sure that only loose jewels are taken; he would signal us if all went well."

"Suppose Kates tries to double-cross you."

"We would shoot the helicopter down immediately."

"Even if it meant war with the Soviet Union?"

"Even if it meant there was a chance of World War Three. These jewels are our national heritage. We will do everything to prevent them from leaving the country."

The ambassador sighed. His intuition, honed by those decades of dealing with Middle Eastern affairs, told him this was going to be a messy business. He moved his queen across the board and said "Check." He watched Feency discreetly over the top of his half-rimmed glasses. Feeney looked startled and began to tug absent-mindedly at his pale jowls.

Fraser concluded that Feeney would never make a good ambassador; a first-rate diplomat needs the ability to think about more than one complex subject at a time.

Then Major Tatrak and the ambassador exchanged glances. In the distance a faint buzzing was audible. It might, or might not, be a helicopter.

Using a key from his key chain, Hiar unlocked the rusty grillwork gate set in the old foundation wall of the palace of Darius. He and Harry ducked through the gateway and Hiar locked the gate behind them. Blinded by the sudden darkness, they moved cautiously along the passage, which sloped gradually downward as they advanced. They moved in a crouch to keep from hitting their heads on the ceiling. When they had gone five yards, Harry took one of the flashlights and switched it on. Its yellow beam licked deep into the tunnel. It was a carefully dug out shaft measuring five feet from its floor, which was the actual bedrock, to its ceiling, which was partly bedrock and partly ancient stone slabs. Its side walls—also the bedrock —were four feet apart.

"The great archaeologist Herzfeld mapped part of the tunnel system between the two world wars," Hiar whispered. "But we still don't know its full extent—and I haven't had to find my way around it for years."

They paused to sort out the equipment. Each man took a flashlight, an Uzi and two extra clips of submachine-gun cartridges. Harry, wanting to travel light, let Hiar take the revolver and the revolver ammunition.

Then they moved forward again, with Harry leading the way, peering along the spear of light that his flashlight thrust ahead of them. He wished the flashlights were stronger—but whoever had provided them had clearly expected them to be used for getting around the surface of the terrace at night; he or she had had no inkling that they would be used for a clandestine advance through total blackness underground.

"Hey," Harry whispered. Twenty or thirty yards ahead of them, something blue was glittering in the flashlight beam. It was a small object, whatever it was, lying on the left side of the tunnel floor. The two men advanced cautiously until they were less than ten yards away.

*"Merde,"* Harry said.

"It's a piece of jewelry. A platinum-and-sapphire brooch."

"Hiar, is there any chance that a piece of jewelry here in the tunnel could be anything but part of the crown jewels?"

"No. These tunnels have been picked clean by looters and sightseers over the centuries. It has to be from the crown jewels."

They moved closer.

"You know what this means?" Harry whispered.

"What?"

"That the robbers have probably been moving the jewels around in the tunnel system. Maybe one of them tried to steal the brooch—and then dropped it for some reason. Maybe it's what I guessed—they've moved the jewels out of the trucks and underground; maybe that's why they wanted to keep us away from the harem. Maybe they've moved the thermite bombs underground, too. What would happen if they were to set off the bombs in one of the tunnels, instead of on the surface of the ground?"

Hiar sighed. "In that event, I imagine that the explosive force might be greatly multiplied." He studied the brooch. "It's an old turban ornament. Must be eighteenth-century. Those sapphires are enormous." He leaned his Uzi against the tunnel wall and bent to pick up the brooch.

"Wait!" Harry snapped. "Freeze. Don't touch it."

"Why? That's a valuable—"

"It might be a booby trap; that's why." Harry studied the brooch, a five-inch spray of blue stones that sparkled in the shifting pool of light. "Look there."

A fresh-looking pile of loose dirt lay two inches from the brooch, adjoining the wall.

Harry said, "There could easily be a wire running from that brooch to a hand grenade or some other kind of explosive charge under that dirt."

"Those vermin, to play like that with our treasures. Should we not try to neutralize it in some way?"

"Better not. We've got to keep moving. Anyway, it may be only a dummy booby trap, put there to make us nervous."

"It has succeeded."

"Never mind, Hiar, let's keep moving."

They went forward in silence, their flashlight beams dancing in the dusty gloom ahead.

"Look. There—up ahead." Hiar said, stepping up the pace.

Harry whistled noiselessly. "Pay dirt."


"Here she is—the whore," Ingo barked. He shoved Gail ahead of him into the harem office. Gumbert looked up, scowling, from the radio. Kates was leaning against a filing cabinet, holding a glass with an inch of whiskey in the bottom.

"She was wandering around, talking to the lookouts one by one," Ingo said. "Like she wanted them to forget their work. Like she wanted to spy on what they were doing."

"Come on, Ingo, don't be such a boy scout," Gail said; her voice had the old metallic tone. "I was trying to pass the time, is all. Just—" She stopped and used her bare right hand to wipe from her face the ounce of whiskey that Kates had splashed across it. She ignored the stains on the white of her blouse.

"What'd you do that for, Colonel? What is this, some kind of cowboy bar?" she said evenly. Her face was paler than before. "I thought we were friends."

"I did, too, honey," Kates said, "but I smell a rat when you pretty yourself up and go around talkin' to my troops. Talkin' to maybe one or two, that's all right, that's human nature. But goin' around my defense perimeter, droppin' in on the lookouts, one after another, I call that some kind of sabotage."

Gumbert looked at his watch and then turned up the volume on the radio that was tuned to Radio Moscow. A newscaster, speaking perfect American English, was reporting about inflation in the United States. He ended with, "And that was the news from Radio Moscow."

Kates reached on top of the filing cabinet, where Hossein had stashed a pint bottle of whiskey. Now Kates, too, looked at his wristwatch, but for a different purpose. "Look, honey," he said, his face dark with menace, "in exactly half a minute I'm going to take this bottle, and I'm going to break it against this filing cabinet. That's goin' to leave a nasty jagged edge. You and I are goin' to take a good look at it. Then we're goin' to wait another half a minute, and you're goin' to think about whether you want to tell us what you were up to just now, why you were goin' around chattin' up my troops. If you don't, I'm—"

"Quiet!" Gumbert yelled. "For God's sake, *quiet!*" He turned the radio up loud. It was playing orchestra music now, a lusty melody with many Muscovite violins—"The Blue Danube."

Kates's face lost its menacing scowl. He smiled. He grinned. He let out a rebel yell. "That's it, that's the signal from Moscow. Shit, that music sounds mighty fine, doesn't it, Rudi? It means that the Shah must have agreed to all the demands—includin' the terms for us leavin' this place, with our share of the jewels."

Gumbert nodded, smiling a blissful smile.

"But how come we haven't heard any announcement on the radio about legalizing the Tudeh party and the other stuff?"

"Easy," Gumbert said. "The Shah must have given the Russians such binding assurances that they were satisfied. Perhaps he has declared the party legal, and the fact has for some reason not yet been broadcast. After all, it is an enormous concession for him to make. At any rate, as we arranged, playing 'The Blue Danube' indicates that the Russians are completely satisfied that all the demands have been adequately met. Including the manner of our departure. That's, um, good enough for me."

"God damn; God *damn,*" Kates said joyously. He clapped Gumbert fondly on one flabby shoulder. "Rudi, you and I just got to be two of the richest old men in the world. And, Ingo, you just got to be the richest down-and-out lion tamer in history. And even you, honey, you've just gotten to be a whole lot richer than a double-crosser like you deserves to be. Now, how about tellin' me what you were up to out there, just between us multimillionaires?"

"You—you never said I wasn't supposed to talk to the men," she said, her voice worried now, falling back on a meaningless, little-girl excuse.

Kates began a falsetto imitation: " 'You never said—' "

"Come on, come on," Gumbert broke in. "We're going to be plenty busy getting ready to leave here. There's no time to pick on the girl, my friend. Besides, she might just possibly be telling the truth."

Kates looked at Gail and shrugged. She turned toward the door.

"Uh, uh, honey," Kates said. "You stay right here."

The royal suite of the Hafiz Hotel was hushed. The court minister sat slumped in his chair in the banquet room, smoking a thin cigar. General Karavi was talking urgently into a gold telephone. He hung up.

"The Bushehr naval base confirms that a helicopter took off from the *Timoshenko* less than half an hour ago."

"I *thought* I heard a helicopter engine just now," the minister said.

"You may very well have; we have instructed it to land on the Shiraz-to-Persepolis highway, five kilometers south of Persepolis, to pick up Dr. Shepehri, the bank's crown jewels expert."

"Why so far away? I thought the helicopter was supposed to be unarmed."

"Because the Russians may try to double-cross us in some way. If we have to start shooting at that helicopter, it is better to do it back there in the open countryside than, say, in the courtyard of this hotel."

The minister nodded tensely. The gold telephone rang again. A corporal on General Karavi's staff moved to answer it, but the general grabbed the receiver first.

The passageway led into a circular, windowless chamber. Lying on the chamber floor were rows of well-scuffed suitcases —the same suitcases that had been loaded into the Maxiwagons and the Jeep Wagoneer what seemed an eon ago.

"We are in luck," Hiar said.

"To say the least." Harry looked at the nearest suitcase, a fat black one, dotted with hotel stickers. He decided it was impossible to tell whether it was booby-trapped. There was nothing suspicious about its exterior, but there was no telling what infernal devices Kates and his friends might have rigged inside. It was, after all, somewhat odd that these suitcases had been left unguarded—although they were, of course, well hidden. Harry supposed that Kates needed most of his limited manpower to guard the perimeter of the terrace.

"Hiar, stand back, please; I'm going to try to open this one."

The suitcase was unlocked. Harry unsnapped the two latch devices that kept the lid shut. Nothing happened. Ever so gingerly he began to lift the lid. As he did so, a strange thought flashed through his mind: the memory of the night he had rifled Princess Troubetzine's steamer trunk in Baden-Baden fifteen years ago. So his life had not changed so very much since then; but now the stakes, and the risks, were far higher. He tugged on the lid. It swung open easily.

Harry peered into the suitcase, then ran his hands along its bottom. It was empty. *"Merde,"* he said.

"Let me try my luck." Hiar opened the next case, moving even more cautiously. "Empty, except for two large pearls— and they are discolored."

They took turns going through the rest of the cases. There was no explosion, and no sign that the cases had ever been booby-trapped. But all they contained were odds and ends— exquisite, precious pieces, to be sure, but still odds and ends: a small dagger here, a dented gold box there, even a dusty ostrich plume.

"This is only a tiny fraction of the loot," Hiar said bleakly. "They have taken everything else with them to some other hiding place."

Harry put a hand on his shoulder. "Come on, Hiar, *courage;* we know they're moving fast, they had to unload these quickly. If we're going to catch up with them, we're going to have to move fast, too."

The tunnel continued on the other side of the chamber. Harry pushed ahead. Hiar followed, breathing heavily now; he was out of shape. Harry hurried onward, heedless of the pain in his leg—feeling stupid because he had not pocketed some of the odds and ends of loot.

# 18

KATES TURNED AWAY FROM GAIL AND MOVED ABRUPTLY TO A window, listening. From the distance came the rasp of a badly maintained electric loud-hailer pouring out a mixture of static and orders in Farsi.

Gumbert smiled. "Relax, Colonel, it's some Iranian general. He's saying he wants to inform all personnel in the area that a Russian helicopter is on its way to the terrace." Gumbert listened some more. "He's saying its mission is peaceful and it's apparently unarmed. He says all personnel are to exercise due caution and be ready to take cover if it engages in any suspicious activity. He says it's expected to be here in a few minutes."

Kates, too, broke into a grin. "Goddamn. That's good news, Rudi. Goddamn." He pulled a blue-and-white bandanna from a hip pocket. Mechanically he wiped his forehead and the back of his neck, although he had not been sweating. "Jesus H. Christ. We're really in business."

"That general sounds tired."

"I'll bet he is, the son-of-a-bitch. In a few minutes we should be out of here. The Shah'll probably give him a medal for not making the situation any worse."

Gumbert gave no reply. He was standing by a window, looking through the binoculars. He gave a kind of sigh, and murmured, in a voice now strangled with emotion, "It's coming."

"The helicopter? Already?" Kates rushed to his side.

Gumbert nodded. "You can see it with the naked eye now

if you look, above the left-hand dome of the hotel and slightly to the left."

"Yeah. Off in the distance. Rudi, old buddy, that is surely the world's most beautiful black dot in the sky."

The dot grew larger. A faint helicopter rotor sound was in the air again, growing louder.

Gumbert turned and took Ingo by one sinewy arm. "All right, my boy. This is it; the helicopter will be here in a few minutes. Take your position as planned."

Ingo grinned, nodded, and trotted out a side door of the harem. He took up a position in a flat, grassy space, which had been leveled and graded after recent reexcavations of the site of Darius's treasury. The space was just southeast of the harem, at the foot of the Mountain of Mercy, near the great cistern. Ingo was wearing a windbreaker and a porkpie hat; he removed them now and held them in his hands, ready to use them as makeshift flags when the moment came to guide the helicopter toward the landing space that Kates and Gumbert had chosen for it months ago.

Then suddenly Ingo began to wave his arms, although the helicopter was still miles away. Watching him, Kates at first assumed that he was simply overexcited, that he was already trying to catch the helicopter pilot's eye. Then Kates realized that Ingo was waving at him and Gumbert. And shouting.

"What's he yellin', Rudi? Can you make it out?"

" 'Cannons.' He's pointing at the mountaintop."

"Pass the binoculars, old buddy." Kates spread his legs to steady himself and studied the ridge line of the mountain. He took out the bandanna, wiped dust off the outer lenses, and studied the mountain some more. He handed the glasses back to Gumbert, saying, "Take a look, old buddy, and see if you see what I see; all bets are off."

"Look there," Hiar said, gesturing with his submachine-gun barrel. "You see the scorch marks on the tunnel wall?"

"Sure, what are they?" Harry spoke impatiently, distract-edly. He was asking himself where the jewels might be.

"You see such marks here and there around Persepolis. They are left from the great fire that wrecked the place. Twenty-three centuries ago, that was, after it was seized by Alexander the Great—"

"Okay, okay, please get to the point."

"All right, my friend. The point is: look how the scorch marks come to an abrupt end—there."

Sure enough, the dark scorched area on the left side of the tunnel wall—which had been carved from the solid bedrock—ended in a neat vertical line. The line was formed by the begin-ning of an expanse of brick which seemed to form a veneer over the bedrock on the tunnel's left side.

"What does that mean?" Harry asked.

"It means the bricks were put up after the scorching took place, but that signifies little, because these particular scorch marks might have been made relatively recently, by campfires, perhaps."

"Okay, but then it's possible that the wall was put up in the last couple of hours? By Kates's people?"

"That's the big question," Hiar said. He put a hand against the bricks to feel whether the mortar was still damp. He gasped. "Hey," he said, "there's no mortar." He nudged at the expanse of brick; some individual bricks moved a little under the pres-sure. "The bricks seem new."

"Easy does it," Harry said. He and Hiar exchanged long glances. "What do you think might be behind the brick?" Harry asked.

"If we are lucky, it's the entrance to a side tunnel contain-ing many billions of rials' worth of jewels." Hiar set down his Uzi and began tugging at the bricks with his deft, archaeologist's hands. He made a small hole, which revealed a cavity behind the brick facing; Harry set down his own weapon and began to help, forcing himself by an act of will to refrain from clawing frantically at the bricks.

"Well, well," Gumbert said to Kates. "I see what got Ingo excited: a black line, rather like a pipe, peeping out from behind those two boulders there, near the ridge line."

"What do you think it is?"

"Heavy machine gun. Almost certainly the Browning .50-caliber M2. What has probably happened there is that the gun crew has had trouble setting the tripod among the rocks up there. They weren't able to keep the entire gun out of sight. They must have moved it very hastily."

"And in the last few minutes," Kates said. "Otherwise, one of us would have seen it before. See anythin' else?"

"I thought I saw the tip of a gun barrel, probably another M2, further to the right. But, um, it seems to have been moved back, or down, or something."

"I saw that one, too. And if we can spot two heavy machine guns, how many more must there be around?"

"Um. Quite a few, I should wager. They probably have some to the west of the terrace, down among the trees."

"What do you think they're plannin' to do?"

"Maybe they only want to increase their options," Gumbert said without conviction. "So that if they think we are welching on the deal, they can start shooting anytime they want. As you know, those M2's fire bullets that are big enough to cut a man or a helicopter apart, but not big enough to do structural damage to the ruins."

"Those motherfuckers," Kates snapped.

"What, the guns?"

"No, that Iranian general and his buddies. You don't really believe what you just said, do you, Rudi?"

"Um. No, not entirely."

"There's only one reason for them to move that kind of fire power up so close, and so late in the game: they've decided to kill us on the ground, or to shoot down the helicopter before it gains much altitude. The Iranians must have panicked. They must have decided it's worth riskin' a war with Russia, and riskin' havin' their precious ruins and their crown jewels destroyed—just for the chance of savin' the jewels. Just for the pleasure of revenge on us. Just for the sake of their pride. Shit." He glared up at the mountain as though it were his personal enemy—which, in a sense, it had become.

"I think you are right," Gumbert said bleakly. "Now what?"

"Now we implement a little contingency plan. I have a plan that will still get us out of here in one piece. And as rich men."

A faint scratching sound came from behind Harry. He whirled, Uzi at the ready—but saw that the noise had been made by a dusty gray cat, which had found its way into the tunnel behind them. Harry kicked at the animal, and it scampered back into the gloom.

Hiar put his hand on Harry's shoulder. "Relax, my friend."

"Okay, Hiar," Harry said with a small smile. "After all, it's only a few billion dollars at stake."

The sound of the helicopter's whirring rotors grew louder and closer. Fraser and Feeney left their chessboard and looked out a window. Sure enough, the Russian helicopter soon appeared. The red star gleamed from its fuselage.

"That must have been the pilot, the man we could see in the front window on our side," Feeney said after it had passed. "He looked young, and I thought I had a glimpse of a khaki flight jacket. This must be a great moment for him; he was probably hand-picked for this mission; if he gets through this alive, he's bound to get a double promotion when he's back at his base. He must think he's taking a place in the history books, striking a blow against the Shah, that sort of thing."

"You're probably right," Fraser said. "He certainly didn't look like the Iranian bank official—he must have been sitting in the co-pilot's seat, where we couldn't see him. The poor bastard."

The suite door opened. It was Major Tatrak again. This time he was so distracted that he had not even bothered to knock.

"Yes, Tatrak, what is it now?" Fraser asked—a little wearily, sorry to be away from the serenity and predictability of his chessboard.

"General Karavi sends his compliments, sir, and asks that you come to the conference room. It is extremely urgent."

Fraser nodded and reached for his jacket.

Outside, the noise of the helicopter faded, then stopped.

"The chopper must have landed on the terrace," Feeney said.

Fraser looked at him with a mixture of affection and contempt and said, "That seems like a logical conclusion."


A side tunnel did indeed run off leftward behind the brick wall. Harry and Hiar pulled down enough bricks to be able to plunge through, then moved cautiously ahead. After twenty yards their flashlight beams fell on a row of six-foot, dun-colored, torpedo-shaped metal objects lying like a sausage chain along the tunnel's right-side wall.

"For God's sake, what are *those?*" Hiar whispered.

"Those are the thermite bombs. The little gismos taped to them must be explosive charges, to set them off."

"Is it safe to walk past them?"

"It should be; the explosive charges aren't wired to anything, and they don't seem to have time fuses."

They walked past, very softly.

"There are only five of them here," Harry said.

"So what? Is that not enough to perform their mission?"

"No, that's enough to spread a huge amount of destruction. But the point is, Kates said at the beginning that there were six thermite bombs. So he has evidently abandoned five of them, in preparation for his departure. And has kept one to take with him when he leaves. As insurance. He told the U.S. consulate that that's what he'd do."

"Where do you think the sixth bomb is?"

"Someplace up ahead, I guess."

"If I were a Christian, I would cross myself now, I think."

There was nothing more to say. They moved ahead.

In the banquet room, the gold telephone rang. General Karavi picked it up.

"Yes, Your Majesty," he said. "Yes, sir. Yes." He put the receiver down slowly. "The Shah simply hung up," he said softly. "He has never hung up on me before. Not in my entire career." The general was obviously shaken, but he pulled himself together. "His Majesty wants action, *action,*" he said. He licked his lips and looked at the circle of haggard faces around the conference table. "Fraser," he said, "does the United States have any suggestions? Karthian's complex arrangements have obviously come to nothing."

Fraser leaned back in his chair. His eyes, meeting Karavi's, were steady, but they had a tired look. "We have nothing to suggest, General, and there have been no suggestions from Washington."

Karavi looked again around the room. "Does *anyone* have anything to suggest?"

Old General Jaddad stirred where he was sitting, on the divan in the back of the room. His thick torso was erect. He moved his heavy lips.

"The time has come to attack," he said, speaking in French. "If the bandits resist, kill them."

General Karavi shook his head. "General, think of the risks involved," he said.

General Jaddad cut him short with a wave of his sallow hand. "This has all gone too far," he said. "The authority of the

Shah has been flouted too long. I know what the Shah's father would have ordered me to do in this situation. He would have said to crush them, like any other rebellious tribe."

"But what about Miss Olsen and Arloff?" Ambassador Fraser burst out, with the indignation he knew Washington would feel. "They are guests in your country, and they may be working against the bandits; you cannot risk killing them; that would be immoral, that would be the equivalent of murder."

General Jaddad did not deign to reply to that objection; he gave a shrug of his heavy shoulders.

The minister of court toyed with his platinum fountain pen. "And what of Persepolis?" he said musingly, "If we attack, we may destroy much of the ruins. We may be blamed for damaging one of the world's great archaeological sites."

"We can take steps to reduce the odds of damaging the ruins," General Jaddad said. "We can start with a few artillery shells, and we can fire them very high, so they merely hit the Mountain of Mercy, without harming the ruins. Then, if the bandits still hold out, we can step up the artillery fire. If the ruins are damaged, so be it. They have been damaged for centuries, after all."

"But we must not forget the jewels themselves," General Karavi said.

"My friend, the jewels are of course a great symbol of our nation's history, and of its cultural heritage," General Jaddad replied. "But we all know that they are themselves largely booty, the fruit of the power of the shahs. We cannot let the present monarch's power be undercut for the sake of a mere symbol. Think of the embarrassment to His Majesty if word of this banditry gets out. We must act quickly. If a few bits of jewelry are damaged or destroyed, that is nothing grave. The authorities can say later that they are away on loan, or that they have been broken up so that the jewels can be fitted into modern pieces. If the loss is greater, well, this country is rich now; we could secretly buy replacements. And if some of the most famous jewelry is destroyed, we can have copies made. Who is to know?"

General Karavi wrung his hands. "Then there is Dr. Hiar, the curator of the ruins," he said. "He is being held captive in there somewhere. Does his life count for nothing?"

General Jaddad spat once again into the wastebasket. "Gentlemen, I know my duty," he said, speaking more loudly now. "And I know yours. If you do not take this action now, I shall report your bumbling to the Shah. When I have made the details clear to him, I am sure his vengeance will be swift and sure. To protect myself against his anger, I have already ordered a few picked men from the Gendarmerie to conceal machine guns on the Mountain of Mercy so that they can open fire on the bandits if need be. General Karavi, I strongly suggest that you show a similar aggressiveness. I suggest that you call His Majesty now, this moment. Tell him that we have concluded that it is necessary to mount a staged attack, beginning with selected artillery fire."

Karavi sighed. He picked up the gold telephone. "Give me His Majesty's office," he said. "Immediately."

General Jaddad leaned back on the divan. He smiled.

# 19

HARRY AND HIAR PRESSED AHEAD ALONG THE SIDE TUNNEL, moving carefully so as to make as little noise as possible. Harry's flashlight beam showed that the tunnel stretched on ahead, sloping gradually downward and maintaining the same height and width.

It seemed dark and quiet—yet the silence meant little, because even if Kates and company were nearby and talking, the bedrock would muffle their voices.

Harry was favoring his bad leg, which was aching again. The air smelled of dampness and cold stone. Harry's flashlight threw yellow ovals of light onto the tunnel walls, revealing Arabic or Farsi inscriptions left by God knows what adventurers of the past. He snapped off his flashlight to test the darkness; once his eyes grew accustomed to the change, he could make out a pale glow of light dozens of yards ahead, where the tunnel seemed to veer to the right.

"What could that be?" he whispered.

"Don't know," Hiar said. "Looks like lantern light, not daylight. Maybe this tunnel links up with some other tunnel, or with an underground entrance to one of the ancient buildings."

Faint noises were audible now from up ahead; muffled thumps and clumps, followed by a man's low cry—which might have been the "Ouch" of a laborer who had dropped something on his foot. The light ahead flickered. It was as though a man had moved across the beam of a lantern.

Harry glanced backward. In the dim light he could see Hiar's eye-whites and teeth: the man was grinning. The Uzi glinted in his hands.

"If we find Kates, please do not kill him," Hiar said softly. "Leave that to me."

Harry smiled but said nothing. They moved ahead, more slowly now. In the quiet, Harry could hear one of his extra bullet magazines clinking against a couple of ten-rial pieces in his pants pocket. He stopped to transfer the coins to another pocket, wondering as he did so whether that was an act of genuine prudence or whether he was really just stalling for time. He wanted a cigarette badly, but he knew that even if he wanted to stop for a few minutes—which he did not—there was no holding Hiar back now.

They came to the bend in the tunnel. Harry stuck his flashlight in his belt and took the Uzi in two hands. He went into a crouch, to make himself a smaller target if shooting broke out. Hiar did the same. They rounded the corner—and found that after twenty feet the tunnel ran into a squarish cavity, which measured perhaps fifteen feet on a side and was lit up by a powerful electric lantern. The floor of the cavity lay three feet below the floor of the tunnel, which meant that Harry and Hiar could only get a partial view of the wiry man who was at work there. He turned toward them for an instant, and, under the porkpie hat, they recognized Ingo. They moved closer and saw that the floor of the cavity was littered with heavy canvas bags —Iranian military mailbags, which must have been stolen from the Shiraz air force base at the same time as the bombs. Now the bags were full of fairly heavy objects, large and small, which made a variety of clinking and clanking sounds as Ingo, panting with exertion, dragged them across the chamber and piled them near the foot of some rusty-looking metal scaffolding, which ran up the cavity's far side.

"Where that man is standing is the bottom of the great cistern, or at least it is as deep as the archaeologists have dug,"

Hiar whispered very softly in Harry's ear. "The crown jewels have obviously been transferred into those sacks. He must be sending the sacks up to the surface of the terrace on board the old elevator that the excavators have been using to remove rubble from the cistern. It runs up and down that metal scaffold."

"Kates must be getting ready to leave," Harry whispered back. "We've got to move fast."

They did. They waited until Ingo turned his back again. Then they stepped to the mouth of the tunnel. Harry called Ingo's name. The man heard, turned, saw the two Uzis and raised his scarred hands. His eyes narrowed to slits; he was like an animal at bay. Harry took his left hand off his Uzi and laid it across his lips, signaling Ingo to keep quiet.

Two miles southwest of Persepolis, an Iranian sergeant in combat boots and fatigues clumped out onto the highway that runs straight toward the terrace. The sergeant carried a red flag and a carbine. He stationed himself in the middle of the highway to stop any military vehicles that might get in the way; civilian vehicles had earlier been barred from the highway. Then the fields on the northwest side of the road began to resound with the rumble and clatter of heavy armored vehicles. In seconds the pencil-shaped barrel of a 105-mm. tank gun poked through the line of pine trees planted beside the highway. It was the turret gun of a hulking U.S.-made M-60A1 combat tank of the Iranian army. The tank pushed through onto the highway, crushing a pine sapling as it did so. Once on the road, it turned left, picked up speed, and charged full-throttle toward Persepolis. Within seconds it was followed by an elephant train of nine other M-60A1's, part of the squadron that Karavi had earlier ordered to be drawn up behind the pines as an emergency reserve.

In the lead tank, the commanding officer, a lieutenant, stood up in an open hatch, Israeli style. His goggles were pushed up on his forehead. He used binoculars to search for signs of movement on the terrace. He was afraid that someone might open fire to try to interdict his tanks' advance. But he saw no signs of artillery or anti-tank weapons, and so his tanks rushed on in single file at nearly their top speed. Their treads carved lengthening herringbone scars on the macadam, which was designed to take the weight of tourist buses but not 53-ton armored vehicles. As the tanks approached the terrace, the bulky ruins seemed to rise before them like a wave. The columns seemed to grow ominously taller. Two black specks in the sky overhead caught his eye. But his binoculars showed them to be not hostile helicopters but large black birds, probably kites. The tanks rolled on.

Harry heard a motor start to whine overhead. He peered up the cistern. Against the patch of sky at its top he could see the rickety elevator moving downward. It was slipping slowly along two rails, agleam with grease, which were attached by the rusty metal scaffolding to the cistern wall. Whoever was at the end of the cistern was sending the elevator down for another load of jewels.

Harry got an idea.

"Hiar, the elevator's coming down again; that means they haven't figured out that anything's wrong down here," he whispered. "Please move Ingo out of sight; take him a couple of yards inside the side tunnel."

Ingo glowered at Hiar and Harry with his narrowed eyes, but under prodding from Hiar's Uzi, he made the move. Harry joined Hiar and Ingo in the tunnel for a moment, took Ingo's windbreaker and hat, put them on and slipped back out onto the cistern floor. Anyone looking down from up above would think Ingo was still standing there, ready to pile on the next load of jewel sacks.

The elevator came to the bottom of the cistern and stopped. Harry laid his Uzi on the elevator floor and loaded on three of the sacks. One of them made a strange, muffled, clacking sound when he dumped it on the elevator's scarred wooden floor; he opened its top and saw it was full of loose emeralds. Christ, if I owned just one of those bags, my descendants would be rich for generations, Harry thought.

"Listen, Hiar, I'm going up on the elevator," he whispered. "Please stay here to keep an eye on Ingo and cover my rear. Now, Ingo, I want you to tell your friends that another elevator load is coming up, and you're coming up on board. Shout it good and loud."

Ingo said nothing. He stood stolidly, his jaw set.

"Go ahead and shout," Hiar whispered. "Or I shoot your feet off, and you die of loss of blood."

Ingo, a connoisseur of cruelty, smiled. He cupped his hands and yelled, "Another load coming up, I'm coming, too." The shout echoed in the tunnel and the cistern, but no one looked down from above.

Harry reached around and jabbed the "up" button on the button panel. The machinery whined again, and the elevator slid upward. The elevator cage had wire-mesh side walls, but it was open to the front and the back. Looking down from the front, Harry could see some loose, spilled jewels glinting faintly on the cistern floor. Looking to the rear, he could see the surface of the old bedrock, laid bare by the original cistern diggers centuries ago. Harry pulled the hat down over his forehead and held the Uzi close to his thigh so that it could not be seen from above. He caught his breath. The sight of the jewel sacks and the knowledge that at long last a showdown was coming left him strangely exhilarated, despite the aching in his bad leg. The awareness that he might soon earn thousands of dollars in reward money gave him a warm feeling that banished nervousness, fear and fatigue. The Uzi's magazine had twenty-five bullets, he reflected, and he still had the two extra magazines. So he could make a lot of trouble, if his luck held out.

The gloom of the cistern gradually gave way to the daylight

as the elevator rose higher and higher. It bumped to a stop at the top, at ground level. Harry stepped off from the rear. Directly in front of him were the clamshell rear doors of the helicopter. They were open. Harry vaulted forward—and found a weird scene. A man in a business suit—it must be the bank official—lay bound and gagged inside the doors. The Soviet pilot was in the pilot's seat. In the co-pilot's seat beside him was Gumbert, and at Gumbert's feet was a torpedo-shaped metal object: the sixth thermite bomb. Standing in the center of the aircraft was Kates. The finest crown jewels of Iran were heaped around him on the floor: besides the jewels in sacks, some of the larger objects were lying around loose: Harry saw old jeweled weapons, a mirror studded with red stones. Next to Kates, her hands cuffed together, was Gail. Her face was shiny with sweat. Kates had his pistol pointed at her gut.

Five hundred yards from the terrace, the tanks fanned out, left and right. Behind them came a column of box-shaped M113 armored personnel carriers, which also fanned out, right and left, taking up positions behind the tanks. When the APC's stopped, two men hopped out of each vehicle. Each pair—a gunner and a loader—hastily set up a tripod-mounted, 3.5-mm. rocket launcher. In the lead APC, an Iranian officer, a certain Lieutenant Saza, waited, looking at his watch, while the rocket-launcher crews got ready. In the U.S. army the crews of 3.5-mm. rocket launchers are trained not to use the weapons at ranges over two hundred yards, but the lieutenant, in the Middle Eastern fashion, was not taking any chances.

# 20

"DROP IT, HARRY," KATES SAID LEVELLY. HE DID NOT MOVE the barrel of the pistol away from Gail's stomach. "Drop the Uzi."

From the distance came the bellow of an electric loud-hailer. It was Ambassador Fraser. His voice was magnified so loud that it echoed eerily off the Mountain of Mercy. "Kates. Now hear this. We still want to talk. You can still surrender. Kates. Now hear this. We still want to talk." He was repeating the message. "You can still surrender. Kates. Now hear this . . ."

Kates remained impassive. "Drop it," he told Harry, "or she gets a bullet in the stomach. It's a bad death. She's your buddy, isn't she? You don't want her to die. So drop the Uzi."

Gail shut her eyes.

Harry looked down at the weapon in his hands. He decided to stall. "You know I can't drop this, it's a submachine gun, Kates. It'll go off if I do. You may get killed."

"Balls," Kates said. "It has an automatic safety grip. It won't fire if you drop it. Go ahead. Drop it now; or the girl dies."

Harry let the Uzi fall. The eight pounds of metal and heat-resistant plastic hit the riveted plates of the helicopter floor with a clunk—which was drowned out as the first shell from the lead tank's cannon struck the Mountain of Mercy behind and above the helicopter with a thunderous *bam*. The gunner was firing very high. Stones and pebbles clattered down on the terrace; one or two hit the fuselage of the helicopter. Keeping the gun pointed at Gail, Kates peered out the helicopter's forward windows, screwing his head around to see where the shell had hit.

"Bastards are shootin' high," he said matter-of-factly, "the way Arab troops do, 'specially when they're green. I guess these guys are green, too." He paused to think for a moment. "No, it must be these gunners have *orders* to fire high, to scare us without damaging the ruins or the museum. It doesn't matter anyhow. We're gettin' out of here in a couple of minutes."

Harry asked, "But what about your other men? Hossein? Faiz? Marcel? The others?"

"I messaged them by walkie-talkie to hold their positions—and to kill you and Hiar if they saw you or him tryin' any funny stuff. I told them the helicopter won't be leaving for a while. That's a lie, of course. But that way they won't try to get on board. That way we'll have more than enough room to carry all the best of the jewels." Kates described his betrayal of his comrades calmly; Gumbert also showed no objection or regret.

In the distance, the ambassador was still repeating his call to surrender. It was abruptly drowned out by the *bam* of another shell. The gunners were still firing high.

Kates gestured toward the pilot. "Georgi here is goin' to fly us out now. He doesn't really have any choice, because in accordance with our original demands, he's unarmed. But I've agreed to give him a five percent cut on the jewels, if his government will let me. And he knows his government will welcome any turn of events that embarrasses the Shah."

The pilot turned around in his seat and grinned a feverish grin. The man was obviously a gung-ho volunteer, obviously out to make a name for himself in a single day.

Kates said, "Let's get ready to take off, Georgi."

The pilot raised the starter switch safety guard and flipped the starter switch to the "on" position. The engine began to purr.

Kates smiled. "In a minute I'm goin' to use the helicopter

radio to broadcast a message to the Iranian officers in the hotel. The message is that I've revoked the original offer to take only the unmarked, loose jewels with us. I'm revokin' it because someone has gotten ready to double-cross us by puttin' heavy machine guns on the mountains. And, now, by harassin' us with artillery fire. So I'm goin' to tell them we're takin' off with all the very finest of the jewels—the crowns, the whole works. And with a thermite bomb on board. If someone shoots us down, Gumbert will make sure the bomb goes off. Gumbert and I have no desire to fall into the hands of Iranian interrogators. Or to face a badly trained Iranian firin' squad. If the bomb goes off, that, of course, will mean the end of the jewels.

"I'm also goin' to broadcast that you and Gail are on board the helicopter. Fraser won't want innocent or semi-innocent Americans killed while he's on the scene. That would be bad for his reputation. So he'll use his influence with the Iranians to try to keep us from gettin' shot down."

The loud-hailer was still blaring Fraser's appeals. He was growing hoarse.

Kates said, "Okay, Georgi, start the rotor blades."

The pilot checked the dials on the control panel, then shifted the clutch handle. The rotor blades began to spin slowly.

Kates gestured at Harry with his pistol. "You go aft and clear those rear doors, so I can press the switch to close 'em. It's time to clear out of here."

Gail's eyes were wide open again. They were ablaze with defiance. She had regained her self-possession. Good girl, Harry thought admiringly, she's got courage to spare.

Another shell hit the Mountain of Mercy. This one caused a small, noisy slide of rocks which went slithering down the mountainside.

Harry went to the rear of the helicopter and pulled some jewel sacks away from the doors. As he moved, his foot struck a bag of pearls—on purpose. Scores of fat pearls poured out and rolled every which way across the metal floor.

"Idiot," Kates snapped. He turned to the pilot and told him to rev the engine and prepare for takeoff. In the instant that Kates's attention was diverted, Harry scooped up the jeweled mirror and jammed it between the left-hand cargo door and the doorframe, next to a hinge, so that the mirror would prevent the door from closing.

"Okay, stand clear," Kates snapped. He reached past Gumbert and pressed the switch to close the doors. There was a whine of electric machinery. The doors began to shut, then stopped abruptly when the mirror got in the way.

"Hey, why won't the doors close?" Fear sounded suddenly in Kates's voice.

Harry said, "I dunno, they're jammed somehow."

"Shit." Kates stumped aft, still keeping the pistol pointed at Gail. He peered at the doors. "Somethin's stuck here on the left side," he said to Harry. "Give me a hand working it clear." Kates wrestled with the mirror handle with his left hand, and as he concentrated on the door, he let his gun hand droop so that the gun barrel was pointing not at Gail but at the floor.

Harry sprang forward on his good leg. He grabbed an antique jeweled carbine by the barrel and swung it like a baseball bat with all his strength. The gold-trimmed walnut stock caught Kates behind the right ear. The old wood splintered. Kates gave a grunt and lurched forward. Then, dazed, he lost his balance. He pitched headlong through the doors and down into the cistern.

Gumbert snarled. His face contorted with hatred, he leaned over and began fiddling with the thermite bomb, trying to detonate it. Gail gasped and gaped at him, uncertain what to do. Harry began to move toward him, saying, "Gumbert, for God's sake, don't be crazy."

Then the pilot switched off the engine, dove from his seat and wrestled Gumbert to the ground, pinning his arms behind him.

"What's this?" Gumbert hissed. "The Soviet government

will kill you for this. You'll—" He gasped and fell silent as the pilot gave his right arm—his shooting arm—a brutal wrench.

The pilot looked up at Gail. "Gumbert has a small pistol in a holster under his left arm—get it," he said, speaking good English, the kind that Iranian officers speak after advanced schooling in the U.S.

Gail did so, grasping clumsily with her handcuffed hands. She trained the gun on Gumbert.

The pilot leaped to his feet and bent over the thermite bomb, checking to make sure it wouldn't go off.

Harry, meanwhile, scooped up his Uzi. "Who are you?" he snapped at the man.

"Relax, Prince Arloff, the bomb won't explode, the jewels are safe—and I'm on your side. I'm Major Tabasi of the Imperial Iranian Air Force. I speak some Russian, enough to fool the bandits. This is one of the helicopters we got from the Russians years ago in an oil barter deal."

"Then how come it has Soviet markings?" Harry asked suspiciously.

The pilot grinned. "They were especially painted on for this top-secret decoy mission. It was even kept secret from the Iranians in the Hafiz Hotel and from the American ambassador and his staff—I'm sorry, but we wanted to make sure they didn't mess things up."

"But look, Major," Gail said, "Kates and Gumbert got a radio signal from Moscow. It meant the Shah was accepting all the demands."

"That was a trick," the pilot said. "Earlier the Russian government played along with the bandits, promising help in order to see what profit it could make from the plot. But then the Russians double-crossed them."

Gumbert put his head in his hands.

"What do you mean, 'double-crossed'?" Harry asked, still wary. He hefted the Uzi in his hands and glanced out a side window to look for signs of hostile activity by the lookouts on the terrace. But the lookouts were not in sight; they had evidently taken cover when the shelling began.

"The Russians wish to increase their power here, but they're not crazy," the pilot said evenly but quickly, wanting to get Harry on his side. "They calculated that the Shah would never grant *all* the bandits' demands. They were satisfied when he agreed to release the prisoners and to make concessions on the oil and gas deal that were worth billions of dollars to them. In return they agreed to help him get all his jewels back. They played 'The Blue Danube' signal to make the bandits think all the demands had been granted—to put them off their guard. And then—" The man winced as another shell went *bam* against the mountainside.

"They're still firing high," Gail said; in her hands the pistol was admirably steady.

Then a man began to scream in Farsi somewhere to the rear of the helicopter. The voice was muffled; it seemed to come from the cistern. Harry peered through the cargo doors into its depths. In the glare from Ingo's lantern, he could see Kates moving slowly and groggily on his hands and knees. He was alive, though clearly in pain: he must have broken some bones in his fall.

Yet the screaming, filled with hatred, was coming not from Kates but from a brown-clad figure standing over him: Hiar.

"Hey, Hiar, don't," Harry shouted. "Let him live. Don't—"

Hiar leaned over Kates, holding his Uzi in both hands. He swung the muzzle down, toward the back of the man's head, and fired a short burst.

Harry turned away. He felt suddenly tired. His bad leg ached like hell. He stepped forward, being careful not to slip on the loose pearls. His main concern now was Gail. But she was obviously all right: even with her hands in handcuffs she had managed to rip off her white blouse and was waving it out a window.

"Cease fire, cease fire," she shouted in the hard, resonant voice that had become music to Harry's ears.

Harry turned to the pilot. "Thanks, Major. I'll keep Gumbert covered. You get on your radio and tell Karavi we're in control of the helicopter and the jewels. Tell them to use the loud-hailer to get the other men to surrender; they have no place to go. And please ask them to arrange for me to talk by telephone to my daughter in the United States. Then somebody better untie that poor banker and let him start counting the jewels."

# 21

WITHOUT ACTUALLY LYING, OR AT LEAST WITHOUT ACTUALLY
lying frequently, Harry had long made it his business to spread
the impression that he met now and then with the Shah. This
was, of course, untrue, although Harry had happened to be
sitting at a corner in a restaurant in St. Moritz one evening in
the 1960s when the Shah had appeared. Flanked by elegant
friends, he had walked out of a private dining room and across
the restaurant, nodding amiably at Harry and the other diners.
The Shah had gone out of the door then to resume heaven
knows what delights in his personal chalet. Harry had never
forgotten that moment. This was not out of any royalist fervor,
but because, to his delight, he had discovered that evening that
the Shah had asked to have the bills of all the other diners in
the restaurant added to his own tab. The maître d'hôtel had
explained: "His Majesty is the host wherever he goes, because
he is the Shah."

That fond memory flitted through Harry's mind as he, Gail
and Ambassador Fraser were ushered into the royal palace, just
to the north of Teheran. After a night's sleep in the Hafiz Hotel,
Harry was still tired and a bit dazed from the succession of
special plane and helicopter flights that had brought him and
Gail here in less than an hour. But Gail was in top form: she
crinkled her eyes at the court minister when he bowed to her
on the palace steps, and more out of habit than anything else,
she held his manicured hand a trifle too warmly and too long.

The minister himself ushered them down long corridors smelling of roses. They led to a high-ceilinged room, which was walled with mirror glass and bookcases filled, Harry noticed, with books on war. Gail gave a little sigh of pleasure and tightened her grip on Harry's arm. Some people's biggest thrills come from beauty, but Gail got hers from wealth and power, Harry reflected affectionately. He gave her hand a reassuring squeeze; he knew that Gail, like himself, was wondering whether they would get rewards and, if so, how much.

A lean, graying man rose from behind the vast desk in the far left-hand corner. His slim figure was reflected a dozen times in the mirrors. The details of his face were familiar from all the close-up portrait photographs Harry had seen. It was the face of a shy princeling who had grown into an immensely rich and powerful king. The eyes were cruel and very, very wary. The grip, when they shook hands, was steel.

"Welcome, Prince Arloff, Miss Olsen," the Shah said in his surprisingly high voice. His English had an odd, Frenchified accent. "We have asked you here," he continued—using the royal "we,"—"because we wanted to extend our thanks to you for your help in preserving our country's treasures."

The Shah uttered more pleasantries, while Harry said, once or twice, "Thank you, Your Majesty," and Gail unleashed the June Allyson smile.

Then the Shah nodded to the court minister rather curtly, as though that notable were only a flunky—which, Harry thought to himself, was what the man essentially was. The minister handed the Shah a small gilt box.

"Miss Olsen," the Shah said, "your role in the drama just ended was rather, ah, dubious, we must say. But in view of your assistance in recovering the treasure, we are letting bygones be bygones, and we wish to present you with a token of our gratitude. We will, of course, be grateful to you for your continuing discretion."

Gail outdid herself June Allyson-ing. She even managed to

blush. Ambassador Fraser smiled with professional sweetness. But Harry thought to himself, So the Shah's giving her, in effect, a pardon for her part in the plot, but he had to do that: if he put her in jail here, sooner or later someone would have raised hell in the U.S. And if the Shah let her go, and the Iranian authorities tried to harass her, she could simply go to the newspapers and tell them about the robbery and its aftermath. So now comes the present to pay her off, to make sure she keeps her mouth shut.

The Shah opened the box and took out a slim gold chain adorned with two round and glittering diamonds. He hung it around Gail's neck while she, not unconscious of the effect of her décolletage, leaned forward more than was absolutely necessary. Then she curtseyed and murmured words of thanks. But her blue eyes were surprisingly cold, Harry noticed. And he realized why.

That necklace was, relatively speaking, peanuts. To be sure, the two diamonds were eye-catching, and their size would make them stand out at any New York discotheque. Well, *most* New York discotheques. They weighed two carats apiece, Harry estimated, which meant they would command a price of about twenty-five thousand dollars apiece—assuming that they were both almost flawless, which was by no means certain. Fifty thousand dollars was nothing to sneeze at, but it was a far, far cry from the dreams of wealth that Gail had confided to him. It wasn't even nearly enough to set her up for her old age. Tired and groggy as he was, Harry felt a wave of resentment sweep through him. The most galling thing about the necklace was that the Shah or, more probably, his advisers had obviously concluded that fifty thousand dollars was enough to *buy* Gail, to make her keep her mouth shut. Well, perhaps it was.

Then the Shah nodded again. The court minister presented him with a white envelope on a gold tray. The Shah took the envelope and hefted it a moment.

"Prince Arloff, you have in truth the courage of a lion," the

Shah said. "We thank you in the name of the Iranian people for your assistance in our hour of need. And we know we can count on you to keep the events of the past few days totally secret, and to use your charm to make certain that Miss Olsen does the same."

The Shah gave Harry a funny little smile—it was almost conspiratorial—and handed him the envelope, which was made of heavy cream-colored paper and engraved in gold leaf with much Farsi script, giving, Harry supposed, the Shah's return address. The envelope was addressed in English, in a social secretary's copperplate handwriting: "His Serene Highness Prince Arloff."

Obviously, the envelope contained paper money or a check or some other legal tender. The ambassador was beaming. Gail was radiant, assuming that Harry, at least, was getting a generous reward. The Shah gave Harry another handshake, a bit less steely than the one before.

Then there was silence in the mirrored chamber. It was time for Harry to murmur his humble thanks. Harry looked down at the envelope. His pride, he supposed, should be hurt that the Shah was handing him a tip like this, as though he were a palace elevator man being remembered at Christmastime. Or the Iranian equivalent of Christmastime. But then, Harry wasn't all that big on pride. He assumed that the proper thing now was to express his thanks and be led away by the court minister—and to open the envelope discreetly back at the hotel. But Harry was not all that big on propriety, either. He ripped open the envelope.

Inside was a gold-leaf-embossed piece of palace notepaper folded three ways. Harry unfolded it. A check fell out and fluttered onto the sumptuous Persian carpet. First things first. Harry leaned down and picked up the check, sensing a hush of disapproval in the room—disapproval of his gaucherie in opening the envelope. The check was written on an Iranian bank and signed by the minister of the treasury. It was for thirty-five million Iranian rials: the equivalent of half a million dollars. Harry's first reaction was: not bad. His second reaction was to wonder how soon he could fly to Switzerland to put the money in his secret bank account. Then he read the letter. It, too, was signed by the treasury minister, and it advised him that, out of gratitude for his discretion, the Iranian government was presenting him with this gift—and also making him the beneficiary of an annuity that would pay ten thousand dollars a year into the bank account of his choice. Hush money, Harry thought. It was obvious that if he should breathe a word about the recent events, the annuity would stop.

Harry thought an instant longer. The Shah and the others in the room were staring at him now; Harry had gone too long without speaking.

"Your Majesty," Harry said briskly, "I can't accept this. As they say in my country, thanks, but no thanks."

The Shah's dark eyebrows rose. The wary eyes flashed and then narrowed, growing warier still. He cocked his head to the side, evidently thinking he might have misunderstood what Harry said.

"Your Majesty, I'll be frank with you," Harry went on. "I did what I did because I thought it was the best way to save my daughter. And because I felt the people of your country should not be deprived of their national treasure. I was successful; that is satisfaction enough. I need no other reward."

Harry thrust the check and the notepaper toward the Shah, but the monarch stood frozen, furious, his hands knotted at his sides. As Harry knew, the Shah was totally unaccustomed to being rebuffed. Now he had lost face. He was clearly outraged. His features were turning scarlet with rage.

Harry turned and laid the check on the Shah's desk. He slipped out the door and strode down the rosy-smelling corridor. Gail followed, looking dazed.

"Wait, wait," the ambassador said, huffing after them. "For God's sake, man, don't make a scene. Don't be infantile."

Behind them the door slammed. Through it Harry could hear shouting, in the Shah's voice, interspersed with soothing sounds from the court minister.

"I've had it," Harry said as the ambassador caught up. "I don't want to be beholden to this guy."

The ambassador, familiar with the layout of the palace, steered Harry and Gail to a small antechamber, crowded with gilded Louis Quatorze furniture. "Wait there a moment at least, my boy," the ambassador said. "Calm your nerves." But as the man took out a cigarette case and lit a Kent with shaking hands, Harry saw it was the ambassador's nerves that needed calming.

"Look, Harry, if you don't take that check, it will be a mortal insult to His Majesty. You'll set back American-Iranian relations for years."

"No." Harry folded his arms. He glanced over at Gail. She was giving him a worried look; she probably thought he was having some sort of nervous breakdown. He gave her a discreet wink. "No," he told the ambassador again. "Nothing doing."

The ambassador put down his Kent and stood up. Harry had the feeling that the man was almost physically rising to the occasion. "Very well," the ambassador said. "Let me see if I can get hold of someone who can, ah, can share some thoughts with you at this important hour of your young life. Would you be so kind as to wait here a few minutes, and let me see what I can do; fortunately, the palace has excellent telephone communications with the whole free world."

I guess that means they don't take the Shah's calls in Moscow, Harry thought wryly. He sat back to wait. The ambassador went off down the corridor. In the distance, Harry thought he could hear the Shah's voice, still fulminating.

Minutes passed. Gail, assuming that the antechamber was bugged, said nothing. She scribbled a note on the inside of a matchbook and showed it to Harry. It said: "HARRY, WHAT ARE YOU DOING? DON'T BE STUPID. TAKE THE MONEY." Harry took the matchbook and scribbled on it a single word: "WAIT." Then he shut his eyes; he wanted to stay awake, but he was feeling drained. After all, he had never made half a million dollars in a morning before. He had never given away half a million, either. He thought his eyes had been shut for only a minute, but it must have been longer when the silence was broken by a muffled buzzing sound. The noise came from a telephone on a side table. He took up the receiver. There was static, but the faraway voices were clear: a succession of secretaries and assistants came briefly on the line, asking, in homey American accents, for him please to wait. Then he heard a soft, drawling voice which was familiar from radio and television.

"Hello, Mr. President," Harry said. "Nice of you to call."

The faraway drawling voice talked on, it paused for laughter, it cajoled, it grew firm. It almost pleaded.

"Yes, sir," Harry said, "I know American-Iranian relations are important to us. The oil. Yes, sir, I know that, and we need Iran as a bulwark against the Russians. Yes, sir."

The faraway voice drawled on insistently.

"Well, yes, sir, I'd certainly take the money, but I'm afraid I'd have to ask one condition." Harry was reverting to the unctuous manner he used as a diamond salesman. He ran one hand nervously through his hair. He was sweating slightly. The enormity of what he was up to was getting to him. He could feel he was losing his cool. Hold your horses, he told himself: remember, this is just another sales job, this man is just another rich and powerful husband. It's as though you were trying to sell him some diamonds for his wife . . .

"What's the condition I'd require?" Harry said, his hand holding tight to the telephone receiver. "Well, um, you know the other American, Gail Olsen, she played a key role in subduing the head jewel thief, this Colonel Kates . . . What's that? You're saying it was your understanding she was handcuffed the whole time? Yes, that was true, in a manner of speaking, but even with her handcuffed hands she managed to hit Kates—a really hard punch. It threw him off balance at the crucial moment. If it weren't for her those jewels might be in Moscow by now."

The familiar voice said, a little impatiently, All right, what was it that Harry wanted.

"Well, I'd have to insist, in all fairness, that Gail get the same amount of reward as I did. Under the circumstances, it's not too much to ask of His Majesty, is it? Then, of course, I'd be happy to accept *my* reward, and we'd certainly promise never to breathe a word—"

"Okay, okay," the slurred voice said, "it might be possible to get the Shah to agree to that. But the Shah was pretty angry . . ."

"And there's another little thing," Harry said, pushing his luck. "What's that? Well, I haven't been able to get through yet to my daughter by telephone. Do you think the White House switchboard could arrange that for me? You think it might be possible? That's wonderful. Yessir, we'll wait here. All day if that's necessary. And if they don't throw us out. Thank you, Mr. President."

And they did wait, long enough for Harry to smoke three cigarettes before the court minister reappeared with two envelopes in his hand. He handed them to Gail and Harry, bowed and disappeared.

"What are you going to invest the money in—diamonds?" the ambassador asked.

Harry shook his head. He put his arm around Gail. "No, sir, we're going to buy two farms, in the Virginia horse country."

Gail said, "Two farms next to each other, that is."

The phone rang again. This time it was Emily.

## About the Author

ERIC PACE, a native New Yorker and a graduate of Exeter and Yale, is a veteran reporter and foreign correspondent for *The New York Times*. Over the years, he has been based in Teheran, Beirut, Cairo, Paris, Saigon and New York, where he now makes his home. The journalistic prizes he has won include the George Polk Award of the Overseas Press Club of America for "exceptional courage" in his reporting from Cairo during the 1967 Arab-Israeli war. He is married to Suzanne Wiedel-Pace, a magazine editor. This is his third novel.